Lucidity

Stephanie Thomas

STEPHANIE THOMAS

ISBN-10: 0692377034
ISBN-13: 9780692377031

To my husband — thank you for being my "hope."

"'Hope' is the thing with feathers -
That perches in the soul -
And sings the tune without the words -
And never stops - at all - "
- Emily Dickinson

Chapter 1

I fall asleep sometime on the way to Echo's homeland of Aura. We had walked a third of the way, and when we were a safe enough distance from the City, an Auran ship finally came to pick us up, relieving us of having to walk the rest of the miserable distance on our own. I rest my head against Echo's robed shoulder and submit myself to the dreams that are threatening to drag me into a deeper sleep. It occurs to me somewhere between the thoughts of the conscious and unconscious mind that I don't know if Dreamcatchers dreamt, and if they did, do they invade and manipulate each other's dreams, too?

When I wake up, we still aren't there yet. It's the first time I take a moment to look around and examine my surroundings. Pulling my head off Echo's shoulder, I yawn, admiring the large windows that allow a blurred view of the land we are racing through. Condensation forms at the edges of the multi-layered panes, which are screwed tightly into the bulkhead of the ship. The inside of it is made for what seems like royalty. We sit on cushions of plush crimson velvet, and the wall décor is done in deep gold intricate carvings. I would have never guessed from what the outside of this piece of junk looked like that the inside would be so grand and palatial.

"Did you sleep well?" Echo asks me, touching the side of my face with his soft hand. It is as if he's never had to pick up anything in his life and work, his touch is so gentle and smooth. It stirs feelings up from the core of me, and dread settles in just as soon as the fluttering in my stomach fades away. I've fled the City, me—the Keeper—and I've managed to leave my best friend, Gabe, behind, too.

The upset must have shown on my face as Echo's smile fades and he draws me into a comforting hug. "You will be okay, Beatrice, I know it."

"Why am I doing this again?" It's my turn to ask the obvious question. At the time I decided to go, I only knew that I had to. I felt it. I am needed in Aura now, to help save them. But I don't know the whole story, and the more I think about Gabe, lying at home in a coma, alone in his hospital bed, the more I want to turn back.

"Because Aura needs you. We need your help, Beatrice. There are things that we just can't see on our own ... and the plague ... " Echo shudders, probably recalling a painful memory. "The women can't have their children anymore, and the people are getting so sick ... and now it's spread to the Dreamcatchers, too."

"But how do I fit into this?" I pull my head away from Echo's shoulder. "I'm just a Seer. And the Dreamcatchers hate the Seers. Why would they want me now?"

"Because you are the Keeper, Beatrice. Your sight is stronger than anyone else's. Perhaps you can help us secure a treaty to bring over more Citizens. Or perhaps you can use your Visions to help guide us back into health." Echo's shoulders round in defeat. "Truth be told, my mother would be able to explain it better than I, Beatrice. She only used me to get to you."

"Your mother?"

Before he can explain anymore, a well-dressed man steps into the cabin from somewhere up front. The door slides open, admitting him, and once inside the room he bows deeply, but I don't know to whom he's bowing. I look to Echo, and he simply nods his head in return.

"Your Highness. We are anxious to welcome you back to Aura after your campaign in the City. Your Queen Mother has expressed that she wants you and your cargo to come straight to the palace and nowhere else." The man's dark eyes slide to mine, filled with contempt. He is intimidating, with dark skin to match his gaze and rounded muscles that stand out on his arms.

Another, smaller, man enters in after this one, dressed in rags and smudged with dirt. In his arms, he holds heavy, silver shackles that spill over the edges of his grasp and nearly drag on the ground. "These are for the Keeper, Your Highness."

"What?" I blurt and sit up straight. I'm not used to being called "the Keeper" yet, nor am I used to the gravity of the role I now fill. Technically, I am the leader of the Institution, where all the Seers live. But the Institution is back in the City, from which I chose to run. So, to say I'm the Keeper at all anymore might be a misunderstanding.

"She won't be put in chains." Echo uses a tone that I'm not used to hearing from him. It leaves little room to argue, and the small man bows and backs out of the room without turning his back on any of us.

"'Your Highness?'" Though I'm relieved the boy with the fetters is gone, I am confused as to why they are calling Echo by this honorific. "What do they mean 'Your Highness?'"

The man looks between us, and then expectantly settles his gaze on Echo, who clears his throat and shyly dips his head down. "I meant to tell you."

"Meant to tell me what?"

"Well, I'm ... I'm a prince. The prince of Aura."

I blink. Echo? A prince? When I look him over again, I can kind of see it. From his platinum-blond hair that's just short enough to get into his eyes, to the straight posture and regal lift of his chin. A prince. Prince Echo.

I realize that I've not said anything, and Echo and this man are staring at me. "Oh. Well … um … " I want to change the subject. Knowing now how important Echo is to Aura, it unsettles me. So, I turn my curiosity on the man instead. "And who is this? Also a prince?"

Echo laughs with a shake of his head. "That is my advisor, Avery. He's been preparing me for my future role as king." Leaning close to me, he adds in a whisper, "He's a little stuck up, so you'll have to excuse him."

"King?" This is too much. What did I get myself into? I sit back down on the couch and run a hand back through my hair, tangling the black tresses between my fingers.

"What's wrong, Beatrice?" I note that Echo has never really called me "Bea" before. Maybe it's a good thing that he doesn't; it would remind me too much of Gabe.

"It's a lot to take in, that's all. I thought you were just a Dreamcatcher, which was already a lot to take in. But now you are a royal Dreamcatcher?" I peer up at him as he sits down beside me and suddenly it doesn't seem so … important.

"There will be more that will be a lot to take in, unfortunately. Aura is very different than the City, and I'm afraid that your reception may not be as … welcomed as it would be among the Seers." Echo takes my hand with a squeeze. "You'll be okay, though. I promise I won't let you go through it alone."

Alone. That is exactly how I've left Gabe. I can't stop thinking about him, and I'm glad that Echo can't read my mind. I try to wipe the worry off my face by keeping my features flat, emotionless, and blank. "Thank you, Echo."

Outside, the landscape is still a blur. I get up and walk over to one of the ship's windows, putting a hand against the cool glass as I peer through. These are the moors, a stretch of featureless land riddled with rocks and tall grass. In my dreams with Echo, we were running to Aura, trying to avoid those who scavenged on the lost, the wandering. Now, as we race through, hovering feet above the ground, we stop for nothing or no one.

As I turn back to Echo, Avery is there beside him, whispering in his ear while keeping one eye focused in my direction. He is obviously talking about me, and the way he regards my presence is untrusting at best. I guess I don't expect much more than this, as I'm a Seer, an enemy to the Dreamcatchers. It isn't going to get any better once we get to Aura, either. Avery is one person, and I can handle one person's wary looks, but having a whole people anxious about my being in their homeland? I'm not sure I'm ready for this.

Echo waves his hand dismissively, shooing Avery away. "While Keeper Beatrice is here, she is my honored guest, and you are to treat her as you would any other honored guest that has come into our home."

"But, Your Highness, she is one of them." Avery regards me with that same untrusting glare.

"She is mine," Echo snaps.

"Yours?" I question in return.

Echo blushes and adds shyly, "My guest, I mean."

I watch him curiously for a little while, but relent with a nod, choosing not to press his statement any further.

Avery doesn't regard me any differently after Echo says this. In fact, his glare intensifies and becomes even more distrusting. He bows and takes his leave, and as he approaches the door to the cabin, it automatically slides open and shuts behind him with a hiss.

"Why did I decide to do this again?" I question my own intentions, plopping back down on the sofa-like bench where we sat before. I tug on the sleeves of my robe, the only thing that remains familiar to me, aside from Echo, whom I'm still learning. Most of the time, it feels like I've known him for as long as I've known Gabe, but then there are moments like this one when I feel completely disconnected and unsure about my decision to follow him.

"Because we need you here." Echo sits beside me and takes my hand into his. His grip is warm and comforting, and I immediately feel better.

Deep in the core of me, the closer we get to his homeland, the more anxious I become, and something that reminds me of pain starts to build. The thing is it's not painful, but a present, dull sensation. I wonder if this is akin to the pain that the Seers feel when they near Dreamcatchers, a pain that I've seem to have grown accustomed to when around Echo. It's just not the same with him for some reason. Echo is different.

I've never been one to fit in, either. My Sight is better than most others back at the City. Maybe I shouldn't use the term "better," but rather "clearer" since most of what I see comes true in some form or another. Maybe it's this difference that makes Echo's presence tolerable to me. I have a feeling that when I get to Aura the story will be much different.

"Echo, how am I going to be able to stay in Aura? Won't it hurt me?"

His eyebrows raise as if I've brought up something that he's forgotten. "Oh yeah. We have something prepared for that." Echo pushes a button to his left and speaks into an intercom. "Avery, please bring back the elixir for Keeper Beatrice to take now. She is getting uncomfortable."

Just as soon as Echo says this, Avery returns, scowl and all, balancing a silver tray on the palm of his hand. Extending it outward to me, the snifter of red liquid barely moves as he offers it. I pluck the glass off the tray and smell its contents. It's a sweet smell that reminds me of the strange citrus fruit that Echo once ate in one of my dreams. I shift my violet gaze to Echo in question. "And what is this?"

Avery leaves as Echo explains away the liquid. "We've made it especially for you. My mother knew that you'd not have an easy time adjusting to being around so many Dreamcatchers, so she had the scientists create a concoction that will dull your nerves and allow you to co-mingle with us."

I stare at Echo then look back down at the glass. "Co-mingle? You make it sound as if I will be staying for a long time."

"We hope you'll stay for as long as it takes to help rid us of the plague," Echo confesses, guiltily lowering his eyes. "At least, it was what I've told my mother."

I sigh and put the drink down on a table beside the sofa. "Echo, I shouldn't stay for too long. I'm the Keeper now. Who will record all the Visions that the Seers have back home? It's my job to make sure that all those Visions don't go undocumented. It's my job to keep them safe. I've already abandoned them for some … some unknown quest that I'm still not sure of." Tugging the hood of my robes over my head, I shift uncomfortably in my seat. "They probably won't even accept me once I go back home. I'm supposed to be there for them ... for Gabe ... and I ran away."

Echo tenses at the mention of Gabe, and I notice it, though he tries to make it seem like it's nothing at all by rolling his shoulders back and lifting his chin. "You're here because of me, and I'd never lead you astray, Beatrice." He squeezes my hand and reminds me that I did come here for him. Or because of him.

"I know, Echo. Or at least, I hope I know this. I must know it if I came all this way to help a people who hate me."

"We don't hate you."

"Okay, fine. Your people hate the Seers. The City. You must if you've attacked us. You nearly destroyed half the City in the process."

Echo lets go of my hand and stands up. Strolling to one of the windows, he puts his hand on the wall and peers outside. "The last Keeper was not honest with us. She betrayed us and kept us at bay when my mother negotiated certain terms with her. There was no choice but to go to war over it." He glances back at me. "We need Citizens just as much as you do. And we need the Seers to cooperate with us. And when they do not ... "

"When they do not? I'll have you know, Echo, that most of us had no idea what was going on. We were being trained for a war that we had little detail about. It's all I've ever known. Dreamcatchers were the enemy, and we had to kill them. The Keeper was so adamant about this, she watched her own Seers be killed so that the others would feed on fear and anger." My tone intensifies as I remember Connie, one of my good friends, bleeding out on the floor of the arena, riddled with bullets like she was nothing to no one. But she was something to me.

"Please don't get upset. I'm just telling you our side of it."

"And I'm asking you that before you go telling me your side of anything, you remember that I'm the Keeper. I'm not one of you. I have a people to protect. A city. And I'm here with you instead."

Echo looks away from the window and back at me. Walking to my side, he puts a hand on my arm and glances down into my eyes. I feel him staring through me, and for a moment, I feel as if he's inside of my head. I close my eyes, squeezing them tightly and open them again, frowning. "What are you doing?"

"I'm feeling what you are feeling."

That doesn't tell me much. Since when could he do this? Aside from when he was in my dreams? Then, I remember what I've known all along, and maybe have forgotten around Echo: Dreamcatchers can enter other's minds and kill us through touch. Echo has always been in my dreams, waiting for me there—calling for me. But now that he's actually in my world and out of my head, I've neglected that he is just as dangerous to me in person as he was in my mind.

Not that I think Echo would ever hurt me. Recalling his lips on mine, the gentle way in which he touches me, comforts me … protects me … I could never imagine Echo causing me any harm.

Still, it makes me uneasy having him inside my thoughts, and I pull away. "Stop. I don't want you to do that with me, do you understand? I don't … I don't like it. I'm not just another Seer. I'm the Keeper. I deserve that respect, just as I'll respect your position as a prince."

Echo pulls his hand away, wounded. "I'm sorry, Beatrice."

Immediately, I regret scolding him, and with a sigh, I pull Echo by the sleeve, urging him to sit back down beside me. We sit in silence as the landscape whizzes by outside, still one plain, blurry vision through the windows. Nothing needs to be said between us as Echo takes my hand again and cradles it in both of his. Immediately, I feel comforted once more, and I know that even if I'm venturing somewhere new, and I'm leaving the familiarity of the City behind, I still, at least, have Echo.

And he has me.

The intercom crackles and Avery's voice transmits through the speaker. "Your Highness, we have about ten minutes before we approach the Port of Aura."

Echo blinks out of his thoughts and clears his voice. "Very well, Avery. We will get ready to disembark." Turning to me, he nods toward the glass of elixir. "You should take that now. We're almost there."

I don't trust the potion, but I don't tell Echo this. I manage a smile and decide that for today, I'll drink the elixir. But for the days after that, I don't intend on being drugged while in the nest of the enemy. I toss the drink back and it tastes as sweet as it smells and goes down smoothly.

"Thank you. I'd hate for you to be in discomfort because of me."

"It's not your fault that the Seers are sensitive to Dreamcatchers."

"No, that would be the fault of those who originally created us." Echo brushes a strand of my jet-black hair back into my hood. "At least that's one thing we'll always have in common, right?"

"What's that?" I ask.

"We've both come from the same creators. People who had no business meddling with the gifts of the Maker." Echo smiles down at me, his body protectively close to mine. "I won't let anything happen to you, Beatrice. This won't be easy for you, but you won't regret it either. We need your help."

"I still don't understand how I can help you."

Echo's smile remains constant. "You will. My mother will explain everything to you in due time."

The ship glides into a port and gently lurches to a halt, hovering over a disembarking point. In the City, we don't use ships, though we're aware of the technology. The streets and tall buildings don't allow for their use, and so most have decided to stick with automobiles and helicopters. Glancing out the window, it's immediately apparent that ships are the main mode of transport in Aura, with all different types of vessels lined up around the tarmac. I look around, ducking my head down to try and get a glimpse of the city itself, but I can't find it.

"You can't see Aura from here. The Port of Aura is kept about twenty miles away so that the pollution doesn't taint our air and stain our buildings." Echo pushes a button on the wall, and the soft whisper of hydraulics precedes the hull door opening. It extends downward into stairs that stop short, hovering just above the ground. Echo walks down first, then holds his hand up for mine to help me down as well.

There are others on the tarmac. Others who have their eyes on us specifically. Or maybe, they just have their eyes on me. My robe blows in the constant flow of wind that pushes sand across the tarmac in ribbons. I put a hand up to my eyes and speak over the howl. "Is it always so windy?"

"Yes, but Aura is surrounded by high walls to break the flow of the wind. It's much more bearable there." Echo tugs on the hood of my robe, keeping one of his hands by his eyes to shield and protect it from the whipping winds. "I bet you are glad that you wore this now, aren't you?"

"I always wear this, Echo." For the first time, I laugh, and Echo puts his arm around my shoulders to escort me to a white limo with golden rims that is parked not too far from where we are.

"Wow. Fancy, aren't we?"

"You have no idea." Echo opens the door for me with a grin that promises I've seen nothing yet.

Chapter 2

Echo was right. I hadn't seen anything yet. As the limousine cruises up to the gates of Aura, I can't do anything but stare out the window in complete awe. Aura is the complete opposite of the City. I immediately understand where their city gets its name from, with its golden-hued buildings and sparkling, translucent glass windows. Everything glitters, even the sand as it whips around the tall walls that protect the city from the dry gusts of wind.

I place my fingers on the limo's window and press my forehead to the glass as I try to get a better look. I can feel Echo's eyes on me as I react probably as a child would at the first sight of something they've never seen before. There are no skyscrapers here, no crowded, jumbled row homes with sooty exteriors. The buildings are no more than two floors high, allowing for a precious view of the almost purple mountains that peek up in the distance.

"Echo … this is beautiful … "

"Thank you. This is the home of the Dreamcatchers. After the City banished us, we had to travel a long way to find a place where we'd be safe from attack. We chose this area because it's so dry, hot, and humid, that we don't know who'd willingly want to come out here. Besides us, of course." Echo scoots over on the leather seat to sidle up closer to me. "It is beautiful though, isn't it? This is my first homecoming, to be honest. I've never been out of the city for this long."

The gates click back when they are fully open, and the limo pulls forward once more. As soon as we are moving again, I can see the crowds of people who line the main street, which leads directly to an impressive palace that stands center of Aura, just like our Institution does in the City. The people are all dressed in white, some with different colored trims on their robes. They reach out for the car, calling for Echo, wanting to see their prince.

We pull around a circle in front of the palace, and the courtyard is also filled with Dreamcatchers, cheering for Echo's arrival. He brushes a hand down his robe, smoothing the wrinkles from the soft fabric. "Are you ready?"

Then, a sudden fear grips me. "Do they know I am with you?"

Echo's pale blue eyes meet mine. "No."

I want to slap him, and it takes everything in me not to lose my temper. "What?"

"They don't know you are with me. I did not tell anyone I was bringing you home. It is a part of my strategy."

I lock the limo's doors. We stare at each other for a long while, my chest rising and falling in anger. "How could you put me in this situation, Echo? I am the Keeper. I'm the leader of your enemy. You are putting me in great danger, and you know you are."

Echo, in his ever-calm way, reaches out and helps pull the hood of my robe up over my head. "You will be fine because you are my guest, and it is a law in Aura that we must treat our guests with utmost respect." He pauses. "Not that we get many guests … ever."

Now, I do smack him. My hand makes contact with his arm, and I scowl. "You better not get me hurt."

"Listen to them. They are too happy to see me. I doubt they'll even take notice of you." Echo unlocks the doors and slides across the seat to the other side where he can exit first. "Driver, we are ready."

The chauffeur exits the vehicle and appears again beside Echo's door. As soon as he opens it, the sound of cheering flows into the car and I hear Echo suck in a deep breath. He exits first, and when I see his hand lower back into the limo, I reach out and gently rest my palm against his, using the offered support to help me out of the car.

As my feet touch the floor, my black robes fall all around me like darkness covering the day, and I'm free of the limousine. Lifting my chin, my eyes move from the ground to the people, and I swallow as the cheering comes to an abrupt stop when they see my violet irises. Almost all at once, they take a step back, and no one makes a sound.

I tighten my grip around Echo's hand, sure that in the next moment they are going to rush us and kill me where I stand. Here I am, their sworn enemy, the representation of the Keeper before me who persecuted them, ran them out of the City and killed many of them, including their princess. I stand before them as if none of that had ever happened. I know, if I were in their place, I'd certainly want to see myself dead, too.

Muttering very quietly to Echo, I tug on his hand. "Let's go."

Echo seems to sense the danger as well, and he half drags me through the throng of people and toward the palace stairs. As soon as he's in view of the guards who stand by the main entrance, they move at the same time, stiff and rigid, and escort us the rest of the way. Before I know it, we are out of the humid outside and standing on a gold and white marble floor of a vast welcoming room. I've never seen anything like it before, and much like I did when coming to the city, I openly stare, almost forgetting about the awkward silence that has replaced their cheering outside.

"This is where you live?"

Echo nods his head, letting go of my hand to walk ahead of me. He spins around, arms out by his sides, gesturing to the room. "Well, not in this room, of course, but yes, this is the Dreamcatcher Palace. My great grandparents established it when they established the city of Aura."

I look up, peering at the paintings that have been carefully created on the ceilings. Most of them depict tales of the Maker with people from a time way before ours. A large chandelier dangles from the middle of the room with crystal teardrops hanging off its many tiers. Candles flicker in their sconces hung around the perimeter of the room. "Everything is so … so golden here. It's like some sort of—"

"Dream?" Echo chuckles, holding his hand out for mine again. "Come. I don't want to keep my mother waiting. I'm sure by now she's probably heard of your arrival."

"You said your mother knows I am here?" I take his hand and follow him down a long hallway with mirrors placed on one side to reflect the beautiful view of the windows opposite of it.

"Mother knows everything. Whether she believes it or not is another story. Her abilities are far more than mine. She knows my thoughts as soon as I step into the room, and she knows well that I thought about bringing you back to Aura to help us."

We round the end of the hallway where two ornate white doors with gold leafing stand closed in front of us. The entrance is flanked by two guards holding guns across their chests. I look up at the doors, then to the guards, and finally back to Echo. "This is it?"

Echo offers me an encouraging smile. "It will be okay, Beatrice."

I sure hope so. Even the guards look at me in contempt, when they probably should be standing at attention. Echo pays it no mind, though, and we walk by them and into the room beyond.

The welcoming room is nothing compared to the throne room. Seated on an embellished chair set on a dais is a beautiful woman dressed in a white, silk gown that hugs close to her form. Her hair is so blond it's almost violet, and it's done up in pins with crystals that sparkle when they catch the light. The throne is situated in the middle of the vast room, which has little else in it besides two cushioned chairs to her left and to her right. On the right hand chair there's a long white rose that rests across the seat.

I hesitantly continue to follow Echo into the middle of the room, where he half bows, never letting go of my hand. His mother's pale blue eyes never leave me and hardly meet her son's presence at all.

"You've brought me the Keeper, my son?" Her voice is soft and gentle, and though her gaze is stern, there's no hardness in her words.

"I've brought you Seer Beatrice, the current Keeper of the City, my Queen Mother." Echo tugs on my hand, and I take another step forward.

"She's a pretty little thing, isn't she, my love?" The queen rises to her feet, the dress rippling around her the way water does when it's disturbed from its still state. "Too pretty to be such a threat to our people."

"She is not a threat, my Queen Mother. She's not like the Keeper before her. She came here to help us with our … our situation."

The Queen smiles the most beautiful smile. I can't take my eyes off of her as she steps down the dais and approaches her son, and consequentially me as well. "Oh, did she? And what made her want to do that? Because I know very well that it would be the most unacceptable thing to do, according to her people."

"Me." Echo states simply.

I've not said a word, nor do I intend to. I listen with interest to the exchange between mother and son, figuring I have no place in their conversation just yet. Standing tall with my chin held up, I try not to look as pathetic and lonely as I feel right now. If only Gabe could see me, standing in the face of the enemy, poised and collected. I wonder if he'd be proud of me for keeping my mouth shut, or if he'd roll his eyes at the fact that I refuse to say anything just yet.

The queen circles me like I am cattle waiting to be bought and sold. I lift my chin just a little more to show that I'm not intimidated by her. While she might be Echo's mother, it's not easy to ignore seventeen years of being told that this woman who is standing in front of me is my enemy. That I should want to kill her and watch her bleed all over her precious marble floors. To turn her silk white dress into a satisfying crimson.

Reaching out, she grabs me by the wrist for just a moment before I pull my arm out of her grasp. "She has many violent thoughts inside of her head, I feel," the queen assesses and stops circling me when she's in front of us once more. "I can feel them coming from her. She is radiating violence."

Echo looks at me with a glance of betrayal. I shrug one of my shoulders and finally speak for the first time. "Would I be able to read the minds of your people and yourself, I would probably come to find the same thing." I pause, not sure what I should call this woman in front of me. I recall the words "your highness" used in the fairytale books that we were allowed to read when we were young, and I go with that. "Your Highness."

"This might be true. It is not every day, or ... ever, if I dare say, that we have the Keeper inside of our walls. And for my son, the beloved of his people, to bring her back home, hold her hand even ... well, it is much to take in. I do hope that you forgive my people for their thoughts, just as I shall try and look over the fact that you wish to turn my dress the color of blood."

I say nothing.

"So this is the girl for whom your sister foolishly got herself killed?" The queen's blue eyes focus on Echo, waiting for an answer. There's a tension between them that can't be broken, and obviously this is because of Paradigm.

Before the battle between the Dreamcatchers and Seers broke out, Paradigm, Echo's young sister, snuck out of Aura and made her way to the City in order to eliminate me, or at least, that was her plan. She had found out about her brother's plan to find and convince me to somehow stop the fight before it even began.

Paradigm's special ability was to be able to fit in, much like a pattern. She could mold herself to belong to others, convince them that she was a part of them. Unfortunately, though, because of my Vision, she failed and was caught and put in front of a firing squad. It was then she told us that the Dreamcatchers were coming, and it was from that moment on when everything got to be too serious.

Echo didn't answer his mother's loaded question. He walked over to my side and stood by, tall and unified, as if protecting me.

"And what do you plan to do with her here, Echo? You've gone much out of your way, endangering good Dreamcatchers, like Enigma, in order to get your hands on this little Keeper of yours."

"Beatrice will know what to do," Echo finally replies, but I have no idea what he is talking about.

"What to do? About what?" I immediately ask the question before he can go any further with this plan of his.

"About the plague." Echo turns himself on an angle to look down at me. I can see his face under the edges of my hood, which is still pulled up over my head, shrouding my face. I feel comfortable and protected inside of my robes, as if the Institution itself had managed to wrap its arms around me and remind me where I've come from.

"How would I know what to do about that?" I look between them both, though the queen is no longer looking at either of us. She moves like she walks above the ground and approaches a tall window, made in the old French style, long and narrow. In our history books, we've learned that the windows were made that way to allow the panes to be thrown back and for the air to circulate through the room. The heat and wind outside doesn't allow for this option, though, and the windows are kept tightly shut.

She puts her hand on the glass and peers outside, and when I look to what she's focusing on, all I can see are the tall tops of green and brown cacti and some thick leafs from the palm trees that survived the war. Her hands are small and slender, like that of a child's, and her long, stark blond hair falls down her back in thick tresses. She shines in the sun, as if she were part of the sun herself.

"I figured that maybe you'd See it. That is what the Seers do, is it not? And aren't you the Seer with the best Vision?" Echo asks these questions of me, and a part of me wonders if he truly doesn't know the answer to them. I've never had a Vision of this place before, nor have I ever seen a plague.

"Echo, I don't even know what it is that your people are going through. How would I be able to … I didn't even know what Aura looked like before now … "

"And do you need to know these things before you See them? Isn't it possible that if you stay here for a little while you'll figure it out?" Echo stands in the way of my view of his mother, who still stands by the window and watches outside, waiting for something.

"I don't know. But that doesn't mean I'll ever see anything that has to do with here." I step forward and lower my voice. "Is this why you brought me here, Echo? In hopes that I'd See something? You know I can't control my Visions. You know that."

Echo shakes his head, his hands pulling up into the comfort of his long bell sleeves. "I don't know how your gift works any more than I understand my own sometimes. All I know is that our Citizens are dying, and without them … we'll fall apart, just like you'll fall apart without yours."

"It is true, Keeper Beatrice." The queen turns away from the window and looks back at me and Echo. "We are in danger. There have been reports of Dreamcatchers having caught the illness now. It is only a matter of time before it spreads amongst us and we can't heal it anymore."

I still don't understand how I fit into this picture. I swallow as the pressure builds and I'm beginning to feel as if I'm being pulled between the both of them. "So, what am I to do? I can't cure plagues. I am just the Keeper, and I can't even do that job when I'm here, in Aura."

"You can get us more Citizens." She makes her way back over to where we stand, her dress' train dragging on the floor behind her. "Healthier ones. We can use them to heal ourselves after purging Aura of the infected."

My mouth opens, gaze shifting between Echo and the queen. "Excuse me?"

"The Citizens belong to the both of us, Keeper Beatrice. We are both made by them, and we both need them to keep our powers balanced." The queen starts to continue, but I cut her off, maybe a bit rudely.

"We don't use the Citizens to resurrect and heal ourselves, though. We don't use them to tap into any special abilities. The Dreamcatchers kill them in order to become more powerful. The Seers stay around them in order to balance our Sight."

"No? You don't kill them?" The queen barks a laugh at this and snaps her fingers. A servant scurries from somewhere near the side of the room with a digipad in his hands. He offers it to the queen, head dipped down so that no eye contact is made. The servant is a Citizen; I can tell by his dull brown hair and scraggly physique, despite the finery of his clothing.

The queen turns the digipad on and slides a few of the screens around until one is made visible from under the others. She pushes the face of the digipad and the picture begins to play, showing a short clip of a Training Games session. One of the ones from when the old Keeper made us use Citizens as targets. "What is this, then, Keeper?"

I frown almost immediately. "We didn't choose to do that. We were made to do it. They were convicts, criminals that she had brought in for target practice." I glance away from the digipad and train my violet gaze on Echo. "If this is how you wanted me to help you, Echo, I don't think I can."

"Oh, darling Keeper," the queen begins, handing the digipad off to the servant who brought it to her. She brushes her hair out of her face and approaches her throne once more, her walk slow and languid. "It is much too late for thoughts of home. Now that you are here, you are going to stay until we figure out a way to fix our little dilemma."

Panic sets in. "Are you keeping me your prisoner then?" I direct the question to Echo, at whom I immediately feel most angry. How dare he bring me into this unsafe situation, pitting the future of his entire people on my shoulders when I can't do anything about it. "Huh, Echo? Is that what I am to you now?"

I see the same sort of panic set in Echo, and it comforts me. "Mother, just let her go back home. She can't help us, so why keep her here?"

The queen sits back down and folds her hands in her lap. She looks younger sitting on a chair that is much too big for her, but is meant for only her to sit in. "Because, Echo, my love, this is how diplomacy works. You either achieve it through compromise, or you force it through ultimatums. Keeper Beatrice here is going to get us what we need, or else she won't be allowed to go back home." She looks over her nose at me, chin dipped downward, dangerous. "And she has something she wants very much at home, don't you, Keeper Beatrice?"

Gabe. I have no idea how he is doing since I left his bedside and ended up here. The guilt of it mixes with the panic of being kept a prisoner, and my eyes narrow in anger. I feel as if I need to protect Gabe, to keep him out of this, but against my will, he's been dragged in, and all at once, it's too late to not have him involved. "Leave him out of this."

"Do you see, Echo? This girl does not love you the way you love her. Now, she will come to love you through some means. It is integral for an alliance to be formed between our people. We need their Citizens, and it is not fair that they should get to keep them all." The queen remains perfectly poised upon her throne, like a perfectly dressed princess doll placed in a seated position.

"Love me?" I stare at Echo, who colors and turns his face away from mine either to hide it, or to address his mother full-on.

"Mother, no. Let's just let her return." Echo protectively steps in front of me like one would if trying to shield another from something harmful. The harm here being his very mother, who looks nothing like danger would, but there's still something very dangerous about her.

"That won't be happening, Echo, my love. Keeper Beatrice will stay here until she has the Visions we need from her. And she will return home only when she's a princess of the Dreamcatchers and has no choice but to favor both the Seers and the Dreamcatchers equally."

"A princess?" Echo and I say in unison.

"Yes. A princess. At the end of the month, you two will be wed, and the long awaited for alliance between our people will be reached. We will live together again the way we used to before the Dreamcatchers were persecuted and sent out of the City all those years ago. We will both have use of the Citizens, and they shall belong to no one in particular." The Dreamcatcher Queen sits up a bit taller now that her plan has been laid out in the open. She smiles a pretty little smile, surely amused by the startled looks from me and Echo. "We will be equal, and the Seers will no longer be the ruling hand."

"Wed?" I turn to Echo. "Echo? What is this all about?"

"I don't know. She never said anything about any of this until right now. This … this isn't how it was supposed to go, Beatrice, I swear."

Marry Echo? All I can think about is Gabe, comatose back in the City. All those times I kissed Echo in my dreams … the time I blindly followed him here, to the home of the enemy. What did I think was going to happen? Did I think they were going to welcome me with open arms? And now, I'm being held their prisoner. I am being forced to be the bride of the enemy if I want to be able to return to the City any time soon. And even that's not a guarantee.

"Mother, I'd like to talk about this. Alone."

"Very well, Echo. Take your bride to her room and you can come back down here and have whatever discussion you'd like to have with me. You can put her in the guest rooms for now. I will send a contingent of guards to make sure she doesn't try to get very far, should she choose to run."

Where would I even run to? The Port of Aura is miles away, and I have no idea how to get to a vehicle in order to flee. I don't even know my way out of the palace, let alone the city.

Echo takes my hand, as if sensing my obvious unease and the multitude of questions that pour through my mind, and I calm just a touch. He leads me out of the throne room without saying anything else to his mother, and as we walk away, I can feel her cool stare locked on me, untrusting but victorious. She has cornered the Keeper, and I'm sure she's proud of herself, probably just as much as I feel as if I failed not only me and the City, but Gabe most of all.

Chapter 3

Echo takes me down another long hallway and to a set of pink-hued, ornate doors. We walk in silence, which is probably for the best, since I'm dying to scream and yell at him for putting me in this situation. Nothing graceful could come from my mouth right now, so I savor the quiet.

He turns the handle and pushes on the doors, and they give way into a large, beautiful bedroom with a baby pink, canopied bed dead center of it all. I'm shocked at the grandeur of something obviously meant for a child to inhabit. The teddy bears on the cushioned bench at the foot of the bed are all lined up, arms outstretched toward me and Echo.

"Leave us," Echo commands the guards, and they look at me, then at each other in hesitation. "Was I not clear? Leave us. Now."

The guards eventually salute and make their exit, closing the door behind them. I remind myself to breathe since the anger has closed itself around my throat like two hands trying to squeeze the air from me. When I can form words, the first three to leave my lips come out shaky. "How dare you!"

"Beatrice, I didn't know she would do this."

"You told me that you needed me. You didn't say that there is absolutely no plan, that you are relying on Visions that I can't promise, and that your mother, who very clearly hates me, now wants to force me into an alliance by making me marry you!" I snap back at Echo, closing the space between us as I point a finger into his chest. "You tricked me."

31

"I didn't ... listen ... "

"You tricked me, you made me leave behind my post in the City, and worst of all, you made me leave Gabe all alone in his coma."

"I didn't make you do anything." Echo's tone goes from being apologetic to defensive and he steps away from my touch. "You followed me here. Willingly. You wanted to help, remember? You said you wanted to help."

"You didn't say I was going to be your prisoner until I can figure out how to cure the plague!" I blurt.

"That wasn't my idea. It's my mother's idea. She's a very stern woman, but she's very passionate about her people. She doesn't want to see them suffer anymore." Echo turns around and starts to circle the bed in the middle of the room.

"Who? The Dreamcatchers or the Citizens?"

"Both, I guess. We cannot be without the Citizens, so in that way, she's probably upset that they must suffer, too. But ever since a few Dreamcatchers have come down with the illness as well, she's been a bit panicky." Echo picks up a porcelain doll from a nearby bookshelf and delicately holds it in his hands. "That, and ever since the execution of my sister, things haven't quite been the same between us. I think she blames me for it. I know she does."

I watch Echo as he stares down at the doll, and it dawns on me that we are in her room and those are Paradigm's dolls and teddy bears. This is her bed, her writing desk, her balcony window. I become wary of my surroundings and walk over to Echo's side, attracted to the comfort that seems to emanate from him. "It wasn't your fault."

"She wanted to find you because of me. I should have never told her about my dream. I shouldn't have said anything about my plan to find you, either." Echo sighs and turns to look down at me, the doll still in his hands. "She hated the thought that I would want to find a Seer to fix our problems here. She was jealous that I wanted nothing more than to dream of you."

I blush and worry on my bottom lip as I try to find words to say that would make sense right now. "It wasn't your fault," I say again, this time without looking at him.

"You say it so easily, Beatrice, but do you really believe it? That it wasn't my fault?" Echo puts the doll back on the shelf, sitting her neatly beside the others, all with carefully painted faces and vibrant glass eyes.

"Does it matter what I believe? If anything, it was my fault. If I wasn't who I am ... you'd have no interest in me anyway. You would have never found me, or caught me, or anything. I'd be just another Seer." I reach out and tug on a ringlet of chestnut that has been neatly tied behind one of the dolls' heads. "Right? So ... we can share the blame."

"If you want. It still doesn't help that now I have my mother and you angry with me."

"Then you shouldn't have lied to me about the situation." I glance about the room. "I don't want to stay in here. It's not right."

"I think that's the point. My mother probably wants you to be as uncomfortable as possible. The Keeper took her daughter away from her, and so now she gets to take the Keeper away from the City." Echo sighs and takes my wrist in his hand. "Beatrice ... I don't want this any more than you do." He pauses as his cheeks color. "I mean ... not that I wouldn't want to marry you ... but ... Let me talk to her, okay?

I clear my throat and go back to staring at the dolls. "Fine. Talk to her." Peeking to Echo, I watch as his blush fades away and turn to face him once more. "I'm sorry I was mad at you. I guess I thought that I'd be walking into something more … definite. Something I really could help with … "

Echo brushes a thumb down my cheek, just like he used to in my dreams, under the tree with the long branches. "You'll help. I just know it. It's who you are, Beatrice. It's a part of you." Leaning down, Echo brushes his lips against mine in a quick kiss that sends tiny sparks of excitement through my fingers and up my arms.

I gently nudge him away from me, breaking the kiss. Mixed with the excitement is the undeniable guilt that I feel for leaving Gabe behind, and I can't help but to think of his kisses, even if it's Echo doing the kissing. "We'll see, Echo. We'll see."

He smiles at me, unfazed by the breaking of the kiss, and makes his way to the double doors that lead back out to the hallway. "Keeper Beatrice is to be left undisturbed for the rest of the night. I'll bring her dinner later," Echo informs the guards in his princely manner which I can't help but find ever so handsome. He looks back at me one more time, smiles, then exits the room after I smile in return.

Now left alone, I study the room one more time and tentatively sit on the corner of the bed. Pink, gauzy curtains have been tied back to the posts, and with a simple tug of a ribbon, I let them fall close, one-by-one. Sitting in the middle of the mattress, enclosed by the curtains, I take a deep breath and wipe my face with my hands. "What did I get myself into?" I ask no one, flopping back onto the bed. It doesn't take long before the long day catches up to me, and I fade into a much-needed sleep.

***

In the infirmary, Gabe's room is left undisturbed. Nurses buzz about everywhere else, but the door to Gabe's personal bed remains closed, shutting out the busy noises of the hospital outside. He lays in bed, covered up to the neck with thick, white blankets that seem so bright against his tanned skin. Monitors are hooked up to his frail form, and they all beep in their own rhythms, each noise meaning something completely different in its cacophony of pulsating sounds.

I sit beside Gabe, one hand on his own cold and sweaty hand. The nurses say he can hear me, but I feel funny talking to someone who can't talk back, so I don't say anything to him. Instead, I watch the way his eyes roll behind his eyelids, and I wonder what he's dreaming about. Hopefully it's something much more pleasant than the last thing he had to face in his waking moments: his own Keeper betraying him in a final act against her Seers.

"I'm so proud of you," I whisper to him and put my head down on his arm, snuggling it close.

The truth is, I am scared, and I hate coming here. I hate seeing him like this, and I hate the way he can only listen, and I hate how he can't say anything back. I want to hear his voice more than anything in this broken world. I want to listen to him speak my name, to call for me down the hallway on the way to the cafeteria for ham day. Maker, I'd give anything just to have him back.

Then, the machines all start to sound in unison, their high-pitched squealing alerting the nursing staff outside. I stand up from the chair beside the bed and am quickly pushed back in a sea of infirmary personnel to the point where I can't see Gabe anymore.

"Gabe?" I call for him, as if he's going to reply, and of course, he doesn't. The nurses push a machine into the room and power it up beside the bed. One of them is telling me to stand back, and I realize only then that I've been pushing into the crowd, trying to figure out what is going on.

"Gabe!"

But he doesn't answer back.

And I don't know what is happening.

***

When I wake up, I feel awful. My head is throbbing and my body hurts. I stumble out of the bed and flail across the room until I crash into a side table and knock it and all its contents on the floor. Holding my head in my hands, I swear something is screaming inside of me, a high-pitched squealing that threatens to crack me in two. It takes everything in me to call out, "Echo!"

I yell his name over and over again until I hear the doors open, and that's when I fall to the ground, unable to take it anymore. A young woman kneels by my side and puts her hands on my shoulders, trying to get me to hold still. Another pushes something cool to my mouth until I have no choice but to open it and drink whatever it is that she's offering me. The taste is familiar. It's the serum.

Echo's voice cuts through the piercing noise. "Beatrice? Are you okay?"

The screeching starts to fade, but my headache remains. It's the sort of headache I get after having a Vision, and by the way the two girls are staring at me, I can only figure that my eyes are glowing now as well. I catch my breath and put a hand back to my head, rubbing it fiercely. "It's getting better … "

Wrapping his arms around me, Echo pulls me into an embrace, rocking me as the turmoil slowly begins to unravel, releasing me before disappearing all together. "I let you sleep for the night, so you didn't have the chance to drink more serum before the last bout of it wore off." Brushing my black hair out of my face, he looks down into my eyes and asks, "You had a Vision?"

That's when I remember the beeping noises from the monitors by Gabe's bedside. The last thing I want is for my dream to have been a Vision, but the glowing of my eyes makes it very apparent that that is what happened. "Gabe is in trouble."

"What?"

"He's in trouble. Something is going to happen to him, Echo. Something bad." I drop my hands back to my sides and sigh sadly. "And I'm here."

Echo shifts uncomfortably as I talk about Gabe, and there's a pause between what I say and what he says. "Well … I … I hope that whatever happened … doesn't … happen." It's obvious that Echo doesn't want to discuss Gabe. He stares at me, marveled by the glow of my eyes. "You are beautiful like this."

Normally, I would probably turn red at those words, but I can't help but to think of the wall of nurses surrounding Gabe's bed, and I sigh. "Why couldn't it have been a silly dream?" Tears well in my eyes; I can feel them swell the more I think about Gabe and whatever danger he is in.

Echo rocks me back and forth to comfort me, and it works. I calm myself, knowing that there's nothing I can do here. If I want to get home, I'll have to be rational and think about a way out of this situation. Crying in the arms of the Prince of Aura isn't going to help me get back to Gabe. "I guess this is as good a time as any to introduce you to your two servants for your stay here." He nods his head toward the two young women who stand nearby, each of them staring at me, probably because they've never seen eyes glow the way mine do.

"Hello," I greet them quietly, noticing also that they are both Citizens, with their almost-black hair and dark eyes.

"This is Irene and Jamie. They will take care of you while you are staying here with us." Echo lets me go, unwrapping himself from around me. I almost immediately miss the comfort of his arms, and I want so desperately for him to go back to holding me. "And it would probably do you well not to cross with my mother again any time soon. Not if you want to leave Aura in the near future. She's still quite upset and set on our marriage."

"You two would look beautiful together," Irene blurts, only to be slapped on the arm by Jamie. Covering her mouth with her hands, Irene offers an apologetic look without saying anything else.

"Excuse her, Keeper Beatrice. Irene has a habit of saying whatever comes to mind." Jamie curtsies, which throws me off guard. I've never had anyone curtsey to me before. It's unnerving, and I almost immediately wish she never did it because just a moment after, Irene does the same.

"Yes, excuse me, Keeper Beatrice," Irene echoes as she rises from her curtsey.

I look at Echo, and he grins. "They've brought you a change of clothes too, if you'd like. It'd probably be easier if you didn't stick out as a Seer in that black robe."

Looking down at my robe, I frown. "There isn't anything wrong with my robe, Echo." But I understand his point and instead of arguing to stay in my own clothes, I relent with a nod. "Very well. I'll get changed then."

"And when you're done, you can come to breakfast. You've slept all through the night." He nods his head to the two young women who seem too eager to help me into clothes that aren't my robe, then takes his leave.

When Echo is gone, Irene and Jamie immediately get to work. They bring in a clothing rack with a few dresses hung on wire hangers, and already I can tell that I'm going to dread this.

Irene bounces forward and offers to take my robe from me by reaching out and simply grabbing it. "Off with this ugly thing!"

Mortified, Jamie steps forward and carefully pries the robe out of Irene's hands. "Irene! Stop being so rude will you? This is the Keeper. She's in charge of all the Citizens back in the City. Don't you know that? You can't just treat her things so roughly."

"It's really not a big deal, I promise. I just … " I give the dresses another wary look. "I'm not so sure I'm up for those. I don't wear dresses very often, you see … just my robe and a jump suit for the days when we have the Training Games—" I stop myself, realizing that I'll never have to take part in Training Games ever again if I didn't want to. Now, I'm the Keeper, and it's my job to make sure everyone else is training. But training for what now that the battle between the Dreamcatchers and the Seers is over? Or, is it really over at all?

Irene ducks her head down in shame. "I'm sorry, Keeper Beatrice." Admonished, the young woman picks a dress from the rack and holds it out for me to see. "They are very beautiful though, aren't they? You'll look much like the queen in these."

The very thought is unsettling. I don't want to look like the queen. I want to look as different from her as I possibly can so that no one confuses me with the impossible woman, not that we could be easily confused. With my midnight black hair compared to her almost violet-blond tresses? No, a dress wasn't going to make us any more alike.

"May I ask you some questions?" I ask as Irene puts the dress aside, then taps on my arms, signaling for me to hold them out by my sides. Like a busy little bee hovering around a flower, she buzzes around me taking my measurements.

"Sure!" she squeaks and goes right back to her measuring.

"You are both Citizens, right?"

Irene stops her measuring and casts a look to Jamie, who nods her head. "We are, Keeper Beatrice."

I don't really need to ask the question to know. The Citizens of Aura look much different than the Dreamcatchers, whose features are mostly light, with startling blue eyes that can't go unnoticed. The Citizens, on the other hand, have dark features, with brown or black hair and dark, muddy-brown eyes. Occasionally, back in the City, one could find a Citizen with light hair and dark eyes, but they weren't very common.

"And there's a plague that is spreading among the Citizens here, is there not?" I put my arms down when Irene is done taking my measurements. Just as soon as she's out of the way, Jamie steps forward with the amethyst-purple dress in her arms, which she lays out on the rose pink-covered bed.

Mentioning the plague brings them both to a stop. Jamie lowers her eyes, which begin to fill with tears, and I immediately regret asking about such a touchy subject. "There is, Keeper. It's the most horrible plague. No one has heard anything of it, and the rumor was that you'd help us get rid of it somehow."

"The rumor?" Brushing my hand over the light fabric of the dress, I think through this, and realize that I've suddenly become their savior, just like I had for the Seers and Citizens back in the City ... before the invasion. Before I left them behind. "Please remember that rumors ... well ... they are just that, rumors. I can't promise you I can do anything. I can't promise the answers will be shown to me."

Tears finally fall from the corners of Jamie's eyes and she sniffles with a nod, her nose and cheeks turning red from being upset. "Yes, we understand, Keeper Beatrice. But, it is still okay for us to hope." She slips the buttons loose that run down the back of the dress in a straight line. Picking it up off the bed, she gathers it up by the waist and holds it by my face. "Arms up."

Irene picks up Jamie's story where she left off, watching as her companion pulls the dress down over my head. I slip my hands through the short sleeves and lift my chin up over the high collar with the ornate, silver button. "The Citizens live in the Camp just outside Aura's walls. The plague has spread so quickly that it's nearly wiped out the whole community. The Breeding tents have been quiet since no new babies are being born. Or, if they are born, they don't live for very long. Family dwellings have been suffering, and sometimes whole units are wiped out in just a matter of days."

Jamie chokes back a sob and moves behind me to button the dress up. Her fingers tremble against my back, and I wait for Irene to explain the young woman's reaction.

"Jamie just found out a week ago that her whole family unit had … well … they died in the plague," Irene explains, moving around me to help her fellow servant with the buttoning.

"All of them. Even my little brother, and his fifth birthday was just a couple of weeks away." Jamie sniffles and steps away from the dress when it's fastened. They both come back around to stand in front of me, and for the first time, I look at Jamie now that I know the burden that she's been carrying around with her. I wish there was something I could do to ease her pain, but I know there's nothing that anyone can do to make her feel better. I don't understand the bond that others have with families, since I've never had one my own, but I do understand what it feels like to lose someone, and memories of Connie and Mae's pretty smiles flash through my mind.

"I am sorry to hear that, Jamie. It must be very difficult for you to keep working here when you know that Citizens are suffering elsewhere." For a moment, I think about Gabe suffering back home while I'm being pampered in some elaborate boudoir that doesn't even belong to me.

I follow Jamie over to a small bench-like chair that is situated in front of a vanity table with an oval mirror. Sitting before the mirror, I watch through the reflection as they take out hair-dressing supplies, including brushes, combs, fancy hairpins, pomades, and other materials.

"We hear stories about the plague through the palace. About what happens when someone comes down with it … " Jamie bites on her lip, unable to go on.

"They get very sick," Irene picks up, handing some oil over to Jamie, who starts to brush her fingers through my hair, preparing it for whatever it is they are about to do with the long, black tresses. "First, they get a fever … and then, they start to moan and scream for relief from the pain. Then, the blood comes." She casts a glance at Jamie as she continues to share the details. "Through the nose and the eyes. And then they start to cough it up. Some say that once the blood comes, there's nothing that can be done, since the body inside has already started to come apart."

"And once the blood comes, it only takes a few hours for them to die. But it's a long, agonizing few hours of immense pain. Only a few have come back from the fever, but no one has come back from the blood." Jamie puts a hot iron aside and wipes her nose with a handkerchief that she pulls out of a hidden pocket in her dress. "It only took a day for my whole family to die. One day they were fine, and the next day my mother came home with the fever and it was all over."

"You mentioned a Breeding tent? With babies? What is that?" I try to change the subject away from Jamie's family, if only so she doesn't have to think about them bleeding from their eyes and nose until there's no more blood in them to be bled.

"The Dreamcatchers have set up Birthing Tents, where women spend their whole fertile lives growing and giving birth to new Citizens or Dreamcatchers." She pauses a moment and looks away from me. "Or Seers, but those children are disposed of just as soon as they open their pretty violet eyes."

This isn't very surprising to me. In the City, much the same thing happens. If a child is born a Dreamcatcher, they are given to the Institution to dispose of. It is something else I wish to change, something that will have to wait until I get back home. At least I can have them sent to Aura to be raised, instead of killed on the spot in the City. Perhaps it is something to think about mentioning to Echo, to see if the opposite could be done here.

But the thought of Birthing Tents is a little much for me. "So, that is all those women do?"

"Yes. Most of the Citizens who are in family units have their own children as well. But to keep the population strong, we have Birthing Tents. The more Citizens we have, the more work can be done." Jamie curls my hair and piles the ringlets up on top of my head. They are fastened with silver pins that are ornamented with tiny purple beads. With my hair out of my face, the raven wings tattooed around my eyes and down my cheeks are much more prominent, and they make my still-glowing violet eyes seem even more radiant.

It hits me what Jamie is getting at, though. The Citizens here are much more than a source of stability for the Dreamcatchers. "So, you are all servants to the Dreamcatchers?"

Irene giggles, finding something that I've said to be amusing. "Servants? No, Keeper Beatrice, only a few of us are servants. All of us are slaves."

"Slaves?" I turn in my seat, nearly ruining my hair in the process. "Slaves?" I look at them both in turn.

"Yes, Keeper." Jamie urges me to face forward again. "We all have different jobs. Most of the Citizens are laborers. They work out in the fields to maintain the production of the crops. Some of us are servants, like Irene and me. Some are trainers, and others are merchants. There are mothers, and teachers, and all sorts of professions … but we all are bound to the Dreamcatchers. We are here to serve them."

Echo never told me that the Aurans used the Citizens as slaves. I'm coming to find out that Echo has been keeping much from me. The thought of the Citizens not being able to live their lives freely infuriates me, and I wave the both of them away so I can stand. "So you are telling me that you are all being made to live in the Settlements, which are now plagued with some deadly epidemic, and you are forced to work for the Dreamcatchers for the rest of your lives?"

Jamie and Irene nod at the same time, the expressions on their faces revealing that this is the only life they've ever known, which means slavery has been in place in Aura for many years now.

Irene reaches up to fix one more piece of my hair, then claps her hands together and smiles at her creation. "You look beautiful, Keeper Beatrice. Doesn't she look so beautiful, Jamie?"

Jamie, now without any tears, smiles as well. "She does. Are you ready for us to bring you to breakfast now, Keeper Beatrice? We would not wish to keep Prince Echo waiting for too long." The two exchange a knowing look and Irene lifts a hand up to her mouth and giggles behind it.

"No, we wouldn't want to keep him waiting," I mutter, not very pleased to have to face Echo again with all of this new information on my mind. There are a few more pieces of information I need to find out, though, and before we leave, I stop the two by the door. "Did you girls live in the Settlements? How did you come to work in the palace?"

"Oh yes. Everyone is born and raised in the Settlements. Girls and boys are sent to different schools to learn. If you do exceptionally well and your behavior and demeanor is right, then you can come to work for the Dreamcatchers in their own homes as servants. Irene and I were picked from our class to work here since we both did so well together." Jamie puts her hand on the knob of the door and turns to smile at Irene. "We've not been apart for most of our lives. I don't know what I'd do without Irene, really. She's like a sister to me."

Irene beams, obviously agreeing. "She's the only family I have, to be honest. I've not seen my parents since I was a very little girl. They worked out in the fields, laboring. I was always left behind in school and would sometimes see them at night if they came to pick me up. It's pretty common for children of laborers. The teachers often end up taking care of us." Folding her hands in front of her with a happy grin, she smiles up at me. "I'd give anything to see them again, though. Just so they know I'm doing such a good job here in the palace. I don't know if they ever believed in me, but sometimes I like to think that they had big aspirations for their only daughter. If only I could show them that I did it, that I got placed somewhere honorable."

"I'm sure they'd be very proud of you, Irene." I put my hand on her shoulder and squeeze it. "You did a wonderful job making me look less like a Keeper and more like … well … one of them."

Irene takes the praise like a child being told she's done something well, bright-eyed and all smiles. Jamie is more subtle and simply nods her head.

I prepare to head back out into the palace, hoping that I won't run into the queen again. With nothing but Gabe on my mind, I try to hold onto a memory of him that is much stronger than the after-effects of the Vision. Instead of nurses swarming around him in a panic, I keep the memory of Gabe on the rooftop, leaning in to kiss me.

How I would give anything to be back on that rooftop. I wouldn't have pulled away from Gabe had I known I might not ever see him again.

LUCIDITY

Chapter 4

Breakfast is tense at best, even if it is just me and Echo sitting at the long table that is meant to sit more than just two people. A holoscreen has been set up on the wall, and news stories from around Aura report the morning's going-ons. Much of it is about the plague, and while the news reporters drone on about the body count for the day, Echo sighs and speaks loudly. "Off." The holo instantaneously switches off, the screen turning black.

I push eggs around my plate with the tip of my fork, not interested in eating. All I can think about is my Vision of Gabe, and the thoughts of Jamie's family perishing in their family home, choking on their own blood.

"What's wrong?" Echo finally asks, and when I look at him, he is watching the way I shove my eggs around without eating them. "You aren't eating."

"I don't really have the stomach for eating right now, to be honest." I let the fork drop to the side and fold my hands in the lap of my dress. "I can't stop thinking about Gabe. Something is going to happen to him, and I'm not there to help him. I feel just awful for leaving him like I did." Though I know Echo doesn't want to hear about Gabe, I don't care. Gabe is a big part of me, and I abandoned him for Echo; Echo's going to hear it whether he wants to or not.

"What happened in your Vision?" Echo surprises me when he asks about it, and I look back up at him. My head still throbs from the after-effects of having the Vision, but through the reflection of his eyes, I can see that mine are no longer glowing.

I shake my head, my curled hair remaining tightly-pinned at the crown. I'm not used to the weight of it, and I realize for the first time how much hair I actually have. "I don't know, exactly. The machines alarmed the nurses to come to the room, and they all swarmed around him before I could see what was going on." With another shake of my head, I settle it in my hands, elbows propped up on the table. "Something's gone horribly wrong, though. He's not doing well, Echo." After a pause, I admit to both myself and him, "I don't think he's going to pull through."

Echo picks up a white mug situated at the side of his plate, fingers curling around the middle. He sips whatever liquid is contained inside, a warm mixture of hearty spices and cloves. "Why do you think that?"

"It's just a feeling ... a horrible feeling that is lingering somewhere inside of me. And when Seers get those feelings ... " I trail off, not wanting to know my own power and how it could play out in this case. I don't want any feeling that I might lose Gabe forever, but it's the one thought that I can't get out of my mind. "I have to go back."

Echo puts the mug down. "You can't go back yet."

"What?" I frown, pushing the plate of food away. "I'm not your prisoner, Echo. I came here on my own, and I'll leave on my own, too."

The hesitant look he gives me tells me that I'm wrong. "My mother won't let you leave. I begged and pleaded with her all of last night to let you return to the City ... that there was nothing you can do for us here, but she's not convinced."

I wait for him to continue, because if I speak right now, nothing pleasant will come out.

"She said that you'll leave when she's ready for you to leave. She said that won't be until after we are married." Echo lowers his head, chin tucked down. Gazing into the mug, he mutters a quiet, "I'm sorry, Beatrice."

But, I am not accepting the apology. I slam my fist down on the table and everything on it jumps. "I am not your prisoner, do you hear me? One day, a Seer is going to see what is going on here, and they will come for me. Is that what you want? Another war?"

"No, Beatrice. I don't want any of this. Why are you yelling at me? I didn't choose for this to happen. I am not my mother." Anger bleeds into Echo's tone, and he begins to lose that patience that makes Echo who he is. After a moment, he reaches out and puts a hand over my clenched fist. "Maybe there is something I can do for Gabe."

I blink a few times, then frown again. "Don't toy with me, Echo. Making this situation worse is not going to help anyone right now."

"I'm not 'toying' with you. I'm being serious. Let me ask around to see what I can do before I promise you anything." Echo's hand squeezes mine. "Beatrice, I don't want to see you upset. It hurts me when you are hurting. This … this is not how anything was supposed to go."

I bite on my lower lip and fight the urge to push Echo away from me. But again, I'm drawn to him like night bugs to a light, and I can't seem to avoid the way he pulls me in, grounds me. "Fine, figure it out. But until then, I want a favor from you."

Echo tilts his head and keeps his hand over my own. Wiggling his fingers into my tight fist, he intertwines them with my own. "Anything you want, Beatrice. I'll try my best to get for you."

Casting a look to the doors of the dining room, I notice the Citizens who are keeping watch, ready to refill glasses and serve more food at the nod of the head. "You didn't tell me that you kept the Citizens as slaves."

"It didn't occur to me that it was something you wanted to know. It's just a way of life for us." Echo follows my gaze to the Citizens by the doors. "They serve us in much the same way that they serve you. The Seers present it differently, is all. You allow them to choose their jobs, and to breed their own children when they wish … and we choose to regulate it." He lets go of my hand and takes up the mug once more. "In the end, though, they are used to breed more of our kind so that we don't die out."

"And you don't think there's something wrong with forcing those people to live like that? To breed them like you are breeding animals for pets?"

"Do you think there's anything wrong with keeping the Citizens barricaded in your City with electric, barbed-wire fences?"

I open my mouth to retort to the comment, but then I shut it again. He's right. We are doing the same things in different ways, and it bothers me all the more to hear it from this point of view.

"See? We aren't as different from each other as you thought." Echo grins, handsome as always. "So, what was the favor you wanted to ask of me?"

"I want to go see the Settlements."

Echo pauses. "What?"

"You heard me, Echo. I want to go down and see the Settlements. I want to see how these people are living. I want to see what the plague is doing. I want to see the Birthing Tents. I want to see it all. Show me." I say it a little too demandingly, but if I'm to be kept prisoner here until I'm forced into marriage, then I'm going to get my way with something.

"But, the plague … "

"I don't care. I want to see it with my own eyes. Maybe then I can See a solution later."

This wins Echo over. "Fine. But we are going to keep this between us … and we'll have to go in disguise. If they recognize me, they could easily try to overcome me."

"Are the Citizens not happy with you right now?"

Echo finishes the spice drink and sets the cup aside. "They are not happy with the way we are handling the plague. They want the royal family to do more for them, but there's very little we can do when we don't have healthy Citizens to … use."

"I see." But I don't. I'll hopefully experience it first hand when I get to the Settlements. "And won't they know we aren't Citizens?"

"They could suspect we are Dreamcatchers, but we go in and out of the Settlements all the time. Some work in the Birthing Tents, others patrol the different districts. It's these Dreamcatchers who are getting sick and bringing the plague back into Aura. I think my mother is about to cut them out of the city to keep the plague from spreading here."

"Well, whatever we have to do, I want to see it for myself, see what I'm supposed to be saving everyone from."

***

Echo is clearly uncomfortable as we walk through the streets of Aura and toward the entrance to the Settlements. Two, long metal barriers swing open as we approach, and from behind my tinted sunglasses, I watch as the guards step out of their dirt-stained stations, rifles held close to their chests.

"Let me talk," Echo whispers to me as we close the distance between us and them.

"Just don't talk all prince-like," I remind him with a smile.

Echo grins as well, which is good, because when we get to the guards, we are all smiles and innocence. "Good day. We've come to visit some Dreamcatchers in the Settlements. We need to monitor their health."

There are two guards, both of whom tower way above us. Their biceps are bigger than my head, and I'm surely no match for the firepower strapped across their broad chests. "And where's your official pass?"

I hesitate for a moment. I didn't think about having a pass. But, Echo is on top of it, and he pulls out a leather badge with what looks like a seal of some sort.

The guards look at each other, then nod to us. "Very well. You may pass."

I smile sweetly at them and wonder what they'd do if they had any idea that they were talking to the Keeper. Our little game of disguise is amusing, and I find some enjoyment in it, despite the gravity of the Settlements. They hand us face masks to cover our noses and mouths, then open the gates.

As soon as we walk in and down one of the dirt paths that serve as a road, the fun seeps out of the experience. Sand-colored tents line the roads with little space in between them. They are maybe big enough to fit eight people in them, at best, and some are smaller than that. Children run up and down the streets in cloth tunics riddled with holes. It smells like urine and sweat, and the baking hot sun beats down on everything.

I swallow back my disgust. At least, in the City, we provide homes to the Citizens. At least they live their lives normally, and not cooped up in a tent city. Slums. "This is horrible." I speak through the mask, which muffles my words.

"There has been an issue with over-crowding, yes. We mean to expand the Settlements and build structures, but since the plague broke out, there's nowhere to re-home the sick and uninfected. We have to keep a sort of quarantine here."

"Why not separate the two and find homes for those who aren't plagued?"

"The few scientists that we have are working on finding out how we can tell who has already caught the plague and isn't showing symptoms yet, and who is healthy. They haven't quite got it down yet, but when they do, we will be separating them as soon as possible." Echo leads me through the narrow roads, and we stop every now-and-then to check on other Dreamcatchers who are watching for any trouble.

"And what will you do with the sick ones?"

Echo looks back at me, his eyes also covered by sunglasses. "Get rid of them."

I stare at him for a long moment, hoping that he doesn't mean what I think he means by that statement. "Get ... rid of them?"

"Yes. In order to kill a plague, you need to kill the source. And unfortunately, the source of this plague ... is ... well ... the infected Citizens."

"Echo!" I hiss lowly so that others don't hear me say his name. "Why don't you work on healing them?"

"We want to. But there aren't enough healthy Citizens to use our power."

"No. No, not with your power, with medicine. Remember that, Echo? Remember when we had medicine?" I reach out and shake him by his arms. "You cannot do that. Promise me you won't."

"It's not my choice, Beatrice." He frowns at being shaken and weaves his way out of my grasp. "And we don't use medicine here. The Dreamcatchers have no use for it."

"But they do!" I wave an arm in any direction. "They are sick! You need to help them!"

My yelling draws some attention, and Citizens peek out of their tents to see what the commotion is. I look down the line of dirty faces and wide, dark eyes, then sigh and return my attention back to Echo.

Echo steps closer to me and looks down over his mask and into my eyes. "This is why I need your help."

"Well, I told you what you could do to make this better." I decide to start walking again; we are drawing too much attention to ourselves. "I want to see more."

Echo catches up with me and we walk in silence for a little bit. I'm glad for it, since it gives me time to think about what I've just been told. It's not easy to absorb. My head starts to throb and I rub at it with one of my hands as Echo comes to a stop before a deep green tent guarded by men with guns. They all look the same to me by now, larger men holding guns that probably weigh more than I do.

"What is this place?" I search the tent for some sort of label, but it's unmarked, and I can't tell what it might be just by looking at it.

"This is one of our Birthing Tents." Echo bites on his lower lip as he looks at it. "Do you want to go in?"

"Do you? You seem kind of nervous." I follow his gaze to the sealed flaps that don't allow for any quick peeks inside.

"I've never really been in one before. I've only heard about them, and … well, I guess that the whole baby thing just isn't my deal." Echo smiles hesitantly and avoids looking at me as he steps forward and shows his badge again. The two guards step aside, and Echo wastes no time stepping into the decontamination chambers.

The tent flaps are sealed tightly behind us, and someone over a speaker starts to give out instructions. "Step forward and each of you enter a personal chamber."

I give Echo a look, which is returned with a nod. "Go ahead, Beatrice. We have to be decontaminated before we can go inside, that's all."

"No one told me about this." But, I suppose that it makes sense. With the plague going around, it would be disastrous if it spread amongst the breeding mothers and their babies.

I step into one of the personal chambers, a small section of the tent with opaque rubber flaps that encircle me into the tiny space. A metal showerhead is directly above me, and thin pipes spider down the sides of the chamber with small jet nozzles.

"Please disrobe."

I touch the mask on my face and hesitate. Though it doesn't completely hide my face, it covers most of it, diverting attention away from my violet eyes. And Echo? What if they realize who he is once his mask is off? Hesitantly, I duck my head down, hopefully blocking it from the view of any cameras, if there just so happened to be any, and I start to undress.

Once my clothes have been removed and placed outside of the chamber, I stand naked, waiting.

"Please take the goggles and cover your eyes," the speaker projects again, so I do just that, happy that my eyes have been shielded once more.

Nothing happens at first, and then I hear the groan of water moving through pipes. Before I have a chance to react, hot steam shoots out of the fixtures. The water comes next, and it's too hot when it first hits me, but I quickly get used to it. It smells like chemicals, and I gag and cough.

"Are you okay, Beatrice?" Echo calls out over the sound of quickly moving water. I can hardly hear him over my own coughing and the noise of the jets.

"What is this?" I call back, concerned about the effects that this will have on me after we're done being decontaminated. Maker only knows what they are dousing me in, and yet here I am, helpless to stop any of it.

"It's just an antiseptic mixed with water, is all. It's okay, Beatrice. I think it's almost done."

Just as Echo says this, the water stops and air is blown out of the pipes instead. It's like a large hairdryer, and the warmth of it is relieving, soothing. I'm dried almost instantly, except for my hair, which remains damp, but not soaking wet. The drying ends and the speaker crackles again as a voice instructs us to reach out and grab the scrubs that have been set out for us.

I feel around for the indicated items, noticing that my clothes are gone, probably because they can't be cleaned off like we can, at least not quickly enough to be returned to us to wear right away. I hurry up and dress in the drab, gray scrubs and step back out of the individual chamber. Echo waits for me just outside, his stark blond hair beaded with droplets of water. I catch myself staring and pull my attention away from the damp looking prince. "Now what?"

"Now we can go in." Echo puts his hand on the small of my back and ushers me forward toward the doors labeled "Birthing Tent."

The tent is enormous, bigger than any other tent in the Settlements by far. There are separate rooms that are lined up down the halls, and nurses, doctors, and guards walking to and from this place and that. I notice that the doctors and nurses are Dreamcatchers by their blond hair and dreamy blue eyes, none of which compare to the devastating hue of Echo's gaze.

"So far, we've managed to keep the plague from the Birthing Tent, if only because everyone who enters and leaves must be decontaminated first. That seems to be working, though the plague can be dormant for a long time before it triggers and becomes active." Echo pauses by a plastic, translucent screen that serves as a window into a nursery, which is split into two parts. One side houses Citizen offspring, and the other side Dreamcatcher babies.

"The Citizen children are placed with families within the Camp." Echo gestures to the Dreamcatcher children next. "These children will be raised by Dreamcatchers. We have a school for them, actually … much like your Institution. Whether or not a Dreamcatcher has a child on their own, or chooses to house a child from the Birthing Tent doesn't matter."

He puts his hand against the plastic window, peering inside. "Some Dreamcatcher children aren't placed, though, which is normal. There aren't enough of us to take in every Dreamcatcher child that is born, so some of the children live in group facilities. Like dormitories." Looking to me, he grins. "Again, like your Institution."

"Yes." I can understand his parallels, but it's hard having it presented to me like this. A factory for children. And of course … there aren't any Seer children mentioned, which makes me feel sick to my stomach. "In a way, I guess."

"We have much in common with each other. If only others could see that. But our people … well … sometimes I get the feeling we will forever be divided. That there are some Seers who don't want to see the similarities, and there are some Dreamcatchers who don't want to see them, either. They choose to be blind."

I rest a hand on Echo's forearm, glancing to all the babies just as he is. "Maybe, one day, we can change that, Echo."

I know he's looking at me then. I can feel his gaze on me, but I don't turn to look up at him. I don't want Echo to think this is some sort of consent to marry him or something. A pact to fix the future of our people. It isn't. At least, it's not just yet.

"Maybe." And then he's walking again.

Somewhere down the hall, a mother is screaming, presumably from labor pains. I've never heard someone in such agonizing pain. I've never witnessed a woman having a child, either. In the City, Citizen women had their children in their Citizen hospitals. There isn't any reason for a Seer to be anywhere near either of those, and there's no reason for us to understand the process, either. Seers can't have children. It's not our place.

"I think a new one is being born. We should wait and see." Echo slows his pace down and stops just outside the room where the mother is yelling. Swearing.

"She sounds like she's in an awful lot of pain." I wrinkle my nose, not so sure I can bear the sounds of someone who is obviously dying or something.

"I heard it's not very pleasant, no."

But, some minutes later, the yelling comes to an abrupt end, and the sound of a newborn's cries fill the air instead. My breath catches somewhere in my throat, and though I can see none of what is going on, I feel something strange blooming inside of me.

And then, I know why.

"It's a Seer."

Echo takes my hand in his and starts to tug me the other way. "Then we should go now." And I know why he wants to get me out of here. Because the next step for this brand new life is for it to be smothered out of existence, just as we smother the Dreamcatchers out of existence back in the City.

"No." I yank my hand out of his. "Get it."

"What?" Echo frowns at me. "You know I can't do that, Beatrice. They will know who we are."

The doctor leaves the room with the tiny infant bundled up in cloth. It's still screaming, drawing in those first breathes of air, little lungs heaving.

"I don't care. You can't kill it. Not while I am here." I point at them. "Get it. I will have it sent back to the City."

"But … we don't do that. We can't do that … it's just not how things work, Beatrice. You don't do that to your Dreamcatchers, and we don't do it for our Seers."

I grab Echo by both of his arms and stand directly in front of him, using my placement in order to command his attention. "Stop him."

Echo looks from the doctor to me and then back to the doctor again. Closing his eyes, he's still, and I'm afraid that he's just going to let the doctor walk away and the Seer baby will disappear forever.

"Echo!" I blurt, not caring who hears me. His name is enough to stop the doctor in his path as he looks back toward us.

"My mother is going to kill me," Echo mutters, but he walks around me, brushing his arm against mine, and moves to where the doctor is standing. "Doctor, I'm going to need to … um … take that," Echo warily begins and shows his badge to the other man. He looks at both of us, and without my sunglasses, it's very apparent what I am. Who I am.

"Prince Echo?" the doctor asks for confirmation, though he never stops looking at me.

"Yes. And Keeper Beatrice. She'll … um … she'll take the baby. And it will be transported back to the City immediately." Echo narrows his eyes at me when he says this, leaving no room for me to argue any other agreement.

"But, Your Highness … we can't … that's not part of the protocol."

"It is now," I mutter and hold my arms out for the child, drawn to protecting it just as I would any other Seer. As their Keeper, I wouldn't let them be summarily killed right in front of me, and I'm not about to let this baby go through the same thing.

"Give it to her."

The doctor hesitates, but gently puts the baby in my arms. I'm not sure how to hold it, but I lift my chin and pretend like I do anyway.

"Thank you," I say.

"This is not right, Your Highness. She's one of them." The doctor continues his protest, taking a step back from me, as if I'll pass my Seer genes onto him somehow.

Echo nods his head and puts his hand to my back again. "And so is the child. It will be sent out of Aura, so you have no worries there." With a tiny push, Echo gives me the signal to begin to walk away now. "Have a good day, Doctor."

I cradle the child close to my chest and shakily walk beside Echo as we near the exit. My knees feel like they will buckle from under me, and my legs feel like jelly. On top of that, my head is starting to pound again, and with my arms full with an infant, I can't stop to rub the tension from it.

Our clothes are waiting for us at the other end of the tent, in bags labeled "HARMFUL." We each pick up a bag and, choosing to remain in our scrubs, make our way out of the Birthing Tents

***

The baby incessantly wails, and it doesn't take long before others are alerted to its presence in my bedroom. I stand beside Echo, and we watch as it flails around on the bed, arms and legs stretching out in any which way. My head is still throbbing, and the screaming and crying doesn't lend to making it feel any better.

Jamie hurries in without her counterpart. "We weren't expecting you back so soon, Keeper," she apologizes without apologizing, then curtsies for Echo. Eventually, her gaze settles on the baby and she lifts a brow in curiosity. "You brought back a baby?"

"A Seer," Echo corrects, then rubs his face with his hand. "My mother is going to kill me."

Jamie approaches the bed and swaddles the infant into its blanket. When she picks it up, it settles, and she rocks it back and forth in her arms to keep it calm. "I've never seen a Seer baby before."

"That's because they are killed before anyone gets a chance to see them." I sit on the edge of the bed and tilt my chin up. "But we can send it back to the City, right?"

Echo meets my gaze. "If that is what you want, I will find a way for it to happen."

"I want to go back with it." I push the issue while I can.

"Beatrice, you and I both know that my mother won't let that happen. She's probably ordered the guards to put you down if you tried." He brushes a hand over his short, almost-white hair. "But, I can manage sending the baby back. Who should I send it to?"

"The Institution."

"You know, it is a girl, right?" Jamie giggles to herself, rewrapping the newborn. "I think she should have a name."

This makes me uncomfortable. I've never really seen a baby, let alone given one a name. Though Jamie holds it in a natural, learned way, I could barely manage to keep it quiet. "They will probably name her when she gets to the Institution," I point out, avoiding the responsibility of giving a whole new life a name. "And then she will be one of us."

But this isn't good enough for Jamie. "I think her name should be Fortuna."

Echo cracks the faintest smile and shrugs a shoulder. "Sounds reasonable to me. She is quite fortunate to not have been carried off and disposed of."

I shudder at the word "disposed." "Okay. Fortuna, then. Prince Echo will make arrangements to deliver Fortuna back to the City, and until then, Jamie, you can care for her." I'm not ready for the responsibility, and it reminds me all too soon of the fact that one day, I'll have to bear my own child to become the next Keeper.

Echo puts a hand on my shoulder, drawing my thoughts away from the subject. Jamie leaves with the infant, slipping out of a side door to a small servant's room connecting to my own. "How's your head feeling?"

I touch my temples with my pointer and middle fingers and rub them in small circles. "It still hurts. I think the Settlements were a little too much for me to focus on all in one day." Echo sits beside me on his sister's bed, and it dips under the added weight. "I thought it would be different, Echo. Don't you ever feel bad that you keep them like that?"

"It's how it has always been, ever since I was a child. I suppose I've not really thought about it because I didn't know of another way ... not until I saw the City through your dreams, and then later, for myself." Echo brushes the wrinkles out of his robes and watches me from the corner of his eye. "Was it really that bad?"

"Yes. And it's even worse that you plan on wiping half of them out in order to get rid of the plague." I add this part in quietly, aware of the fact that Jamie might still be listening.

"I will speak to my mother about that." Echo puts his hand down on my knee, comforting me with just a simple touch. "Okay?"

Nodding my head, I take in a breath, trying to will my heart to stop beating so quickly. We sit in silence for a moment, and I wonder if Echo was truly being sincere when he said he'd send Fortuna back because it is what I wanted. We are both stuck in his mother's game, pawns to a political move that has been forced on the both of us. Will I ever see my home again? Would I really have to marry Echo?

And would it really be that bad?

I watch Echo's hand on my leg, the silence growing larger and becoming more awkward. He leans forward and kisses the side of my head, in just the same place where I had rubbed it before. Tucking my hair behind one of my ears, he smiles at me, and I'm suddenly sure that Echo means everything that he says. He always has. Fortuna will get back to the City, and somehow, some way, this whole situation will resolve itself in the right way, if only because Echo said so and has faith in the outcome.

That's when the Vision happens. I clutch onto Echo's hand as the prophesy draws me out of this world and into another …

***

I am standing alone in the Camp, and it seems empty. The wind blows through the hundreds of tents, which billow and wave in one eerie, uniformed motion. In the distance, I see the shadow of a human figure moving, jerking awkwardly, limbs at strange angles. At first, there is only one, but then another shadow grows behind it, and I realize there are more. Dozens more. Hundreds more.

They are advancing toward me, but I am stuck where I am. I feel sick inside, like something is trying to claw its way out of my center, fingers raking at my stomach. The world flickers on and off around me, like a broken holo, and each time it comes back to view, the creatures have gotten that much closer to me.

They are dead.

Or are they?

Another flicker, and they are right in front of me. They stand lined up beside each other like a wall. A wall of the dead. They are grotesque and dripping with fluids that should be inside of the body and not on the outside. It smells like bile and rotting flesh. One of them is pointing at me, and then the rest of them follow suit, and soon I have a bunch of dead fingers pointing in my direction, as if blaming me for something.

One of them speaks. "Save us."

The rest of them repeat, "Save us."

Their dark hair and dark eyes tell me that they used to be Citizens. The plagued Citizens in the Settlement. They've charged me with saving them, just as I was charged with saving the City from the Dreamcatchers. I want to tell them that I can't save them, that I'm no good at saving anyone, like Gabe, for example. Now he is in a coma, and it's all because I couldn't save him. And worse, I left him there to deal with it all by himself.

But I can't speak. I can only watch them point at me, hundreds of pairs of lifeless eyes stuck on where I stand. Waiting.

***

I start out of the Vision and Echo is just where he was before, but now he holds both of my hands in his own, and he almost looks hopeful. He probably thinks that I've had the Vision that he wants me to have, one that will tell him the answer to this plague. I shake my head sympathetically, and I can see my glowing eyes in his gaze. "I'm sorry, Echo. It was about the plague … but there wasn't anything to tell me what to do."

Echo's shoulders slump just a touch, but he doesn't let go of my hands. "I'm more concerned about you than I am about the Vision. Are you okay?"

I nod my head and find it touching that he's so concerned about the aftermath of something that has been happening all my life. "Yes, I'll be fine. But the Vision … it was not pretty. There was a bunch of dead people, Citizens, and they were all pointing at me, telling me to save them." Rubbing my head again, I try to will away the headache that follows.

Jamie peeks back out from the servant's room, obviously having overheard the conversation. She holds Fortuna in her arms, and thankfully, the child is still quiet and doesn't add any more pain to my headache. "Save us from what, Keeper?"

"That's a good question, Jamie. And, I don't know the answer, unfortunately."

Echo lets go of my hands and rises from the bed. "I'll go get you some tea for your headache. And I'll figure out how to get Fortuna back to the City before my mother finds out we've smuggled a baby out of the Camp."

"She probably already knows, Echo," I say realistically. We didn't exactly sneak the baby out of the Settlements in our retreat back to the palace. And people were well aware of who we were when we left the Birthing Tent.

"In either case, I need to figure out how to get her someplace safe." Echo leans down and kisses my forehead. "I'll be back, Beatrice."

I smile at him before he leaves and touch the place where he kissed my head. How any girl could deny herself such a boy, I don't know. But I can't let him get too close to me, especially when I intend to go back to the City where I belong.

I can't get too close to him.

Chapter 5

Sitting under the tree with the umbrella limbs, Gabe and I share a piece of the native citrus fruit of Aura. The juice has made our fingers and lips sticky, and we laugh about something, and it doesn't matter what, because I am with Gabe, and that's all that matters.

When the laughing tapers off, I lift a piece of the fruit to Gabe's mouth and smile. "I am sorry I left you."

Gabe opens his mouth and comically chomps down on the fruit. He mmm's and shakes his head. "I understand, Bea. You don't have to apologize to me."

I think that this is too easy, that he has forgiven me too quickly, but it doesn't feel wrong. Wiping my hands off on my robes, I reach out and brush his hair back behind his ear. He turns his head to nuzzle into my touch, then sighs happily.

"Don't leave again, Bea. Promise me that you won't leave again."

I hesitate here, staring into Gabe's violet eyes. Everything about him is handsome and familiar. Though we sit in the middle of a field, under the tree that seems to reach for the sky and the ground at the same time, Gabe feels like home, and I don't want to lose that again. I want to go home.

"Promise me?"

I open my mouth to reply, but nothing comes out. I try again, but the same thing happens.

"Beatrice?" He takes his hand in mine. "Beatrice?"

Beatrice ...

***

"Beatrice?"

The intercom crackles with Echo's voice and rouses me from my sleep. I roll over and reach out toward the side table, feeling for the speaker with the tips of my fingers. When I find it, I drag the intercom closer to the bed and press the transmit button.

"Yes, Echo?" I rub the sleep out of my eyes and check the time. It's just past the seventh hour. Too early.

"I need you to get dressed and meet me outside your room as soon as possible."

"I sense the urgency in his voice. "Is something wrong?"

There's a pause. "No. I just need you ready as soon as possible."

I drag my legs out of the bed and slap the button again. "All right."

Echo comes over the speaker again, " And Beatrice?"

"Yes?"

"Make sure you hurry up." The intercom clicks off and Echo is no longer there.

Jamie and Irene enter after a knock on the door. They seem uncertain today, their movements timid and unsure. Irene approaches with a crimson gown that has a high collar, in Dreamcatcher fashion. "Is this one good for today, Keeper?"

I shake my head. "No. Today I will wear my robes. It's what I look best in, and whatever is happening seems important." I won't have them keep dressing me as a Dreamcatcher, like one of Paradigm's porcelaine dolls. "But maybe it won't hurt to wear it underneath."

Irene smiles when I relent and helps me into the gown. I pull my robes over and poke my arms through the long sleeves. The collar sticks out of the top, the deep red contrasting with the pitch black of my robes.

Jamie steps forward with a hair brush in hand, but I wave her off with a flick of my hand. "No need for fancy today. I'm going to leave my hair down."

"Very well, Keeper." Jamie moves aside, and I look at myself in the long, full-sized mirror with the gold-gilded frame.

Approving of my appearance, I spin around to face Irene and Jamie. "Okay, I think I'm ready now." Then, I eye each of them. "Do either of you know what is going on?"

They both shake their heads without saying anything.

"Well, I guess I'll have to go find out myself." I nod my thanks to the girls and approach the door with many questions running through my mind. What has Echo acting so seriously?

When I step outside, Echo is there, as he said he'd be. He has two guards with him, each holding a large gun across their chest. Their uniforms are golden, like most things in Aura. I can't tell, but their helmets might be solid gold.

"What is this about?" I give the guards a look, and they eye me back, their contempt obvious. They don't want me here, and I don't trust them anymore than they trust me.

"You'll see." Echo is wary about something, I see it in the way that he shifts uncomfortably where he stands.

"You're worried."

"I am."

I frown. "I don't like this."

"Most people won't." He doesn't clarify and begins to lead me down the hall. The closer we get to the entrance of the palace, the more I notice that there are more guards here than there were the previous days of my stay.

I anxiously slip my hand into Echo's, but try to keep the jittery feeling buried deep inside so that no one else knows. We round one more corner, then step outside onto a large landing at the top of about a dozen stairs that lead up into the palace. Dreamcatchers have gathered in the courtyard, standing around waiting for something, but I don't know what. I've never been surrounded by so many of them before, and with all their eerie blue eyes settled on me, I clutch onto Echo's hand for support.

I am so distracted by everything else that I don't realize when the queen, dressed in another beautiful gown of white satin, joins us, taking her son by the arm, as if to pull him away from me.

"What is the meaning of this?" Though her words are milky-smooth, there is danger wrapped around each one. She's not pleased with whatever is going on.

The guards work hard on clearing a path into the courtyard, just big enough for a vehicle to come through. The Dreamcatchers have to be kept back with firm reminders from the guards who have formed a perimeter to control the growing crowd.

"This is my wedding present to Beatrice, Mother."

I loosen my hand in his grip, surprised. "If there's a marriage at all."

"Oh, there will be Keeper. There will be." The queen casts me a sidelong glance, as if daring me to challenge her any more.

I don't reply. I have learned that it is more powerful to say nothing rather than say something.

Echo, thankfully, doesn't say anything back to his mother, either. Instead, he whispers into my ear, "I would do anything to make you happy, Beatrice."

I shiver from his lips being so close to my ear and continue to stare straight ahead at the amassing Dreamcatchers.

"Anything. Remember that."

I look up at him, our eyes locking on each other. "I know, Echo."

"I hope you enjoyed the dream I gave to you last night."

"You did that?" Memories of Gabe and I sitting under the tree in the field come flooding back.

"I did. You were missing him so much, that I wanted to give him to you."

"But … but you don't even like Gabe."

"I like you, though." He stands up straight, the whispering coming to an end. A car approaches the palace, kicking up sand and dirt that forms a cloud behind it. Echo folds his hands in front of him, watching his plan unfold before all who are gathered.

As the car gets closer, I realize that it's a white van with a symbol of two hands facing palms down painted on the side. "What does that mean?" I ask, having never seen the symbol before. There is a car behind the van that is unmarked, with dark, tinted windows. "What is this?"

Soon enough, the van pulls around in front of the palace and stops. "It's the symbol for healing." Echo gestures to the vehicle. "That is a medic van."

The doors to the back of the van click, and two Dreamcatchers jump out of the back. The second car pulls up behind the van and stops; no one exits.

There's a tense moment when everything stands still. Even the queen is silent, though she looks stiff and uncomfortable, as if she knows something I don't. All of the Dreamcatchers look that way.

"Anything," Echo repeats again, nodding to the two Dreamcatchers behind the medic van. On cue, they reach inside and firmly tug on something that I can't see. With another tug, a stretcher comes into view. Another medic carefully disembarks the van, holding a pole with IV tubes dangling from the bags that are hooked to the top.

Another tug and the stretcher's wheels unfold and hit the ground. I look up at Echo, confused, and I find that he's already looking at me. Watching me. Studying me. "You are going to heal the Citizens?" I guess, but he shakes his head then nods to the van.

"Go and look."

I unwrap my hand from his and descend the stairs, toward the van. Each step brings me closer to whatever it is that is being kept a secret. And that's when I see what Echo brought to me to make me happy.

Gabe.

"Gabe!" I yell and jump down the last few stairs, nearly tripping on my robes as I throw myself across his lifeless torso. "Gabe! You're here!"

"He still can't hear you," a familiar voice cuts in. I glance up and there beside me stand Brandon and Elan. They don't look too happy. Not as happy as I am to see Gabe again.

I straighten myself, but keep a hand on Gabe's arm. "What … how did you get here? And why?" Casting a glance over my shoulder, I stare at Echo. "He brought you here?"

"He told us that you called us here. So we came because you're our Keeper," Brandon says, all while avoiding eye contact with me.

"Even if you abandoned your post. And us." Elan's words are more serious and cut to the bone. He's always been serious since the attack on the City, since he had to witness things that no boy his age should have to witness.

"I didn't abandon you, I—"

"This is unacceptable, Echo." The queen cuts me off as she steps down from the landing. "How many of them will you end up bringing back here?"

"These ones aren't staying," Echo says.

"You're staying?" Brandon asks me in confusion.

"No." I look at the queen. "I'm not."

"She is ours until agreements are made." The queen regally pulls back her shoulders to stand taller. Prouder.

"You can't do that." Elan frowns. He stares at the queen, unimpressed with her.

"I am the queen here, I can do as I please. And if you don't watch your tongue, Seer, I will string you up at the end of a rope, just like you did with our people."

Elan shuts his mouth.

"Enough," Echo cuts in, the one word carrying weight and authority. "I brought Gabe here so that I could make Beatrice happy. And so I can heal him."

The queen suddenly turns to Echo. "You will do no such thing. It is too much of a risk."

"I don't care, Mother. I am doing it for Beatrice."

"Doing what?" I don't understand past the part where Echo mentions healing Gabe. The Dreamcatchers are known for their capability to heal, but is there some danger in healing a Seer that I don't know about? Why doesn't the queen want Echo to heal Gabe?

The queen, furious now, gives Echo a disappointed look. "Get the Seers inside and secure them in a room. This circus is over. You and I will talk alone." Without another word, she turns and goes back into the palace, guards following behind her. Most of them, though, surround us.

Echo takes a deep breath and turns to me, Elan, and Brandon. "Let's get you guys inside. There's been enough of a show today."

Chapter 6

"What is going on?" Elan asks as we are escorted into the palace. Echo and his mother have long since disappeared down the hallway, leaving us with a retinue of guards who won't let Gabe, Brandon, or Elan go any further than the receiving room.

A medical team is soon to arrive and they approach Gabe's stretcher, which I'm standing beside, holding tightly to his hand. I don't move for them, though it's clear by the way they move around me that they expect me to. "What are you doing?"

"We've been told to take the sick Seer to the healing center, Keeper," a female Dreamcatcher responds. She is dressed in a white robe with the symbol of the healing hands embroidered over the left breast. She must be a healer, but it doesn't mean I trust her any more than I do any other Dreamcatcher.

"He's not going anywhere without me," I insist and step closer to the stretcher, even if there isn't any more space to close between me and it.

"They are our orders," the male attendant adds.

"And I am telling you no."

Elan and Brandon watch the exchange curiously, though Elan's permanent frown is much more serious than Brandon's expression.

The two healers hesitate and trade glances with one another, as if speaking without using any words at all. It makes me wonder, if but for a moment, if Dreamcatchers could have that capability, and I realize that it's not entirely impossible. They could be doing just that.

Thankfully, though, Irene arrives and clears her throat to try and draw the attention to her.

"Who is that?" Elan demands.

Brandon crosses his thick arms over his chest and peers at the girl who seems half his size.

"This is Irene. She's one of my servants." I realize how awkward that sounds only after I say it, and I shoot Elan a precursory glare. "Don't say anything. She's a very nice girl, and she and Jamie are the only neutral company I keep here."

"And what about Echo, hmm? You keep his company, too, don't you?" Elan snaps.

"Echo is different."

"Different in the way that you left us all here so that you could be with him? A Dreamcatcher?"

I frown and hide the fact that it feels like Elan has punched me in my stomach with his words. And though Brandon doesn't say anything now, I know by the way he's regarding me that he feels just as betrayed. And if Gabe was awake? Would he feel this way too? Guiltily, I mutter, "You don't understand."

"So you keep saying." Elan isn't taking it as an excuse.

"And I will say more when we are in private. But this is not the time or the place, Elan. And I won't have any more of it." For the first time, I speak as the Keeper, holding all the authority in my words as the Keeper before me, no matter how jaded she turned out to be. And although I left the City behind, I know Elan still recognizes me in that role, as his mouth shuts and simply nods his head, gaze smoldering.

I return my attention to Irene. "Did you have something to say, Irene?"

The young woman curtsies and addresses us all as she speaks. "The queen would like to invite you to an audience in her throne room. She and our prince are waiting."

Looking down at Gabe, I brush his somewhat greasy hair back from his face and sigh. "Just as I get you back, I need to leave your side again. I'll come back to you as soon as I can, Gabe." And, even surrounded by all the Dreamcatchers who expect me to marry their prince, I kiss Gabe's still mouth and allow for the healers to take him away just as soon as I stand up.

"We shouldn't keep them waiting, I suppose."

***

When we arrive to the throne room, the queen sits on the dais with Echo standing beside her. He looks at me apologetically, and I know right away that this isn't going to turn out the way that I would want it to. Irene and Jamie are also present, standing at the side of the room, waiting solemnly in case they are needed.

Brandon and Elan walk behind me, and with them, I feel more secure than I have before. I am no longer outnumbered, and I am less of a prisoner than I was the previous days. I stop a few feet in front of the throne and my robes ripple around me, eventually settling about my form.

"My son, Echo, has taken many liberties as of late. Perhaps he has forgotten himself after his sister's execution. Perhaps he has forgotten that we are not friends, that we are very much enemies still. We may have come together to eliminate the Beacon and rid ourselves of your corrupt Keeper, but the rift that was before still exists," the queen begins in her smooth voice, her words drifting over us like a lullaby.

Echo doesn't speak, but I know he wants to. I can see it in the way he is keeping his gaze on me. I can see it in his tense posture that his mother has threatened him with something too great for him to beat on his own. Maybe it has to do with us. Or Gabe. I try to encourage Echo's behavior with a slight nod of my head, and eventually, I give the queen the attention she so craves.

"His first transgression was bringing the Keeper back to Aura, a city that has prided itself on rebuilding after a past Keeper had us indefinitely removed." The queen's silky hair drapes around her face, lending an ethereal presence along with the rest of her pale, milky features. She's beautiful to look at, and it's no wonder why Echo is so startlingly handsome as well.

"His second transgression was taking the Keeper into the Settlements and leaving with a Seer child that should have been eliminated at birth. No mercy is shown to the Dreamcatcher children back in the City, and so no mercy should be shown here."

Echo shifts in his place, never taking his blue eyes from mine.

"And his third transgression was bringing more Seers here with the intent to heal one of them as a gift to his future bride." The queen pauses here, and I can feel everyone's eyes on me. "These things will not happen the way that Echo believes that they will."

"And what, exactly, does that mean?" I ask in a neutral tone, since the queen is not denying that they could happen. She's only stating that they aren't going to happen the way Echo wants them to. There's still a chance to save Gabriel.

"It means that there will be a price, Keeper. If you want the child returned to the City, if you want your friend healed, if these two," she nods to Brandon and Elan, "ever want to see their home again, you will pay a price."

I try not to let it register that I would pay any price to save Gabe. I would pay any price to protect my people as well. I can't let her know I am so desperate, and so I don't respond and only wait for her to continue.

"Tomorrow," the queen presses on, "you will marry my son. You will form an alliance between Aura and the City. You will agree that healthy Citizens will be transferred to Aura in order to replenish the sick that we will lose. You will bring forward an heir that has both the capabilities of a Seer and a Dreamcatcher, and it shall belong to Aura. Only then will we uphold the terms of sending the child and your friends back to the City, and of healing the dying Seer."

"Beatrice … " Brandon starts in a whisper, and I turn to look at him, my mind reeling. Never before has the decision been so immediately important, and yet, if I just say "yes" everything can be fixed. Everything besides the fact that Gabe will never forgive me for marrying Echo. And I'd never forgive myself for breaking both his and Echo's hearts.

"What am I supposed to do?" I whisper back to him, turning my back on the queen. "He will die if I don't do this. We all know that he won't ever wake up again."

"And if you do do this?" Elan returns with the question I don't want to think about. "What will you be giving up in order to save two people?" For once, Elan looks sympathetic, and he sighs, not knowing the answer himself. "I don't know what you should do, Keeper."

"It's true … that he won't wake up. The doctors said as much back at the Institution. They mentioned that only the machines are keeping him alive right now." Brandon lifts his gaze to Echo, staring at the Dreamcatcher prince with a certain wariness in his eyes. "But you will be married to him."

I bite on my lower lip. "Do you think Gabe would forgive me?"

"You will be saving his life … how could he not forgive you?" Brandon replies, and he is right. A marriage is so small compared to Gabe's life. How could he hold it against me? I know the choice I have to make.

I have to marry Echo.

Turning back to face the queen and her son, I lift my chin and state very clearly, "I will take you up on your terms. Tomorrow, I will marry Prince Echo in exchange for Gabe's life. But," I narrow my violet eyes at them both, "if Gabe's life cannot be saved, then the whole thing is off."

"Very well, Keeper." The queen smiles pleasantly. "We have a deal."

From the side of the room, Irene claps her hands in excitement, having no idea what this means to me. My chest feels tight, like I'm being squeezed between something too great for me to escape. I've placed myself in a trap, and I've done it for no other reason than to save Gabe.

Brandon puts his hand on my shoulder, as if knowing the very thoughts that run through my head. I lean back against his touch, suddenly feeling dizzy from all of the pressure. My head is beginning to throb again, and I know another Vision is materializing.

Echo can see it too. "Beatrice, are you okay?"

"I need to go back to my room. If you'll all excuse me." I murmur the words and start toward the exit to the hallway.

Brandon and Elan both follow along, but the guards are quick to stop them at the door.

"Let them go," the queen instructs with that serene smile still pulling at her lips. "They are no threat to us."

She is right. The Dreamcatchers are more a threat to us than we are to them. They could, if they really wanted to, kill us with just a touch. But they can also heal us with just a touch as well, and it's the latter I'm more concerned about.

Elan and Brandon stay close behind me as I hurry through the halls and back to Paradigm's room. Jamie and Irene are not too far behind. I need to get away from everyone before the next Vision comes; judging by the headache alone, it's not going to be easy to bear.

I round the corner and push open the door to my room. Once I am inside, I put my hands to my head and sink down onto the floor as the Vision takes control of me. Ever since becoming the Keeper, they've been much more frequent and harder to withstand. They leave me exhausted when they pass, and sometimes I wonder if I will ever recover from the throbbing headaches that follow.

Brandon rushes to my side. "Beatrice, are you okay?"

But his words seem miles away, and I lose grip of the world around me.

***

I am lying in a bed, and nurses are hovering around me, as if I can't see or hear them. But I can see and hear them, and when I try to speak, to let them know, they can't hear me. They are

Dreamcatcher nurses, with their white robes and the healing hands symbol marking them as such.

"So what are we supposed to do with him?"

"Nothing, yet. Our orders were to bring him here and keep him stable."

"I don't see why we should be helping the Seers at all. Since when have we become a bunch of Seer-lovers in the first place?"

"It's the prince," the one female nurse whispers to the other and looks around to make sure no one else is listening. "He's so taken by that Keeper that nothing he is doing makes any sense anymore."

"And just think. If he never would have Caught that Keeper, we probably would still have our princess, too. She would have never tried to stop him by killing her."

I open my mouth to try and speak again, but my mouth doesn't move at all, and I'm stuck lying there, unable to move. It occurs to me that I am Seeing through Gabe, and that these nurses around me must be the nurses that are currently around him. It's a new sort of Sight, one that I've not had before. I wonder if it means Gabe really can hear what is going on around him. Could that part of it be true?

"Prince Echo is normally a very sensible young man. There really must be something about that Keeper that has changed him so much."

"And now look ... we're stuck healing those Seers as if they were our own. It's ridiculous. I should refuse to do it."

"We should. Who would know any better if we just ended him now and said that it was just too late?"

***

"I would know!" I shout with a start, grabbing whatever is close by to me, which just so happens to be Elan.

With a shove, he scrambles away from me and frowns. "Keeper?"

"It's Gabe. They want to hurt Gabe. Kill him even." I try to push myself to my feet, but the force of the headache behind my eyes brings me back to the ground again.

"Calm down, Bea. You need to rest." Brandon urges me to stay down with a gentle nudge, guiding me to the floor once more.

"Who is going to kill Gabe?" Elan is more practical in times of crises. Where I just want to react, he wants to plan, and it doesn't surprise me when he starts to pry for details. "What are you talking about?"

"In my Vision. It was Gabe's Vision ... or ... it was something. I was in his body. I could see and hear the nurses around me, but I couldn't speak, and they didn't seem to know I could see or hear them. They said that they were going to kill me. That no one would know any better." I swallow back tears, not knowing if this is really going to happen or not. But with my Vision, it's very likely. I'm not the Keeper for nothing.

"Irene? Jamie?" I call for the serving girls since I'm too weak to get to the intercom myself. They both appear no sooner after their names leave my mouth.

"Yes, Keeper?"

"Please tell Echo to bring Gabe back. I want him here with me, where I can keep an eye on him. And hurry." I grab one of their hems. "I mean it ... hurry."

"Yes, Keeper," they both reply in unison and scramble out.

I go back to holding my head, resting it against one of Brandon's broad shoulders. "They hurt so much now ... and in the last few days I've had at least two Visions. They were both of something different ... first of Gabe ... then of the Citizens in the Camp, and now this ... "

"What do you think they mean?" Brandon brushes my hair back out of my face. "You know, don't you?"

But I don't know. How do I tell them I don't know when I'm supposed to be the Keeper, and the Keeper should know these things? "I have to think on them a little more. They seem so obvious, but it's the obviousness that makes me feel as if it's something much more complicated than what I think." This time, I pull myself up to my feet, using one of the nearby side tables to assist me. Once I am up, I stumble over to the vanity table and pull the bench out. Once seated, I look back up at my friends and regard them each for a moment. Now that we are truly alone, I can pull my thoughts together enough to process that they are actually with me.

"I am so glad to have you both here. Everything has been so ... so strange."

"You could just come home, you know," Elan says as they both take a seat on the edge of my bed. "Though, it seems like that's less of a possibility now, given the current situation." His mouth turns downward into another frown. "What are you going to do about this, Keeper? Marrying a Dreamcatcher? The people back in the City are going to flip out once they hear about it."

"Then maybe they shouldn't hear about it just yet, hmm?" I shoot back expectantly. "In fact, they won't hear about it. That's an order. When you guys go home, you aren't to say anything to anyone about any deals made with the Dreamcatcher Queen. Not yet, at least. There's still much that I have to figure out, but I'll make this right. I will." I have to. If I'm to be Echo's bride, and if I'm to send off hundreds of Citizens in order to save Gabe's life, there has to be a way to turn this to my advantage. Our advantage.

"As you wish, Keeper," Elan mutters. "I'm not thrilled with having to keep secrets from the City though."

"But you will," I am quick to add. "Because I told you to. The Institution was built on secrets, Elan. One more isn't going to hurt it."

We all glance up at the doors when someone knocks. "Who is it?" I call, hoping with all my heart that it's the healers delivering Gabe back to me.

"It's Echo. Can I come in?"

I turn to look into the mirror, quickly pulling on my hair to straighten it so it doesn't look like I just took a tumble to the ground. Not that I have to be presentable for Echo, but, part of me knows I should be. He's always so presentable to me. "Yes, come in."

The presence of Echo brings an intensity with it. Elan and Brandon tense, not used to being so close to a Dreamcatcher, or for a Dreamcatcher to be so close to me. The prince strolls over to where I'm seated and looks down into my eyes. "You had another Vision."

There are all sorts of things I can lie about, but having a Vision is not one of them. The glow of my violet eyes is not something that can be controlled, and they still continue to shine brightly, despite the time that has passed. "I did. Did you get my request to have Gabe brought back to me? I don't want him in the healing center, Echo."

"Does this have to do with your Vision?" he asks in concern.

"Yes. I don't really want to waste time talking about it. I want him here. And I don't want those healers by him either. I don't trust them." I pause. "Who am I kidding? I don't trust anyone here, to be honest. Except for you. And maybe Irene and Jamie. But other than that … I would rather if my friends could stay close to me. I'm sure you understand."

Echo glances back at Elan and Brandon with the same distrust in his eyes as they hold for him in theirs. "If that is what you want, I can ask. My mother is not being very cooperative at the moment, though, so don't be surprised if she says they have to be held in the brig until their departure."

"They aren't going to be put in jail." I leave no room for argument after my words are spoken. "They will stay with me. And they will all return just as soon as Gabe is healed. As was the deal, yes?"

"Yes. And Gabe will be healed tomorrow, after … after our wedding." Echo stumbles over the words, his cheeks coloring. I can feel the heat rise to my own face, and I duck my head down so as not to embarrass Echo any further. "I've sent for him to be brought back to the palace. He's in a very critical state, though, Beatrice. Are you sure you don't want him in the healing center until tomorrow?"

There's no hesitation when I reply. "Positive."

Echo smiles a little at the quickness of my reply, then reaches down and cups the side of my face in one of his soft, large hands. "You are so beautiful when you are impassioned by something, Beatrice." His thumb brushes over my cheek. "Don't ever lose that passion."

Brandon makes a disagreeable noise after clearing his throat. "We are still in the room, Dreamcatcher."

"Yes, we are. And you should spare us," Elan adds, still frowning, as always. "And take your hands off our Keeper."

Echo's eyes narrow, but only I can see it since his back is turned to the other two. I put my hand to his, squeeze it, and then gently lower it from the side of my face. "Nothing will ever take away how I feel for my friends, Echo. Don't you worry." The gentle squeeze draws Echo's attention away from the negative comments from Brandon and Elan, and he goes back to smiling at me.

There's another knock at the door, and this time, there's a very small chance it isn't Gabe. I stand up from the bench, holding Echo's arm to steady myself. The headache is almost gone, but I'm still shaky on my feet, which is even more apparent once they are on the ground, and I'm upright once more. "Come in!" I call, not bothering to ask who it is this time around.

Sure enough, the two doors part and along with a gust of warm air, two healers escort Gabe's stretcher and small gathering of machines into the room. My heart stops in my chest when I see him again, and it's only by the steady beeping of the machines that I know he is alive. Otherwise, were I to try and figure it out by his pale, raw lips, closed eyes, and still figure, I wouldn't have known.

The two healers bow deeply to Echo, and behind them, Jamie and Irene both curtsy and filter off to the sides of the room to stand out of the way of everyone else. "You asked for the Seer to be delivered here, Prince Echo?"

"Yes. Thank you." He leaves my side and approaches Gabe's bed when the healers leave, and I hesitate then step forward after him, hurrying to Gabe's side. I try not to look so desperate to be back by his side, but inside I know that I don't ever want to let him go again. I never want to walk away from his side.

Brandon and Elan sneak up on the other side of the bed and watch us as we watch Gabe.

"You are sure that he can be healed?" I ask in a whisper to Echo, remembering that if my Vision is true, then Gabe can hear us, and maybe even See us in his coma.

"I'm sure he can be … but I am not sure at what cost." Echo chews on his bottom lip and casually adds, "It could mean the death of me. And it will mean that a Citizen will have to be used."

"Used?" Brandon asks before the rest of us can.

I look up at Jamie and Irene, who are both staring ahead as if they can't hear anything. I wonder if they really are paying attention or not. Do they know what this means?

"Yes, used. Just as you use the Citizens to balance your Sight, we use them to balance our healing power. If it doesn't kill me, it will most likely kill the Citizen." Echo looks at no one but Gabe as he speaks, as if he wants the comatose figure to know what exactly is at risk in trying to save him.

"What do you mean that you can … can die? I thought … isn't that what some Dreamcatchers do? Heal?" I watch Echo, hoping that what he is saying is not true. I've already sacrificed so much just to get Gabe to live again, but at what cost? Echo? Must I give up Echo in order to save Gabe?

Echo sighs and turns himself so he's facing into me. "He's very sick, Beatrice. Little bruises, they are easy to heal. They don't take much energy from us … but cases like these … It's rare any Dreamcatcher will take them on. Even when a Dreamcatcher is so sick, it means we have to use a Seer in order to bring them back to life. But, we don't have Seers to do that. And we try not to use Citizens to bring other Citizens back to life because … well … what's the point? One life for another? No one should have to make that sort of decision."

"But Echo, you can't … I don't want you to … " I'm being torn in half, I can feel it. Do I sacrifice one friend in order to save the other? Do I allow Gabe to live the rest of his life in this vegetative state?

Echo holds my hands in his. "It's not your choice to make, Beatrice. It's my choice, and I am making it for you."

"But you can't … "

"I will. It's what you want, and it's the least I can do for the both of you. If you didn't help us destroy the Beacon, who knows what the Keeper would have done? My mother might not see it in that light, but I do. Gabe almost gave his life in order to save the rest of us. It's only fair that I take the same chances on him."

When I open my mouth to protest again, Echo puts his fingers on my lips until they slowly shut again. "It will be okay, Beatrice.

Brandon clears his throat again, and Echo takes his fingers away from my mouth.

"Sorry," Echo mumbles and looks back down at Gabe. "He's here now. If you four need anything, just let Irene and Jamie know." Echo prepares himself to leave, taking a few steps toward the door. "My mother said she'll have everything delivered for the wedding first thing tomorrow morning. It's to be a televised event. I'm not sure how the people are going to react to it, but she told me that they have no choice in the matter. This … this is the start of a new beginning." He says the last sentence with conviction, and must believe in it just as much as his mother does. "A new beginning, Beatrice."

I'm stuck standing in one spot, transfixed in place. *A new beginning*. I can't even bring myself to smile at Echo, I'm so paralyzed by the three words. Tomorrow is my wedding. A Seer joined forever with a Dreamcatcher. *A new beginning*. A new beginning.

And I might lose Gabe or Echo in the process of starting it.

Chapter 7

On the morning of the wedding, I don't leave Gabe's side. I've not left it the whole night, either. Brandon and Elan both slept in the canopied bed while I sat awake by Gabe's stretcher. And now, as the sun begins to change the sky the colors of pink and orange, I'm still here, my hand in his, wondering what he'd think if he was awake right now.

My eyes are dry from being open for so long, and when I stare down at Gabe, sometimes I see two of him as I momentarily lose focus. I clutch onto his hand tighter, using him to draw me away from the lure of sleep. After the wedding, Echo will be waiting in the infirmary with the Citizen chosen for the healing. I don't want to think about losing Echo or Gabe, and I don't want to think about another person sacrificed in this game of saving lives.

Irene and Jamie enter from their back room and draw the curtains to let the ever-present sunlight of Aura filter through the large, French-style windows. As Jamie pushes them open to allow a humid breeze to wake us, Irene approaches where I stay with Gabe, and she tries to put on her best smile for such an awkward sight. It is my wedding day, and I won't part from this other man to prepare for it. "Keeper Beatrice? We've been sent to prepare you for your wedding now. Would you care to get up and meet Jamie in the bathing room? We've drawn you a nice bath." Her words are hopeful, and it's only because of this that I agree. There's no use fighting any of this, it's what I have to do to get Gabe back, and I'm sure that my marriage to Echo has more than one purpose to it that I'm not aware of.

I stand, my hand brushing down Gabe's arm, then nod my consent to the young woman. "Yes, a bath would be nice."

After Irene escorts me into the bathing room, her tiny feet pitter-patter on the floor back out to the common area, and I hear her urging Elan and Brandon to leave in her ever-so-polite way. Of course they mumble their sleepy dissent before actually getting up to move at all. Jamie shuts the door so that I can't see into the room anymore and takes one of my hands. "I added fresh lavender bath salts to the bathwater so that you'll smell as soft and fragrant as the flower itself."

The scent is alluring and calming, and though it's a small comfort, I am grateful for what I can get in this moment. "Thank you, Jamie."

"Oh, you don't have to thank me now. Thank me when it is all over, for there's so much to do, you'll be saying 'thank you' all day long." Jamie helps me out of my robes until I am standing naked in front of her. This is really the first time I've ever been undressed in front of anyone, and I flush with color. Jamie doesn't seem to notice, though, and is too content on getting me settled into the bath. I step up onto a small stool, then down into the pool of warm, bubbly water, which covers my form once more and makes me feel less exposed. The bubbles are tinted purple from the lavender, which I already feel seeping into my skin, calming me.

"Many people have already showed up to get a good place to watch your wedding, Keeper Beatrice. The last reports I've heard, there were hundreds of Dreamcatchers already gathered in the courtyard, and hundreds more have filed into the streets where large holoscreens have been set up to broadcast the event. They even set up holos in the Settlements so that the Citizens can watch as well."

"I don't understand why so many Dreamcatchers would come out to watch this if they are supposedly so against it," I comment just as Jamie leans over the tub and starts to scrub some shampoo into my hair.

"They are curious, I'm sure. Their prince marrying the Keeper. They are also hopeful that you have brought the cure to the plague with you."

I scoff at this, my eyes closing as Jamie's fingers knead into my scalp, making small circles in the roots of my hair. "I have no cure."

"You might, though." Jamie is hopeful. "You just might not know it yet."

That's true. If the cure can be found in my Visions, I wouldn't know until the Visions actually occurred … and there's no way of knowing when I'll receive one. "I guess I don't fully understand why the Dreamcatcher Queen would take this chance and make it so public when there's so much outcry against it."

Jamie falls quiet, an indication that she knows more than what she should. I grab the edges of the tub and turn around to look her in the eye, to intimidate it out of her. "What did you hear?"

Her fingers untangle from my hair and she dips them into the tub to clean the soap off. "I really shouldn't say, Keeper."

"There's no one here to hear you but me." But we both know that's a lie. Anyone could be watching us through any channel of secret, streaming video. There are probably cameras all over my room, recording my every word and action.

Jamie takes the bait, though, maybe too naive to know that there's hardly a time when I am not watched. "I heard the Dreamcatcher Queen mention that if you were to bear a child that was part Dreamcatcher and part Seer … then it would start a new breed that would be a stronger, better healer. Maybe … maybe one who could save us from the plague."

I turn back around and stare in front of me.

"They even tested the theory once, but it didn't work because the Seer was too weak in Sight, and the Dreamcatcher just an ordinary Dreamcatcher. But with a prince and the Keeper?" Jamie's words are filled with a childish wistfulness that almost makes me want to slap her. Does she not remember I am sitting right here? That she's talking about breeding me with Echo like we were cattle?

Before our conversation can continue any further, Irene bumbles in holding some ornate boxes with heavy locks on them, and some that have drawers that slide halfway open as the girl twirls about in an effort to find a place to put it all. "I've come with your makeup and jewelry and hair supplies!"

"Looks like bath time is over." Jamie grabs a warm, soft towel from a nearby towel rack and opens it up, immediately wrapping me in it as soon as I stand. I pull the towel securely around my frame and tuck an end into the top to keep it in place.

Irene ushers me to a small bench in front of a vanity table, and starts to dry my hair with another towel. She's filled with energy and absolutely radiant with the joy that I should perhaps be feeling as a bride. But I feel nothing but trapped, and the only thing I can do is go through the motions one process at a time. She babbles on about this and that as she drags a comb through my hair and fixes it up. At some point, I hear nothing that she is saying over the hum of the hairdryer, but she keeps on chatting anyway, answering her own questions and stopping to flail her arms about in wild expressions before continuing once more.

They tie my hair back into a loose French braid that ends in a bun right at the left side of the nape of my neck. Lots of pins are used to keep the thick tresses of hair in place, and on top of that, lots of hair spray. When I think that all I'm going to be is a film of spray, Irene is done and claps her hands in appreciation over her work. "Oh, Keeper Beatrice, it will look so lovely once we get the tiger lilies pinned in!"

I force a smile just as Jamie picks up her part of preparing me, which is the makeup. She thankfully doesn't take too long, and when she's done, my face is tinted in colors of golds and pinks, subtle and refined. I look as if the sun has kissed me, just as it has all of Aura, and I understand what, exactly, they are trying to get me to look like. A Dreamcatcher. My dark hair and violet eyes aren't as manipulative, though, and there's no denying, no matter how "bright" they try to make me look, that I'm a Seer through and through.

Finally, it is time for me to put on my dress and apply all the other extra pieces that come along with the ensemble. I'm expecting something elaborate, fit for a royal wedding, but the dress that they bring to me is simple and whimsical. Beautiful. Trumpet-shaped with an overlay of lace and a champagne satin sash tied around the waist, the piece is understated and natural, as if it was pulled from the desert sands that surround Aura.

Both Irene and Jamie have to help me into the dress, and once it is zipped up the fabric hugs my form perfectly. Irene comes back to pin the lilies into my hair, and Jamie applies a few extra touches of makeup to make sure everything is just right.

"You look radiant," Irene whispers in awe.

"Like a sunflower," Jamie adds.

I stand in front of the mirror and regard my bride self. I do look radiant and like a sunflower. I feel as beautiful as I ever have, and I never thought I'd ever be a bride ... ever. Seers do not marry. Especially not the Keeper. But, here I am, standing in my dress, feeling as if I've been dipped into sunlight, and I have no one to share the moment with except for the Citizen servants, who now flitter about me making sure every little detail is in place.

There's a knock at the door, and they both freeze in their place. "Yes?" I call.

"Keeper Beatrice, the queen demands your presence in her chambers immediately. The wedding will begin in fifteen minutes, and she will be escorting you to its locale."

"Of course she would." Who else to lead the circus but the ringmaster herself?

"We are nearly ready!" Jamie nearly sings the words and fusses with a stray piece of my hair.

"I think we are done. We shouldn't keep the queen waiting. She'll be angry with us." The two exchange a look, a secret, knowing look that I don't understand yet. I wonder what happens to them when things do not go the way they are supposed to. Does the queen take it out on the servants?

"Come, Keeper Beatrice. We mustn't keep her waiting!" They both open one of the bathing room doors, and I step through them and into the bedroom as if I were already walking down the aisle. It starts now, this march to my fate. When I leave this room, I won't return until I am Echo's bride. Outside, by the window, I hear a familiar, yet distant sound. A raven. Have they always been here? I detour to one of the windows that look out into the back gardens, and sure enough, there's a raven perched high on a tree branch. It cries again, the caw loud enough to echo through courtyards and down the halls.

I may not come back to this room the woman I am now, but I will come back the Keeper. They can force me to marry Echo by using Gabe as a mere pawn in their game to save their people, but they can't force me to unbecome what I am.

The raven's call sounds again, and I push forward to meet with the Dreamcatcher Queen.

She is waiting for me in the cubiculum, her attendants fluttering about her like a disarray of errant butterflies. She wears as gown that is just as beautiful as mine is, ever so sure to outshine the bride on this occasion. Again, she reminds me of the storybook queens kept away in the fairytales that the Caretakers read to us when we were little. In her right hand, she holds a small vanity mirror set in a gold frame, and she pats her hair in place with her left. Finally, she turns to regard me, her gaze careful and hateful at the same time.

"Is she ready?" the queen asks past me to Jamie and Irene.

But I choose to answer. "I am."

The queen's ice blue eyes shift to mine. She hands the mirror off to a servant and brushes by a few more of them to get to where I am standing. I think she's going to strike me, and part of me wishes she would, but I know the sting of it would be much, much more than physical. She could take my life with just one touch, and I'm ever more aware of it now that she's standing so near.

"When we go out onto the balcony in just a little bit, you will meet with the Dreamcatcher people who are loathe today to hear that you will be marrying my son." The queen's attention flickers to the double doors that lead out onto the enormous palace balcony that oversees the main courtyard. I can hear the bustle of people outside, the muffled noise of someone speaking through a microphone, and the general chaos that comes along with having a large crowd in a place not big enough to hold them. "But they are hopeful, too, because not only does that mean that the Keeper is ours—"

"Which it doesn't mean at all," I am quick to cut in.

The queen doesn't stop to debate the matter, though. "Not only does it mean that, but it also means there's a possibility that a child will be born from your union. One who will be strong enough to cure the plague. From everyone."

There's the truth of it. It's why she so desperately wants me, so she can put me in her sick experiment to find a way to heal and live forever. Of course, she thinks that this is the outcome, but no one really knows what a Dreamcatcher and Seer would produce should they have a child. Whatever it is … it is not natural.

And it is not coming from me.

An overly dressed and too-fancy attendant approaches the queen, his pants gold and baggy with bells tied on chains wrapped around his waist. Maker, it is tacky, and though I want to laugh, I only let my mirth for the entertaining man show through a gaze given to my two Citizen servants, Irene and Jamie. They hide their smiles behind their hands and try to pull themselves together.

"I am being told that now is the time." The queen touches me, wrapping her arm through mine to escort me to the balcony. I stiffen, waiting for the pain, for the blackness, for everything that they told us about a Dreamcatcher's kill in the Institution, but nothing comes aside from the impatient tug. "Come on, child."

For whatever reason, I think back to the Keeper, standing by the Beacon, blurting at me that I'm her daughter, that it is my job to protect the Institution and the Seers ... to go with her. What would she think of me now, on the arm of a Dreamcatcher, being marched down some metaphorical aisle to my Dreamcatcher prince? Shouldn't it be she who gives me away? I don't know much about marriages and weddings, aside from what I've seen on the holovisions and read in books, but I thought it was someone's job to give me away.

And why do I care so much?

While I am too busy thinking about what was and what will be, we have made it to the balcony doors, which are opened wide for us. A sheet of light almost blinds me as it bursts through the space, illuminating me to everyone on the outside, but casting a glare over everything I see. It takes a moment for my eyes to adjust, and when they do, I am standing at the top of three stairs that lead down onto the balcony where Echo is waiting for me. He's dressed in his ceremonial robes with golden trim to replace the normal crimson, and the way the sun casts down on him, he looks as if he stands in a protective, summery halo.

The crowd goes silent just as soon as my image is broadcast across the millions of holos in Aura. Those who are physically gathered in the courtyard shift together in one press to get a better look at me. I feel their eyes on me, hating me, admiring me, and generally not knowing how they should react.

Echo smiles. Is he trying to be reassuring? I can only stare at him and wonder.

The queen steps down the stairs, and I have no choice but to follow her. She tugs me along as if I'm going to turn and flee at the last moment, and I actually laugh a little, finding it to be a ridiculous notion. Where could I possibly run to now?

Out of the corner of my eye, I see Brandon and Elan standing off to my side in a throng of wealthy, miserable Dreamcatchers who can't stand to be so near to them. I take a deep, calming breath, knowing how much my friends must also hate me right now. I sincerely hope they understand why I am doing what I am … this is all for Gabe. I need him back, and if this is what I have to do … then I'm doing it.

Before I know it, the queen lets go of my arm, puts my hand in Echo's, and kisses her son's cheek. She turns outward to face her people, and a loud, almost deafening cheer goes up for her. Echo's fingers twitch and squeeze around my own, and I lift my violet gaze to him and can't help but to feel sad that his wedding should have to be as forced and political as it is.

But I am also grateful that it's Echo I am being forced to marry. He has become more than just a friend to me throughout our ordeal, and I've never had reason to not trust him in the past. This is another case of me letting him hold my hand and take me into the unknown.

I tighten my grip on his fingers and steel myself.

"Today, people of Aura, we will be making history. Today, we will be marrying the Keeper to my son, Prince Echo. We will be forever closing the rift between the Dreamcatchers and the Seers, despite the wishes of those at the Institution. The previous Keeper made it her goal to create a chasm that would forever keep our two people apart. This chasm was made out of fear and jealousy that the Dreamcatchers were becoming too powerful. So, when they cast us out, put up their shields, and turned their backs on us, the Dreamcatchers went west and, with the help of my great grandparents, founded Aura." The queen begins the ceremony with some biased background of our shared history, and it doesn't surprise me. The crowd reacts, grumbling at first, but when their home city is announced, they break into wild cheering once more, too proud of their accomplishment.

"And now we must protect Aura. As long as we have the Keeper with us here, we will be safe. We will also get the many things we've demanded for years, such as new and healthy Citizens who will hopefully help to curb the plague. So while I know you are upset that our only heir, Prince Echo, must give himself away to one of them, I want you to remember the benefits of this marriage."

Echo leans over and whispers something close to my ear. "Are you sure about this, Beatrice?"

"It's the only way to get Gabe back." It is a cold reply, but I say it with an intensity that Echo can hopefully understand.

The queen steps back so that she's facing the crowd, and we turn slightly to face her. She holds her hands out and puts one over each of our heads. "In the eyes of all these witnesses here today, I, queen of the Dreamcatchers, do hereby proclaim my son, Echo, and the woman who stands beside him, Keeper Beatrice, to be wed. May they forever live out their days as husband and wife, and may their union be fruitful and blessed." She lifts Echo's chin so that he has no choice but to look into his mother's eyes. "Do you accept my blessing, my son?"

"I do," Echo whispers quietly.

"Will you protect and honor your wife until the end of your days?"

"I will."

I swallow back tears. How could I do this to Gabe?

The queen lifts my chin next. "Do you accept my blessing, Keeper Beatrice?"

I am doing this for Gabe.

"I do."

"Will you protect and honor your husband until the end of your days?"

"I will."

Everything is quiet. No one makes a sound. The wind rustles through the crowd, and expensive silks brush together, sometimes causing a whipping echo that dies as soon as the wind does. I can hear my heart beating in my ears, and Echo's palm pushes against mine, sensing, maybe, the panic beginning to fill my chest.

A too-large raven startles almost everyone as it appears overhead and bellows out its cry. It perches on the edge of the balcony, and the queen takes a step away from the black bird, confusion set in her gaze. When I look up to see the holoscreens, the cameras have all focused on the arrival of this strange omen, and people point and whisper as they regard the projected images.

"I present to you, people of Aura, your prince and his new princess, Keeper Beatrice." The queen is quick to draw the attention back to the wedding, and her announcement brings a confused cry of celebration that doesn't quite sound sincere. The words "PRINCE ECHO MARRIES KEEPER BEATRICE" flash across the bottom of the holoscreen, scrolling in an endless marquee.

From above us, servants fling white and gold rose petals that shower down and get everywhere.

"This is when I kiss you," Echo whispers into my ear while I'm busy staring up at the rose petals, some of which brush down my face and onto the ground.

I forgot about the kiss. It is insult to injury, but it's what the people want … it's how the wedding finally ends.

I also forgot about how much I enjoy kissing Echo, and when he leans down to press his lips against mine, I make no extra show of kissing him in return, aside from squeezing both of his hands in my own. I also don't pull back right away, and allow the kiss to go on as the crowds cheer around us. It's a dizzying sensation, and just before I allow myself to get lost in it, I remember Gabe back in the palace nearly dead on his stretcher. I break the kiss and manage a shy smile, if only so the camera crews can make good on it.

"Are we done now?" I shout at Echo through the endless cheering. He nods his head and leads me back up the stairs and into the palace, safe from the cameras and holoscreens and thousands of people who are both angry and fascinated with our union.

The queen stops behind us, putting a hand on Echo's shoulder. "The formal reception will begin in a few hours. That gives you two some time to settle from the ceremony."

I blush almost immediately, knowing that what she really means is much, much more. Echo bows his head in a formal gesture to his mother. "I think Beatrice and I are going to go for a walk instead. Somewhere private, where we can be left alone."

"As it pleases you, my son." She kisses Echo's cheek and turns on her heel to walk off down the long, mirrored hallway. An entourage of people follow after her, and I honestly don't know how she manages it all day long, being tailed by so many people and not having a break for herself.

"Come on, Beatrice." Echo wraps an arm through mine and pulls me close to him so we can walk together. "Just so I don't forget … " He begins and looks down at me, his white-blond hair even more radiant when he's dressed with golden accents. "You are a beautiful bride."

I smile and shyly lower my eyes away from his gaze. "Thank you." It's all I can say. I let him walk me to wherever, and I happily follow him, because I have nothing else to do here. I am his prisoner and his bride at the same time, and I only have Echo to confide in. He is my husband now and until the end of my days.

And perhaps it takes until this moment to realize for how long that actually is …

Chapter 8

The next day, they decide to revive Gabe in the back room of the healing center. The Citizen they are using has a name, but I don't bother to learn it. I don't want to learn it. I don't even want to look at her, but she's dragged across the room in front of me, and I notice her feeble, knobby knees that poke out from under her hospital gown and the way her golden hair tangles around her face. She can't be any older than I am, and in just a moment she will probably cease to exist.

Echo must sense the knot growing in my stomach and pushing its way up my throat so I can't breathe. I feel his fingers brush against mine, but I don't want to be touched. I haven't let him touch me since the wedding, when we turned to face the room of awestruck Dreamcatchers, hands joined together, newly married. I can't bring myself to think of Echo as my husband yet. Not with Gabe still in a coma. And even after … how am I supposed to tell Gabe that I belong to Echo now? To the Dreamcatchers? To the enemy?

I also forget that Echo is the one doing the healing. He insists.

The Citizen woman is tied to an unforgiving metal table, and I look away. This has to happen for Gabe. I need him back. I'd do anything to get him back … I just didn't think I'd go as far as possibly taking another's life. Or Echo's. When did I become so desperate and cold?

I look down at the silver wedding band on my finger and twirl it with my thumb as the Citizen screams in protest. Eventually, they gag her, and her screams muffle then die out.

Gabe also lies on a metal table, hooked up to the same machines that keep him breathing and stable. He looks so pale, and if I didn't know by the constant beeping of the different apparatuses, I would easily think him dead.

Echo steps forward just as his mother enters the room. She's wearing a pale yellow gown that makes her blend into the rest of the sunny accents of Aura. "Echo, I will remind you that this is a terrible idea."

When Echo looks at the Citizen, the woman stares up at him with wide, pleading eyes, and he doesn't break contact with the frantic gaze. "It is not stupid if it will save his life, Mother."

"You don't have to care about his life. He's just some Seer boy who should be on his way back to the City." I hate how she talks as if I am not here, but in this moment, I don't feel entirely here anyway. I feel like a bug on the wall, observing some sick scene that I can't stop and can't look away, either.

"He is Beatrice's, my wife's, best friend. And that means something to me, even if it doesn't mean anything to you."

Does it mean something to you, Echo? I look to my new husband and try to find some sort of truth in that statement. I don't know why, exactly, he wants Gabe to come back to us. He says it is for me, swears it is for me, but I know inside he is dreading the competition.

Echo puts his hand on the Citizen and she stiffens almost immediately. His eyes turn a crimson color that I haven't seen since the last time he killed a Citizen to heal himself. It frightens me, and I take a step back away from the tables.

"This is ludicrous," the queen announces, steeling herself to where she stands.

Echo looks to his mother, but defiantly reaches out with his other hand and pushes it down on Gabe's naked chest. Gabe jolts up, his back arching, then crashes back down on the table and starts to convulse. Echo struggles to keep his hand on him, and he stiffens in pain, his eyes glowing a fierce red. He grits his teeth together and grunts in misery, and all the while, the Citizen girl lies still, her body becoming limper and more fragile. I even think she's turning grey, and I can't stand to look at her any more.

"Echo … " I start, wanting him to stop. But I don't want him to stop. I want Gabe back.

I need Gabe back.

Gabe cries out, and it's the first time I've heard his voice since the Institution. Echo cries out at the same time, and I notice that every time Echo yells in agony, Gabe does too.

"What is happening?" I blurt at the queen, expecting her to tell me that this is normal, a part of the process. But she looks just as concerned as I do, and my question goes ignored.

Eventually, Echo forces his hand off of Gabe, as if it was being sucked into his chest by an unseen force. Echo then crumples to the floor in a lifeless ball.

And Gabe opens his eyes.

The Citizen doesn't move.

None of us do.

I don't know who to run to first, and my legs are stiff, fixing me to my spot. I'm paralyzed with fear that I just lost Echo to Gabe. Why did I let him go through with this?

Gabe turns his head and surveys where he is. He is confused, I can see it in the way his brows knit together in concern, so I step forward, deciding to approach the both of them at one time.

"Beatrice?" Gabe whispers, his voice rash and wispy from being silent for so long.

I stop beside Echo, but before I can check on him to make sure he is okay, his mother rushes up behind me and shoves me out of the way and into Gabe's gurney. I catch myself on the edge, just short of smashing into Gabe's frail body, then look down at my no longer comatose best friend. "Gabe."

The Dreamcatcher Queen rocks Echo's lifeless body in her arms and actually begins to sob. That is my husband, possibly dead, and yet, all I can concentrate on is Gabe, who looks as confused than ever.

"What happened?" he asks.

The doors to the healing center open, and Brandon and Elan step in. Both of them scan the scene, and when they notice Gabe is alive, they hurry over to his side, caring little for Echo's lifeless body, or the way his mother cries out his name.

"Echo, come back to us ... come back to us. This girl is not worth it!" The queen means me, and I am starting to believe the same thing. I'm not worth it. I'm not worth Echo's life.

"Excuse me," I whisper the words to Gabe and the same guilt I felt when I left him floods over me again as I choose to go to Echo. Kneeling to the ground, I try to reach out to put my hand on Echo's head, to brush back his hair, to just touch him and feel that he's still warm, but his mother won't let me. She jerks Echo away from my fingers, and if she were a cat, she'd probably hiss at me to keep me at bay.

"Leave us!" the queen blurts in her rage. "He should have never brought you back here ..."

"But he did," I deadpan.

The queen's icy glare meets with mine. "And he shouldn't have. Bringing the Keeper into Aura with the silly dream that she'd be able to save us all? My son believes too much in people, Keeper Beatrice. His mistake this time was believing too much in you."

"Keeper Beatrice?" Gabe asks, probably having no idea why I am being referred to as such.

I frown. "I never said I could save anyone, and I never gave him that idea. He came to me and told me that I needed to save him, and he needed to save me. It wasn't the other way around."

"I don't care how it really went, Keeper. You took my son away from me."

"I did no such thing." My words are deep and to the bone.

The Dreamcatcher Queen doesn't bait me any further. I stand back up and look down at Echo's lifeless body, and I find myself yearning for him just like I yearned for Gabe when I thought he was lost from this world as well. Tears well in my eyes when I least expect them to, and my heart feels as if it is being ripped down the middle.

The Citizen on the table hasn't moved for a long while either, and Brandon goes as far as poking the girl in her arm, but immediately retracts his hand. "She's cold."

"She's dead," the queen hisses now.

"Dead? So we killed a Citizen in order to save Gabe?" Elan narrows his eyes on me, as if I'm at fault for this.

"Echo said there was a small chance that she would live … that she'd most likely not make it… " I start, but it is Gabe who cuts me off next.

"Someone died to save me?" He sits up, his chest bare and covered with beads of sweat. "Someone … died?"

"Gabe, we had no other choice. You were going to die ... " I put my hand on his arm to steady him. "You were going to die."

Gabe yanks his arm away from my fingers. "Where are we?"

"Aura," Elan helpfully points out. "With the Dreamcatchers. You should ask Beatrice why. It's really an interesting story."

Brandon shifts in his spot and doesn't look at me any longer. All of them seem to have turned themselves against me, and when I look from one face to the next, they avoid my gaze.

The only person who doesn't look away from me is Echo, and that's because his mother is still holding his lifeless body in her arms. I stare too long at him and my head begins to swim with pain. My fingers barely brush against the metal table in time to grab hold of it so I don't end up falling. A Vision.

I can hear them talking, but their words sound like they are under water. One moment, I am standing in the middle of a ring of people who have nothing but anger for me, and the next moment, I am in blackness, and there's nothing. I am nothing, and it is silent.

***

The haze begins to clear, and Echo is there. He stands in front of me and seems surprised, as if I am not supposed to be there. Or maybe it is him who isn't supposed to be here? The surprise melts away into a gentle smile, and he holds his arms out for me, and I have no other inclination than to go to him.

I want him. I wrap my arms around him and hold him close to me. I bury my face into his chest and hide my eyes, my soul, my everything from everyone. Only Echo can see me now. He is mine, and I am his, and we are joined in marriage and dreams and Visions. I trust no one other than Echo, because he's only ever trusted me.

But somewhere in the distance, I hear someone calling my name. Gabe. I can barely make out his voice, but I know it's there, even if Echo doesn't seem to show any indication that he can hear Gabe, too. Echo's hands are on my back, then slide up my neck and onto my cheeks, and he draws me into a passionate kiss that should never end up breaking. I don't want it to. I kiss him back, again and again.

And Gabe calls louder and louder until his voice breaks like someone rising to the surface of the ocean to breathe in the fresh, salt water air. Echo disappears, and everything turns black once more.

***

When the Vision ends, I wake up on the floor. My head is throbbing. I must have fallen after all. I look up, and can barely make out the faces that hover over me, the most prominent being Brandon, who lightly slaps my cheek with his hand to get me to come around.

"Beatrice? Are you back?" he asks and taps my cheek again.

"Please stop slapping me," I mutter and rub at my face with my palm. My eyes are sensitive to the light, so I close them again and lie in place, unwilling to test my resolve so soon after these Visions I've been having. "I'm fine. It was just a Vision."

"Of what?" Gabe asks, though his tone suggests he is still upset with me.

"You." I half lie. "I heard you calling for me."

"I was calling for you." Gabe rolls his eyes and lays back down on his stretcher. I'm sure that all of this is probably a lot to soak in for someone who has just come out of a coma.

"Well … that's what it was." I drag my elbow up and push myself into a sitting position. It's now that I realize that the Dreamcatcher Queen and Echo are gone. "Where'd she'd take Echo?"

Elan responds while holding his hands out to help me to my feet. "She is bringing him to another healing ward. When you were in your Vision, he woke up … but it's not looking so well."

I remember how he kissed me in my Vision, and suddenly have an urge to go to him. "I should be with him."

"Why?" Gabe coughs and Brandon pulls a blanket up over his recovering friend. "Why do you care so much about some stupid Dreamcatcher?"

"Because he saved you, Gabe." I frown at him and his ungratefulness. "He risked his own life in order to bring you back to us. To me."

Gabe rubs his head, his greasy, long hair falling in front of his eyes. "I don't understand. Why would he care about saving me? He's the enemy. He's a damned Dreamcatcher, the same ones we are supposed to be killing and eliminating and keeping from getting to the City. The same one—"

"That she married," Elan cuts Gabe off and slices to the heart of the matter.

There's a silence that settles over the room, shrouding it in emotion. Gabe's gaze meets my own, and he searches my eyes for an answer … an explanation, neither of which I've prepared myself to give.

LUCIDITY

Chapter 9

Now that I'm married, I'm expected to live with Echo. This means that Gabe can't be housed in my—no, Paradigm's—quarters any more. After his healing, they've taken Gabe, Elan, and Brandon to a holding room, where the guards can easily watch the three of them, as if they were going to do something.

I am anxious to see Gabe again, but I'm not allowed to go to him right now. Instead, I am being forced to take part in this silly moving in ceremony that Dreamcatchers go through after they marry. The tradition is based on the old tradition of the wife moving in together with the husband in a new home. Here, the wife moves into wherever her husband lives.

Attendants carry boxes of wedding gifts past me and into Echo's room. They are deposited in a designated corner, and after a while, I begin to wonder if the line of servants would ever end. Echo is not here because he's still recovering from Gabe's healing. I haven't been allowed to see him, either. I am separated from everyone I know, and am left here, a new princess, monarch to the enemy.

Already, it is boring. I try to walk away, but just as I turn to make my escape, Jamie and Irene appear, both with bright fabrics draped in their arms. Before I can open my mouth to excuse myself, they block my way and start chattering.

"Look what you got, Keeper Beatrice!" Jamie starts.

"Aren't they beautiful? You are so lucky!" Irene only realizes after that she's speaking so informally, and she corrects herself with a blush. "Uh—Your Highness."

"I am nobody's 'highness.'" That is something I just can't deal with. It's bad enough I've been born into the unfortunate position of being the next Keeper; I certainly do not want to adopt another title on top of it. "Just call me Keeper Beatrice."

Jamie and Irene both curtsy at the same time and reply together, "Yes, My Keeper."

That's better, I think to myself. "I was just on my way out. I wanted to see if I could visit Echo." And I do want to visit Echo, since I now worry for him just as much as I worried for Gabe when he was incapacitated.

The two servants exchange a glance, and Jamie shakes her head. "I don't think anyone is allowed to see him just yet, Keeper Beatrice. The queen wishes for him to heal alone."

There's something they aren't telling me; I can sense it.

And they know I can.

"He's not doing very well, My Keeper," Irene whispers at last, even when Jamie glares at her for maybe saying too much. "They tried to heal him twice already, but he's just not coming around."

This is terrible news, and I take a deep breath and watch as the end of the servants drop off a few more gifts before departing. Echo's room is not like Paradigm's at all. It is stately, with its royal blue walls and crown molding. There are polished pieces of dark-stained furniture, so polished that they reflect the image of the items around them. I take a good look at where I'll be staying, and when my gaze moves to our marriage bed, I blush and quickly look away. At least I won't have to worry about that for a little while.

It's a horrible thought to have since my relief stems from Echo's pain and suffering—pain and suffering that was ultimately caused by me. "Well, I want to try. What sort of wife would I be if I just sat around here and didn't even try?"

My mind is made up, and I brush by the girls, who are left in my wake carrying the burden of all those fancy bolts of fabrics. I'm afraid that the guards will stop me on my way out, but strangely, they are not here. Perhaps they have not had their posts adjusted yet. They are not used to the fact that their enemy Keeper is now lodging with their prince.

Still, I must be careful. I don't rush around corners, but I stop, my slippered feet soft on the marble floors, and I peek around the bend to make sure no one is there. Once I determine it is clear, I start on my way again. I realize, as I am meandering about the palace, that I have no idea where I am going, or where Echo is being kept. Is he back in the healing center? Did they move him into the palace?

These questions swirl through my mind as I aimlessly continue my search. I could probably escape now, if I wanted to. I could find a way back to the spaceport, but then what? No one from Aura would willingly take me back to the City. And the journey back across the Outlands was treacherous, probably even more so if I was on my own.

On top of all of that, I can't leave Gabe, Elan, and Brandon behind. And without me, they'd all probably be killed. I am the only reason why they are alive. The queen doesn't need them any more than she needs a common Citizen. I have to constantly remind myself that I'm walking amongst the enemy. If it wasn't for the serum that I took every morning, I'd have the pain to keep me aware of the fact that I am swimming in a sea of Dreamcatchers, but I don't even have that.

I finally find Echo in a cozy room tucked away in his mother's side of the palace. The wing is expansive, with a décor that would be expected of a queen. Everything is a dusty color of gold, or the yellow-orange of a sunrise.

When I knock lightly on the door, it's Echo who responds. "Yes?"

I peek my head around the corner and find that my husband is in much better shape than Gabe. He is lying in a bed draped with royal blue sheets, and fluffy pillows have been piled high around his head. His healing must have gone over better, since there's color in his cheeks, and his eyes are as blue as ever. "Mind a visitor?"

"Doesn't Gabe need you?" Echo doesn't say this with any conviction. It's a simple question, an honest one, and yet, I don't answer it honestly.

"He's fine." He kicked me out. He won't talk to me. He's not fine at all. "I was worried about you. No one would tell me where you were. I had to search the whole palace to find out."

Echo rolls his eyes and pats the edge of his bed, inviting me over to sit. The mattress is soft and cushiony, and I could easily crawl into it, slip under the covers and will myself back to the City. At least through my dreams. Dreams that Echo probably knows about in some capacity or another. "I don't know why my mother is being how she is. I chose to heal Gabe on my own—it's not like you made me."

"It will always be my fault. As long as I am here and married to you, it will always be my fault." I put the back of my hand to Echo's forehead to check for a fever. He doesn't look feverish at all, but it's what people do to sick people when they want to show they are concerned.

Echo sucks in a deep breath and his hand reaches up to mine, and he pulls it away from his forehead to hold it instead. "I know you don't want to be married to me."

He is right. I don't want to be married to him. Not because I don't like him, or love him, even, but because this is not my calling. I'm not meant to be a wife. Seers aren't wives. Keepers aren't wives. I'm not supposed to fall in love.

And though I know all of this inside my head, there doesn't seem to be a way I can express it in words without crushing Echo entirely. I don't want to hurt him. Hurting Gabe is torture enough.

"I never expected to be married." It seems the diplomatic way of saying everything that is running through my mind.

"I understand, you know. We can be friends and just … let everyone else see us as husband and wife."

"We are husband and wife," I point out bluntly.

Echo squeezes my hand. "You know what I mean."

"Gabe is upset with me." The words tumble out of my mouth before I can stop them. "He's upset that I'm married to you, and he won't talk to me. He asked me to leave his cell, and I've not been back to check on him since."

Echo's lips purse into a concerned frown and he lets go of my hand to run his fingers through his blond hair. "Well, it's normal for him to be angry about it. He's probably shocked. By many things. He's woken up and found out that you're not just his friend anymore, you are his Keeper."

As always, Echo is a voice of reason. Gabe has woken out of a coma to find out that his whole world has been shaken like one of those snow globes that the Citizens collect, and each little piece of white is something in his life that has been rattled out of place.

"Give him some time, Beatrice." Though he offers the advice, I know it pains him. I feel like Echo loves me just as much as Gabe does, and every time I bring Gabe up, it's like turning a knife inside of Echo's guts. He doesn't want Gabe to come around like I do. And he probably is happy with me being his wife.

The thing about Echo is, he tries to please everyone at once. He is trying to please Aura, his mother, his sister, me ... but he's never watching out for himself. And that's a dangerous place to be.

"I will have to, won't I?" I'm miserable just thinking about the fact that Gabe doesn't want me near him. What would he do if I left here and went back to his cell? Would he still turn me away? The anticipation of rejection is enough to keep me from going there to find out. I don't want to be turned away again. Not by Gabe.

Echo tugs on my arm, and I lie down, resting my head on his chest as he cradles me close to him. "It'll be okay, Beatrice. I promise you that this will all work out. I promised you that I'd get Gabe back, didn't I?"

I can hear his heart beating through his chest, and it's strangely calming. I let my eyelids flutter shut and invite the comforting darkness, wishing I was back home in my bunk, before the Dreamcatchers invaded, before I became the Keeper. Life was much simpler then, my days filled with the Training Games and classes.

Echo rakes his fingers through my hair, and when I open my eyes, black strands fall across my face. I blow them out of my vision with a puff of air, then tilt my head up to look at Echo, who may have been staring down at me this whole time. He hooks a finger under my chin and lifts it just high enough so that he can lower his lips to mine in a gentle kiss.

I kiss him back with a need that surprises me. Before I understand what is driving me to do this, I turn toward Echo so that the kiss can blossom into something more. Maybe I'm thirsty for affection, a break from the whirlwind my life has become. I grab at his robes and the kiss only parts when Echo pushes my shoulders with his palms so he can look up into my eyes.

"Beatrice?" He says my name with concern, as if asking if I am sure about what we are doing.

"Don't talk, Echo. Just let it be." I don't know where this part of me is coming from. It's a part which wants to be accepted and loved without all the politics behind it. Echo feels safe to me. For so long he's existed only in my dreams, but even then, his presence was comforting and real. Now that he has me here with him, it's even more real.

He obeys and leans back down to kiss me, and our lips graze each other's just as his mother walks into the room and stops in the doorway, surprised. It's the clearing of her throat that brings the kiss to a definite end.

"Mother," Echo greets her in a somewhat disappointed manner that dares me to smile.

"I see that you are feeling better. And that your … wife … has found you." The queen's icy stare narrows on me, and I instinctively clutch onto Echo.

"I am feeling much better, yes."

"And her paramour? How does he feel?"

Now I sit up, my fingers uncurling from Echo's robes. "Gabe's not my 'paramour.'"

"I suppose not, since you now lay with my son." The queen looks between us.

I blush furiously at the thought of laying with Echo at all. Her words are a double-edged sword, and it cuts through me just as she planned. I want to withdraw, but I know that is what she wants me to do, so I stay where I am, heavy with guilt. What was I thinking? What will Gabe think?

Echo cuts in where I don't speak. "Mother, it's not really your concern as far as my relationship with Beatrice goes. I'd appreciate it if you could keep your comments to yourself."

The queen looks as if Echo has slapped her, and she crosses her arms in front of her chest, resting her slender fingers against her pale skin. "Very well. But I will have you know that your relationship is every bit of my concern. It is what will fix what the Seers have broken. It will align us with the City, our original home."

"Yes, I know." Echo has probably heard this speech more than a billion times. His hand finds my forearm and he presses his fingers against it in a hidden and much needed gesture of support.

"The Keeper is our princess now. Let the City figure out what they should do without her, I don't care. But she's not leaving here until she finds a way to both stop this plague and restore our people's dignity." She leaves on that note, giving me no time to reply. Their dignity? What did that have to do with anything?

Echo laughs shallowly and wraps his arms around me. "Well, that certainly ruined the moment, didn't it?"

I want to laugh, but the queen's words echo through my head and keep me from doing so. I push myself off the bed and brush my hands down my black robes, which I still stubbornly wear, despite the queen's wishes. "I should go." When I look back at Echo, there's a clear flash of disappointment that flickers over his features. I stare at him for a long while then leave before the tension between us shatters me.

Chapter 10

When I get back to the cell where Gabe, Elan, and Brandon are being kept, it's lights out for them. They aren't exactly locked in there like prisoners, but there is a guard posted in the hallway, just in case any of them decides to make a break for it. The guard shoots me a disapproving look, much like every other Dreamcatcher in Aura, and just like every other time, I ignore it.

I push the metal door open, perhaps one of the only doors in the palace that uses a material that is a little more our time than the wooden doors from long ago that they use. A sliver of light grows the more I open the door, until it finally illuminates Gabriel, who is not asleep like Elan and Brandon are. He is staring at the door, and maybe he has been waiting for me to come this whole while. Or maybe he is just thinking about how to escape.

"Gabe?" I whisper and shut the door behind me. He doesn't answer back, not even when I fumble about to find his bunk, which is only half occupied, as Brandon and Elan are sleeping in another bunk on the other side of the small room.

Finally, I reach my destination, and without an invite, I slip into the bottom bunk beside Gabe, who doesn't move away from me, but doesn't make any move to be closer to me, either.

"Gabe?" I ask again.

Still, he doesn't answer.

"Listen, I know you are mad at me … and that this is all very confusing for you since you've woken up out of your coma …
"

"I didn't just 'wake up,' I was healed. By your husband." He says the last word with a conviction so intense that my heart immediately feels heavy in my chest, as if it were sinking down between my lungs and toward my stomach.

This seems like a good place to explain things, though, so I swallow back my fear and start to do just that. "They are keeping me prisoner here." That's what comes out of my mouth first. Let him understand that I am not staying here out of my own accord, even if I made a promise not to leave until the Citizens were freed and the plague was gone. I will have to explain that to him later, because right now it feels like I am running out of time, and Gabe can, at any moment, dismiss me from his life forever.

"I thought about you all the time. You were in my dreams, my Visions, everything. So, somehow, Echo arranged for you to come to Aura to be healed. I had no idea ... but his mother ..." I grit my teeth together and shoot a look toward the door, wondering if she'll make an appearance. She seems to be everywhere and anywhere, just like the Keeper back at the Institution. "His mother decreed that the only way you would be healed would be if I married Echo. So I did, because if I didn't, you'd be dead."

"Being dead would hurt less than this does, Beatrice." Gabe's voice cracks in a rare show of emotion. My heart drops further inside me.

"I'm sorry, Gabe, I really am ... but I didn't want you to die. I couldn't think of living in this world without you ... and I can't think of myself as being any sort of reasonable Keeper without your help." This is a rather radical thought, that the Keeper should need help from anyone at all. Sure, the previous Keeper had her attendants and officers, but she didn't have an advisor. I need Gabe when I get back to the City. I just can't do it without him.

Gabe's violet eyes find mine, and the longer I stare into them, the more the sadness begins to swell up inside of me, wrapping its tendrils around every inside part, squeezing the life from them.

"Get out." The words slice through me.

I can't move. Did he just tell me to leave? Is my time really up already?

"I can't deal with this, Beatrice. My head is swimming, and it's too much to hear that not only are you the Keeper, but you've abandoned the City and married a Dreamcatcher."

"I didn't abandon the City."

Gabe frowns. "Then why are you here and not there?"

I pause. The words awkwardly tumble from my mouth. "I had dreams and Visions and they all called me here."

"Echo called you here!" Gabe blurts in a loud whisper, careful not to wake the other two, even if I can see the rage boiling in his gaze. "This has nothing to do with a Vision. He put it in your head that you had to be here. He is manipulating you to believe that you are needed to cure the plague, and you aren't, Beatrice. You aren't."

When he touches me, he grabs me by my arms and shakes me until my head bobs back and forth. "Why can't you see any of this? You are smarter than this, Bea, and you are acting like a ... a ... heartsick little puppy."

I push his hands off me and frown. "Stop it. I am not acting like some puppy. I am trying to help these people, Gabe. If you saw the way they have their Citizens living ... if you saw the Birthing Tents and the families huddled in shanty houses ... I can't just leave them here." After a pause, I continue in a much gentler tone. "As Seers, it is our duty to protect the Citizens, right?"

Gabe grumbles something indecipherable.

"And that's what I am doing. They might not be our Citizens, but they are Citizens none-the-less, and they don't deserve to be enslaved and bred and used for healing." My chest rises and falls like I've just run a marathon. Having this conversation is just as exhausting,

"Whatever you want to call it, Beatrice. All I know is, I want to go home and forget any of this ever happened." Gabe rubs his forehead with both of his hands, smushing his palms against his eyes.

I swallow, then pull on the bottle cap necklace that is hidden under my robes until it comes out. "Just remember." Reaching out, I pull one of his hands away from his eyes so that he's peeking at me through the tussled hair that falls in front of his face. "This is only temporary. I might be a princess to these people now, but I am first and foremost a Seer. The Keeper."

Gabe's eye blinks and he pulls his other hand away from his face.

"I'm your Beatrice." The words sound so pathetic, and are whispered just barely enough to be heard. Even as I say it, I can't help but to think how I can belong to two people at once. How do I give my heart to both of them without hurting the other?

And I know what my answer is.

I can't have them both.

Gabe sinks back down in his covers and pulls them up to his shoulder, not minding the part that I am sitting on. "Goodnight, Beatrice."

That's my cue that it's my turn to leave. I lean down and kiss Gabe's forehead before he can stop me, then stand and creep back out of the room and into the brightly-lit hallway. The guard gives me that same, annoyed stare, and I glare at him back. I'm in no mood now.

I have to figure out whom to follow.

***

I arrive back to Echo's quarters and find that he's not there. Thankfully. I don't think I could handle the pressure of our first night together, or the disappointment when I turn him down.

I slip out of my robes and let it fall on the ground in a puddle of midnight fabric. Then, I wiggle out of my underclothing and into a set of pajamas that have been laid out for me on top of the covers of the bed. Irene and Jamie must have been by, judging by the turned-down sheets and a light snack of berries set onto a side table.

I pop one into my mouth before crawling under the covers. I lay back, my head sinking into a pillow which nests around my face and makes me feel like the walls are closing in. In a way, I feel safe, buried in my blankets and pillows.

But when I close my eyes and try to will myself into sleep, that is when a Vision grabs hold of me. I grip onto the covers as the bright light washes out my true vision and replaces it with my gift instead.

***

Paradigm stands before me. She is wearing the same polka-dot dress that she did when she was executed. Even the dark bloodstains are there, shiny and moist, as if the execution had just happened.

The smaller girl crosses her arms over her chest and regards me like a mother would a chastised child. "Beatrice, what have you done?"

I don't answer her, since I have no idea what she is talking about. What have I done? What has her family done?

"They've done nothing." She answers my question, somehow in tune with my thoughts. "But you, you've come to Aura and turned it all upside down. Or at least, that is what you plan to do."

"It is what needs to be done," I tell her, because outside of my Vision, Paradigm doesn't exist. Outside of my Vision, she is nothing and has no power to tell anyone what I share with her here. "Aura needs to change. The Dreamcatchers need to change. We all need to change."

"The Dreamcatchers will die." Paradigm's arms fall back to her sides. "They will die if you don't stop your crusade to free the Citizens and instead find a way to cure the plague."

"And how do you expect that I do that?"

"You need to gather the leaves."

"What? What does that even mean?"

"You need to go into the Outlands and gather the leaves. They are purple-ish and curl up at night when the sun goes away."

I purse my lips together in thought. "So you are telling me that I have to wander out into the dangerous Outlands to find a purple leaf?"

"You will need more than just one leaf to help rid Aura of the plague, Keeper Beatrice." Paradigm steps closer to me and pokes me in the chest with one of her bony, pale, dead-like fingers. "Do not let my brother die. You may have killed me, but I'm not letting you kill him."

"I didn't kill you," I blurt almost immediately, but in just that moment, Paradigm is gone, and the blackness starts to swallow up the light of the Vision, and I wake once more.

***

I sit up, holding my head in my hands. It throbs, and I can't take much of the pain any longer. There's an intercom located on the table, and I press the button, not knowing who will pick up.

Thankfully, it's Irene. "Yes, Keeper Beatrice?"

"I've had a Vision ... I need something cool to drink, and some medicine for my headache."

"I will bring you the serum, I'm sure it's wearing off by now. You are up very late!" Irene chides me in a too-cheerful tone. "Be right there, Keeper Beatrice!"

The plant with the purple leaves. I have to scour the whole of the Outlands, anywhere between here and the City, to find a plant with purple leaves that curl up without the sun. The task is already daunting, and I've not even set out on it yet.

On top of this, I have to ask: Do I trust my own Vision? How did Paradigm get into my head? And how did she know where to direct me? Some mysteries of Visions will never be solved, and I sink back into the pillow and ponder how, exactly, I'm going to find this purple leaf plant.

Chapter 11

The next day, I decide that I have to tell the others about my Vision. Unlike the other Seers, I am not required to share any of my Visions, and as far as I know, the previous Keeper never shared a Vision of hers with anyone.

Echo is well enough to attend the meeting, and it's the first time that he and Gabe have been in the same place since the healing. We gather in a room designed for meetings, with a long, wooden table and several chairs set around it. Gabe, Brandon, and Elan sit on one side of the table, and Echo sits opposite them. I remain standing, and the queen will take her place at the head of the table, should she ever bother to show up. So far, she is late, and we are all waiting on her.

Gabe stares at Echo, unafraid to show the intense distaste for the Dreamcatcher, or any Dreamcather at that. Echo meets his gaze some of the time, but mostly he is watching me with curiosity in his eyes. Surely, he is wondering why I'd call them all into the same room, especially when there's four of us and only one of him.

"Can we get started?" Elan asks impatiently.

"I think my mother should be here."

"Do you need your mommy for everything?" Gabe cuts in, crossing his arms over his chest.

"I saved your life. I'd think you'd be more grateful," Echo calmly replies without a touch of anger rising into his words.

"Grateful?" Gabe laughs, and it's the sort of laugh that shoots a chill up your spine.

I step forward and sit where the queen would sit. "I think it's best if both of you just don't talk to each other for now." Casting a glance to the door, I wait to see if it will magically swing open with the queen waiting outside, but there's no such luck. "I guess we can get started."

But just as soon as I get the words out, a servant bursts through the door, out of breath and flushed. "Prince Echo ... " She can't catch her breath, and everything that bubbles out of her mouth is in broken sentences. "Queen ... she ... and first ... but then ... and the plague ... spread."

Echo tilts his head, latching on to the last few words like a fish to a hook. "What about my mother and the plague?"

Brandon leans his elbows on the table and cradles his chin in one of his hands. "I think she's trying to say that your mother has the plague?"

Echo glares at Brandon, and the servant nods her head, "Yes ... it spread ... into the palace. You must ... go back to your quarters and be quarantined." She looks to the rest of us. "All of you."

"Hell no. I'm not going anywhere with you freaks." Gabe pushes his chair away from the table and stands up. "This is stupid. I want to go back to the City."

"Is she okay?" Echo ignores Gabe's comment in order to find more information about his mother. I stand when Gabe does, but I walk over to Echo's side, waiting to hear of any further news.

"No." The servant girl looks at us all. "It's spread. It's worse ... "

"Worse?" I question.

"Forgive me for saying, Your Highness, but I don't think she will live much past the day. She's vomiting blood and can't keep anything down. They've tried to heal her, but it is not working." The servant bows down low in a sign of deep respect. "I need to be quarantined now. The guard will be coming to escort you to quarantine as well." Before any of us can stop her, she races out, probably just as quickly as she raced over here.

"So, she came from the queen … then to us … without being quarantined?" Elan rolls his eyes. "What sort of sense does that make? She's exposed us all now."

Echo doesn't say anything. He stands there in a state of shock, then runs both of his hands through his hair, tugging at the roots. Eventually, he sinks down into his chair, his eyes lowered, defeated.

It breaks my heart, and I move behind him and hesitate to put my hand on his shoulder for fear that any sign of affection will set Gabe off. I withdraw my hand before it touches Echo, but I stay close to him to let him know I'm there. "I had a Vision."

"Is that why you called us here?" Brandon glances around and adds, "Is there going to be any food?"

I frown at Brandon's latter question and shake my head. "This is serious, Brandon."

Admonished, Brandon nods his head with a quiet, "Yes, Keeper Beatrice."

"Keeper Beatrice," Gabe mutters after Brandon.

I sigh and continue with my thought. "I had a Vision about the cure to the plague."

This is when Echo looks up at me, his eyes flashing with hope. "You had the Vision?"

"A Vision, yes. I don't know if it is accurate or not, though —"

"Of course it is. You are the Keeper. And everyone knows your Visions always come true in some way or another." Elan shatters my humility with his words. Sometimes I wonder where this boy's manners went, or what made him so angry at the world.

Echo grabs my wrist and tugs me closer to his chair. "The cure? Well, what is it?"

The urgency and strength of his grip distracts me for a moment, but I soon come back to my thoughts, violet eyes meeting his. "It was your sister who told me. She said that there's a plant in the Outlands … "

Gabe starts to laugh now, that same, sinister laugh that doesn't represent anything funny. "The Outlands?"

"Yes, Gabe, the Outlands. There's a plant with purple leaves that curl up without the sunlight. She said I had to find the plant and bring it back. It is the cure. I don't know how … but it is."

"Then we should go!" Echo decides almost immediately, jumping to his feet. He's but centimeters away from me, and the closeness brings a blush to my cheeks, especially since he's still holding on to my wrist. "Let's go."

"Oh no. You aren't going anywhere with her." Gabe stands as well. His physique is hardier than Echo's, and where Echo is thin, Gabe is bulky and toned from training. He could probably pummel Echo, but Echo could also kill him with just one touch. I pull my wrist away from Echo and stand between them, holding my arms out to keep them from getting any closer to one another.

When I turn to address Echo, I notice a thin line of blood that has begun to trail down from his nose. He's bleeding, or rather, his nose is bleeding. "Echo, are you okay?"

"Yes. Why?" He puts his hand up to his nose and pulls it away, only to find his fingers smeared with crimson.

Panic surges through me, but I can't let Echo see it. If he sees it, he will panic as well. But, as I watch him, I come to understand that he's already filled with a sudden and intense anxiety. He wipes his nose again.

Gabe thankfully doesn't say anything spiteful, and instead, I whisper quietly to Echo, "We should get you back to your room. Gabe will go with me. You can trust him to bring me back." Slipping my hand into Echo's non-bloodied one, I calmly face the others and say, "I am going to walk Echo back to his room, and when I return, we will figure out a plan on how to find the leaf." My eyes meet with Gabriel's but briefly, a silent plea for him to behave and be patient.

"Fine. But hurry up," Gabe huffs and plops back down in his chair, arms crossed over his chest. He's not staring at me or Echo, but rather at our hands. I feel his eyes on me until the very moment when I step out of the room.

Echo and I walk back to his quarters in silence. He keeps a hand over his nose, which has continued to bleed, albeit slowly. I know what this means. The servant was right. The plague has spread into the palace. I have no idea if it can effect Seers or not, but I don't care in this moment. All I care about is the fact that Echo's mother is dying somewhere in some room, and Echo has come down with a plague symptom. I could lose him, just like he is going to lose her.

When we are safe inside his room, Echo dismisses all of his servants, and they scurry out like mice in the dark when the lights turn on. I hurry and grab a towel from the washroom and quickly return to his side. Reaching up, I dab the cloth against his face as I look into his eyes. "Hold this and pinch your nose. It will stop."

"No, it won't, Beatrice." Echo's words are so stark and naked that the truth of it hurts.

"Don't talk like that. It can just be a simple nose bleed, and you will get better, and don't worry, okay?" The words leave my mouth in one sentence with no room for breathing. I help Echo over to his bed and when he lies back, I cover him with the luscious navy blue sheets. "There you go."

Echo stares up at me over the towel, which he still holds to his nose. His icy eyes are desperate and scared, and it's the first time that I've ever seen him look that way. Echo has never been frightened around me. Even during the invasion of the City, he was brave and strong. Relentless. But now, he looks so small and helpless, a victim to something he can't control.

I run my fingers through his hair to calm him, then reach with my other hand to take the towel away from his face. His nose has stopped bleeding, for now. The bleeding will become worse, though, and will continue to worsen until the plague has run its course. As I comb my fingers through Echo's hair, I realize I'm doing it more to calm myself than to calm him. I can't lose him.

"You have to find the leaf," Echo whispers.

"I know, Echo. And I will." My voice cracks, despite myself. "I will."

Echo lifts his hand and rubs a thumb down the side of my face and over my jawbone. Then, he lifts his other hand and cradles it around the back of my head, drawing me down to where he lies. His lips press to mine, and I drink him in as he kisses me with an urgency that I've never felt before. Warmness spreads through my body as Echo draws me into the bed, closer to him. So close to him. Too close to him.

But I move with it. I go to him. I let him wrap me up in his arms, and when he pushes me back onto the bed, I let him do that too. I kiss him back every time he kisses me, and when he brushes his hand down my middle and rests it on my stomach, I don't stop him.

All I can think about is how I might come back, and he might be gone.

Between kisses, Echo mutters against my lips, "You have to come back."

"And you have to be here when I do." My lips graze against his, barely touching at first, but then he's kissing me again, and I'm lost inside his every touch. I don't want him to stop. I don't want to lose him. I don't want to walk away from this room and leave him behind, sick and dying.

But ultimately, I have to. And it's too important to ignore it for a wash of kisses that will do neither of us any good.

I gently push Echo away, breaking the connection between us. "I should go now, and you should rest."

Expectantly, Echo looks as if I just pulled his whole world out from under him. I roll out of the bed and fix up my robes by brushing my trembling hands over the fabric. My lips are numb and tingle from the needy kissing, and I can feel the warmth that has blossomed inside of me spread like fire over my skin. "Don't worry, Echo ... I will come back. And you can stay in my dreams."

"I already planned on it." Echo smiles, but the smile fades when another line of blood starts to trail down his nose and over his mouth. He quickly grabs the towel and puts it to his face. He apologetically peeks out at me, and I lean over to kiss his forehead one last time. "I'll send your servants in to attend to you on my way out."

"Beatrice?"

"Yes?"

Echo pulls the towel away from his face. "Please find that plant."

I will. I hear myself say it in my head. *I will, Echo. I will.*

But the Outlands are so vast and dangerous, and I have no idea if I will make it back to Aura or not.

For some reason, I say, "I promise." Then I hurry and leave the room.

Gabe, Elan, and Brandon are right where I have left them, and judging by their rather curious stares, I know that I probably look as tousled and flushed as I feel. I clear my throat, avoid Gabe's gaze, and sit down at the end of the table. "Here's the deal," I begin, getting to business before anyone can say anything about my state. "Gabe and I will go to find the leaves. If we find them and return, we will use them to barter our freedom and safe passage back to the City. If we don't find them or don't return ... "

"Then all these Dreamcatchers will die." Elan taps his fingers on the table. "Part of me doesn't want you to find those leaves, to be honest. That will be one less problem for the City to deal with. Or maybe they will just fall apart without their queen."

"Elan, try to be a little more open-minded. One of them is Beatrice's husband now..." Brandon reminds not only Elan, but Gabe, who visibly winces at the words.

"You are wrong. They won't fall apart. They will fall under the rule of Echo," I correct Elan.

"And if he dies?" Elan rests his elbow on the table, a bit too nonchalantly.

"If … if Echo dies … " I start, the words leaving me in a whisper. "If he dies, then Aura will probably be turned over to the queen's advisor. I didn't catch his name, but I've heard from Jamie and Irene that he wishes to cull the Citizens, capture healthy ones, and breed them anew. I can't let that happen." I lean forward and put my palms on the table as I regard the three in front of me. "I won't let it happen. Because even if you hate the Dreamcatchers, which we've all been raised to do, we are still sworn to protect the Citizens. So it is as much your job as it is mine to make sure that the queen and Echo don't perish before we can get back."

Elan frowns at me, but thankfully, there's no smart remark to follow.

"We will take care of things here, Beatrice. Don't you worry," Brandon assures me. Another day in another place, I might have found it to be funny, Brandon standing up and taking some authority over a matter. But right now, I am grateful for his support.

"Thank you, Brandon." Drawing in a deep breath, I look back to Gabe, meeting his gaze head on for the first time since I've come back to the room. "We should get ready, then. See if we can find some mode of transportation to get to the Outlands."

Gabe rises with a nod of his head. "I'm ready when you are, Keeper Beatrice."

I give Gabe a look. "You don't have to call me that."

"But I will," Gabe replies and starts for the door, even if he has no idea where to go.

With a sigh, I walk after him. This is going to be a long journey, and not only do I have to carry the weight of a hundred of lives on my shoulders, but I have to manage Gabe's insecurities as well. Maker help me.

LUCIDITY

Chapter 12

Ships come and go from the tarmac, and their thrusters force the air through my hair, which whips around my face and gets in my mouth and eyes. Even Gabe has to drag his hair out of his face as we wait by a port that sells speeder bikes. Neither Gabe or I know how to ride one of these, but we aren't about to tell that to the weary Dreamcatcher rental agent, who keeps staring at us in contempt.

"We are here on orders of Prince Echo himself. He sent us with this." I hand out a note that has been signed by Echo. It is worth hundreds of Aura's currency, and the amount is enough to widen the renter's eyes. I take this as a sign of approval. "So, we can have two bikes?"

The man nods his head and gestures over to two dirty and dusty speeder bikes. "You can have my best ones, Keeper Beatrice. Just don't break them."

Gabe smirks. "We won't."

I smile as well, despite the heaviness of our mission. "Thank you, sir." I heft the burdensome canvas backpack back onto my shoulders and start for the bikes. The bike agent tucks his note away in his pocket and happily whistles as he walks back into his office. Now, it's up to us to figure out how to work these things.

"How do you think this works?" I grab onto the handles and swing a leg over the seat, straddling it. The ignition button is under my right thumb, so I push it and give it a go. The whole bike shakes under me, then rises, hovering inches off of the ground. "Huh."

Gabriel follows suit, but he takes his initiation a step further and twists the throttle. The bike races forward, nearly crashing into a ship of some sort, but Gabe manages to reverse the thrusters before it can collide with the larger, metal object.

"Gabe!" I hiss at him.

Gabe laughs and shrugs his shoulders. "What? I'm just trying to figure this stupid thing out, is all."

"Well don't break it before we can even use it." I look over my shoulder and nod at the end of the port. This section is designated as the launch pad, and the bigger ships use it to take off and over the walls of Aura. "Think we should head out that way?"

"What way did you come in?"

"I came in that way, but I was on a ship." I look about the tarmac and notice a road that leads off to the side and toward the gates. "Maybe we should take the road with the bikes."

"Sounds better than being blown away by some incoming metal hunk of crap." Gabe turns the handles of his bike, then twists the throttle and speeds off toward the gate. He's far ahead of me in just a blink of an eye, and I'm amazed at how quickly the bikes move.

I pull my hair back into a pony tail, pull my hood up, open the throttle and speed off after Gabe, who has left behind a trail of kicked up dust and sand in his wake. It doesn't take long before I catch up with him, and we speed off through the gates, which barely open wide enough for the both of us to pass by the time we get there.

Just as soon as we are outside Aura's walls, we are officially in the Outlands, a vast desert space between here and the east coast, where no one but Rogues live. These are Citizens who didn't make it to the City after the collapse of the nation, Citizens who live off of the land, stealing whatever they can from the very few travelers who pass by. They attack and kill each other, as everything is free game in the Outlands. There are no rules. Civility does not exist.

In school, we've been taught that the Rogues lack the intelligence of those who have made it through to the City. They have regressed into a desperate people who don't know how to read or write, nor to co-exist with too many others. The barrier around the City serves to protect it not only from the Dreamcatchers, but mostly from stray Rogue groups who have a sudden urge to attack. They never win. Their numbers are too small.

But now, it's just me and Gabe, and our numbers are much, much smaller than the hundreds of roaming Rogues that are scattered across the Outlands. The odds are against us, and I know Gabe is just as aware of it as I am. Making it back will be a great accomplishment. Failure is not an option.

As we ride, I notice a shadow that has been following us the whole way from Aura. I look up over my shoulder and notice the raven who has followed me, and keeps following me. The raven is all-knowing and all-seeing. I remember the words from the Institution and look to Gabe to see if he notices, but he's too busy speeding ahead, darting in the direction of nothing.

We continue through the Outlands like this for hours, racing against the darkness which blossoms overhead and turns the desert black. Eventually, Gabe's speeder begins to slow down, and I close the throttle to come to a stop beside him. We'll only have the speeders until the gasoline runs out, and then we'll have to trek the rest of it on foot. It's best we don't use them for too long anyway, it'll only draw attention to us, and I'd rather not deal with any Rogues.

Gabe swings his leg over the bike and his feet hit the ground with a thump. He's dusty, and when he pulls his glasses off, there's an outline of clean skin where the lenses were protecting his face.

I laugh at him, and of course, this makes Gabe frown. "What are you laughing at?"

"Your face." I realize that comes out as a whole other insult, then laugh again. "I mean … your face is all dusty … " I reach up to pull off my glasses, as I'm sure the same effect has happened to me. "See?"

Sure enough, Gabe laughs as well, then slings his backpack off his back, letting the heavy canvas bag roll on the floor. Inside is our shelter, a tiny tent that is the color of sand. Inside my pack are the provisions and anything we might need to survive through the night. Or nights. So far, I've yet to see one plant anywhere, so it's not looking too well.

"Do you even know how to set up a tent?" I ask as I watch him pull the collapsed structure out of the bag.

"Watch this." Gabe smirks, sets the tent onto the ground, then pulls a string. The thing immediately expands into a tent form, needing no further assembly.

I roll my eyes skyward. "That's cheating."

"That's just smart." Gabe pulls the flap of the tent open and steps inside. I take one last look around at the vast space around us, then duck into the tent as well.

It's cozy for two people, barely enough room for the both of us to sleep. Include our packs in the mix, and we're sardines. Gabe ruffles his hair and dust flies everywhere. Thankfully, he hasn't put down the blankets yet, or they'd be soiled with filth. Not that it matters, since we are just as soiled as any sheets could be.

I'm exhausted, and there's a strange air between Gabe and me. As he goes on arranging our tent for the night, I watch him and run my fingers through my hair to try and eliminate the knots. It's another small and stupid waste of time, since as soon as we get back on those speeders, it will be knotty again.

"So, we'll have to take turns sleeping, I figure. Can't risk us both being asleep at the same time and have someone sneak up on us." Gabe naturally falls back into his leadership role, despite the fact that in this moment I am his Keeper and thus lead him. "So, do you want to sleep first or second?"

"First. You can sleep second." I am exhausted, and I want nothing more but to dream, if just to see if Echo is okay. If he shows himself to me at all. "Is that okay?"

"Sure." Gabe props his backpack behind him so he can sit up comfortably. He has a gun beside him, and I tilt my head, wondering where it came from.

"You brought that?" I never even thought about weapons, but Gabe, being the fighter that he is, probably thought about it before anything else.

"I brought two. Did you think we were just going to walk around here unprotected?" Gabe pats the gun like it was a pet. "I'm not letting any Rogue hurt you."

I smile at his protectiveness, then lay my head down on his lap to sleep. I want to be close to him like this, since I haven't been since he fell into his coma. Gabe's body becomes tense at first, but the longer I settle there, the more at ease he becomes with it. Eventually, he resorts to soothingly brushing his fingers through my hair.

Silence lingers between us for a long, pregnant moment. Finally, Gabe breaks it by asking the most uncomfortable question. "Do you like being married to him?"

I close my eyes and relish the feeling of his fingers raking over my scalp. It sends shivers down my spine, and I shudder. "I don't know. I've only been married to him for a few days."

"Wouldn't it have been nicer if you just said 'no?'" Gabe's other hand rests on my hip, and I bend my knees to curl up against his legs.

"I wouldn't lie to you. I never have."

"True." He gives me that much.

There's silence again, and I visualize a wealth of questions buzzing inside Gabe's head like a swarm of captive bees with nowhere to go. I wonder which one will break free?

"Have you guys … had your wedding night?"

I definitely did not expect that one. I push myself up so I can twist my body around and look him in the eye. "Firstly … that's not really your business. Secondly, no. And I won't. I didn't choose this marriage, Gabe. I did it for you."

"Well, I think it is my business in a way." Gabe reaches out and tugs on my necklace, pulling it free from under my jumpsuit. "I thought that we were more than just friends. And then you've gone off and married some Dreamcatcher."

"To save you." It is like he is not listening to me, and I quickly become frustrated. "And we never said what we were. We never really had that talk … did we?"

He lingers on the answer, which affirms my words. "Still … " he mutters.

"If you want to hold Echo against me, then that's fine. But I want you to remember that I was—am—being held captive by the queen, that she's using me as a political pawn to protect her kingdom, and that I entered into the marriage knowing that you would be alive at the end of the day." I rest my head back down in his lap and close my eyes again. "That was all that mattered to me."

Gabe's gentle touch returns, and he combs my hair through to calm me. "Okay, Bea. Okay."

I allow myself to drift into a sleep after that, with nothing but Gabe and Echo on my mind. I feel safe where I am, curled up beside Gabe, alone in the world with no city to manage or people to please. It doesn't take long for me to dream.

***

Echo is standing under the tree with the limbs that umbrella out then curve up toward the sky. It's where we normally meet in my dreams, and it always seems calm and detached from every worldly thing.

When I go to him, he holds his arms out for me, and I step into his familiar embrace. He smells of warm spices, a cologne he usually doesn't wear. When I turn my head to face his neck, I can also detect another scent—the smell of sickness, though he doesn't appear to be sick.

For a while, he doesn't speak, he just holds me to him like a child clinging to a teddy bear.

"You've already been gone for too long." Echo finally breaks the silence.

"It's hardly been a day yet, Echo. I'm sure you're doing fine without me." But is he? When I left him, he was starting to

show symptoms of the plague. How much worse could it have gotten?

"My mother has died." His words are abrupt, sad.

" ... what?" I pull back and look up into his eyes. "Dead?"

Echo's gaze strays from mine as tears well in his eyes. He struggles not to let them fall, to not appear weak. "Yes. She passed away last night. They've announced me as King, but I refused a coronation ceremony. I just ... I am not up for it." He avoids letting me know that he is sick, but I know. I know. "I do nothing but worry about you now."

I wrap my arms around him in a comforting embrace. "I'm in good hands, you don't have to worry." That's assuming that Echo believes that Gabe is good enough to protect me. I used to think that he did, since he never concerned himself much with Gabe. Until Echo's feelings for me intensified, and mine for him. Until I became his wife, a princess to his prince. Now, the two are at odds with each other, and I am stuck between them, unsure myself of whom I should choose.

"He better bring you home safely, with or without that leaf."

"He will, Echo. He will."

Echo reaches out and cups my cheek in his hand. I stare into his blue eyes, which seem a little dim, their evanescence lacking.

"We will be home soon ... and then ... then we'll have to talk about what happens next."

Echo simply nods then leans in and sweetly kisses my lips. Even in my dreams he is a good kisser, and I crave more from him ... I want more ... but I'm woken with a sudden, jarring shake ...

***

"Get up," Gabe commands.

"What is happening?" Everything around me is blurry as I wake up and readjust to my conscious surroundings. That's when I hear the voices and the footsteps. It's also when I realize that it's too late.

The tent is pushed in from the outside, and Gabe protectively throws himself over me, smushing my body into the ground as hands press through the canvas, reaching blindly for our limbs.

"Get them out of there. Let's see what they have." There's a voice that is louder than the rest, and the next time I hear it, it's right by me and Gabe. "Seems like there's two of 'em in there." Hands finally clamp down on my arm, and someone else struggles with the zipper to the tent.

"Gabe!" I don't want to be separated from him, but they are pulling me, and eventually I'm dragged out of the tent and dropped onto the arid ground. It doesn't take long before Gabe gives up and allows himself to be pulled out as well. Two of these people hold Gabe by his arms, and it doesn't take much, since he doesn't struggle.

The people standing around us are dressed in tight, leather leggings with leather tunics that match the color of the sand and dirt. They look rough, like lost brambles that have been blown across the Outlands, picking up whatever grime they've tumbled over. Their skin is dark, tanned from many hours spent in the sun. These must be the Rogues that I've heard so much about, but have never met face-to-face. One of them, a male, stands in front of the others, his hair long and corded. At a second glance, I notice that there are trinkets that have been woven into his locks, some of them look metal and others look like bone or plastic. When he crouches down in front of me, I can make out a bronze key and a coin with a hole through the center.

"What do we have here?"

This is when I hope Gabe is bright enough not to mention I'm the Keeper. The Rogue grabs me by the chin and tilts it upward so he can look into my eyes. "Can it really be?"

"Looks like a Seer, Boss." One of the others chimes in helpfully.

"A Seer indeed. It's been a long time since we've seen any Seers come through here." The Rogue drops his hand from my chin and yanks me up to my feet. "You'll be a welcome sight back at the camp. There's much we can do with you. Maybe try to ransom you back to your corrupt City. Maybe sell you to the Dreamcatchers to do whatever they want with you … or maybe … " He rubs his goatee in thought. "We can keep you and make our own little army of Seers. Wouldn't that be something? Rogue Seers?"

The group of them laugh the same sardonic laugh. All-in-all, there's seven, two females and five males—too much for Gabe or I to fight. That, and they've already confiscated our weapons. One of the females holds our guns, one tucked under her armpit, the other hanging loosely in her hand against her side.

"What do you want from us?" I ask the leader of the bunch.

"What do we want from you, darling?" He laughs and grabs my wrist, tugging me to walk alongside him. I look over my shoulder and Gabe is pushed forward, a sign that he should go, too. The whole group follows, and we leave our tent behind. I say a quiet prayer to the Maker for this small favor. At least, if Echo sends out someone to search for us, he'll find our tent. Hopefully, that will be a sign enough that we are in trouble.

"Yes. What do you want?" I repeat myself a little more slowly this time, just in case he didn't hear me.

"We'll figure that out later, when we get to camp. For now, it's just fun to say that I've found two Seers. And one of them is pretty at that."

I try to yank my hand out of his grip, but he only grasps me tighter, his nails digging into my skin. "Now, you want to behave, honey, or we're going to have some real issues you and I."

"I'm not your 'honey.'"

"You are whatever I call you."

I wriggle my wrist in his grip, trying to abate the pressure of his fingernails. "And what do I call you?"

Over his shoulder, he flashes me a grin. "That's a question I can answer. You can call me Lee."

Not so far away, behind a rock structure, we arrive to a line of speeder bikes that have been hidden out of plain sight. Lee slings a leg over the seat and then pulls me down in front of him. When I look behind for Gabe, he is struggling with his captors, which I'd expect from Gabe. He's not one to go down without a fight. He catches my gaze, and I shake my head at him. There's no point fighting now. We're stuck, and we're going with these Rogues whether we want to or not.

"Ready to go, darling?" Lee asks as he starts the bike and it hovers over the ground.

Ready as I'll ever be, I think to myself. But before I can answer, he speeds off toward the blinding sunrise.

Chapter 13

We ride for what feels like hours, and probably is. The sun is hot and unbearable, and I'm sweating uncomfortably under my jumpsuit. Lee is hunched over me, his hands on the handles of the bike, his breath by my ear. I think he's enjoying this a little too much, but there's nothing I can do.

Finally, I make out something in the distance, a group of tents, hundreds of multi-colored tents ... a little tent city. They ride the speeders right up to a watch post that consists of five guards holding machine guns. The bike slows down to a stop just before the entryway into the camp, and Lee hops off, pulling me down off the bike with him.

"Found something good, did 'ja?" one of the guards calls down from the little post, which can't be more than ten feet up in the air.

"Something real good." Lee smiles and brushes his dreadlocks back behind his shoulders. They are covered in dust that has been kicked up from the speeder, and when I look down at myself, I notice that I've been blessed with the same, dirty appearance.

"We'll get someone to put the bikes back. Go on in." The guard motions with his gun to pass, and we continue into the camp. It reminds me much of the Citizen Settlements back in Aura, except these people aren't slaves, they are misplaced from society. Rogues. There are children running through the dirt streets, and the smells of humans and food and the general odor of living close to each other wafts through the air. Once we are inside the camp, I can't see where it ends, not even when I take the time to stop and tiptoe in an effort to get a better look at my surroundings. Lee pulls me off balance, though, and I almost stumble into him.

"Keep up, honey."

"You can call me Be—"

"Beth!" Gabe cuts in, calling the name out in my direction. "Beth, is he hurting you?"

It only takes me a moment to figure out why he called me "Beth." He's protecting me and my identity. What would they do to me if they found out that I was the Keeper? I'd never see home again, probably.

"No, Gabe. I'm fine," I reply calmly.

"Beth, huh? A pretty name for a pretty girl." Lee motions ahead of us, gesturing down the road. "We are taking you to the leader of the camp, Moses."

"Moses? That's a unique name." It seems vaguely familiar to me, as if I've heard it once before, perhaps in a class or a book.

"It's the name of a prophet from the Bible. He was given the Ten Commandments. He also freed the slaves of Egypt." Lee steers me around a puddle of filth, and a group of kids nearly collide with us as they round a corner and bound off down another alley. "So, our leader likes to be called Moses, because he's gathered us, freed us, and given us rules to live by that aren't the rules of the City or of Aura."

Moses. The Bible. The book was banned from the City long ago when we took up the faith of the Maker, the one who guided the scientists to make our abilities which blessed us with the gift of Sight. I've heard of the Bible only in my history classes and thought it had long since disappeared.

"You still didn't tell me what you want from us. You already took our stuff, why not let us go?" I press on, thinking of Echo and how he's probably rapidly perishing from the plague back at the palace. I think of his mother, who is most likely already dead. I need to find that plant, and getting caught by these Rogues isn't helping.

"Because it's been many years since we've found Seers outside of the City. Moses will be interested to hear about why you are wandering around the Outlands. There has to be a good reason, honey, because no one comes out here just because they felt like it."

"And after we meet with your Moses? Then what?"

"That's up to him, sweetheart."

I really hate him calling me all these pet names, and I grind my teeth together in annoyance. When I glance back at Gabe, I see the same annoyance written all over his face, and it makes me feel a little better that I'm not the only one who is letting it get to me.

We finally get to a large tent that looks to be made from a deep green velvet. The flaps have been pinned open, but the inside is darkened with a shadow that keeps anything from being seen. Two guards flank the entrance, and as we approach, their legs part and they block our entry.

"We're here to see Moses. It's very important."

"Everyone wants to see Moses. Did you make an appointment?" one of the guards responds.

"No. We just got back from a raid and we found some pretty interesting stuff. Like these two Seers." Lee motions back at me and Gabe, then smiles a smile that is almost bigger than his face. "See?"

The guards glance at us, then look back at Lee. "Fine. You may enter, but I can't promise he is taking any visitors. Especially unannounced ones."

"Yeah, yeah. I'm rude! But everyone pretty much knows that." Lee barks a laugh, and his little posse of Rogues chime in with their fake guffaws in a show of support.

The guards never take their eyes off of me or Gabe, though, and even when we pass into the tent, I can feel their gaze burning into the back of me.

When my eyes adjust to the lack of light, I realize that we are standing in some sort of antechamber to the tent where Moses must really be. The room is outfitted with large pillows to sit on and tables with short legs that sit close to the ground. There are sticks of incense burning, and the thick smoke irritates my eyes, not to mention my lungs as I suck in deep breaths of what smells like lavender.

A woman with the same sort of dark corded hair that Lee has appears in the doorway of the second larger tent. She wears a beautiful suede dress that clings tightly to her form, leaving very little to the imagination. I catch Gabe staring at her, and there's a piece of me that ignites with jealousy. That woman is really nothing to look at. She's all meat and bones anyway.

"You wish to see Moses?" She must be stupid too, because for what other reason would be we standing out here?

"We do, lovely. Don't you look sweet today, too?" Lee lets go of my wrist long enough to brush his fingers down the woman's cheek.

She blushes, her ruddy skin turning a darker shade of brown. "You may come in."

Lee grabs my wrist again and Gabe and I are escorted into the larger tent. This one is much more impressive than the previous tent, with knickknacks and all sorts of furniture and artwork strewn about. It's a mess, but a somewhat organized mess, and I have no idea where I want to look first, there's just so much to look at. I stop just inside the door, and Lee lets go of my arm again, allowing me the time to admire my surroundings.

"Beautiful, isn't it?" A gentle, soothing voice comes from somewhere to my right. I turn that way and an old man stands up from a chair that looks to be made from bone ... or tusks? I've heard of such things before, but no one has seen an elephant since the War. How could he possibly have tusks in the middle of the Outlands? "All of these things were once lost to the survivors of the War. The City won't allow them, since they are things of the past ... things that make us remember when all they want you to do is forget. The City is all about looking forward, not looking behind—that's where they get everything wrong."

"Are those tusks?" I ask.

The man nods his head. "They are. One of my groups of raiders found it on a journey up north. Came across an old museum that had lots of different things for the taking." He smiles and gestures for Gabe and I to sit down in a pile of velvet pillows situated on the floor behind us. "I am Moses. Welcome to my humble abode."

"Bet you never thought we'd find us some Seers, Moses. Did you?" Lee puffs his chest up proudly, which I find to be ridiculous. "They call themselves Gabe and Beth."

"A good find, indeed. It's been many years since I've spoken to a Seer. Many years since I've seen them. As the decades wear on, less and less try to escape the City, because they forget there's a world outside of those barricades, so welcome, Gabe and Beth." Moses doesn't sit down and imposingly towers over Gabe and me, regarding us both like we are one of his prized objects. In particular, he watches me. "So, Seers, tell me how you ended up way out here, walking in the wrong direction?"

"What's the right direction?" I wonder.

"Away from the City, not toward it. That makes me believe that you are coming from Aura, but that can't be, because why would two Seers want to have any business with the Dreamcatchers? Especially after we just learned about the attack against your people and the loss of your Keepers."

Keepers. He means me, too.

"To be honest, we are looking for a plant," Gabe blurts out, giving away our true intentions without giving away too much. "Some of our Seers are sick, and we heard that the only way to cure them is to find this plant."

"Well, we didn't hear it but we Saw it in one of our Visions." I try to play it up as much as I can. It's not too far off the mark. A shiny bauble catches my attention when it deflects the light from a nearby lantern. It's curious why one would have a fire in a tent filled with precious things.

Moses smiles at my curiosity, admiring it from where he sits. "That is called a sun catcher, though it catches very little sun here in these confines."

"Why not put it outside, then?" I don't remember seeing any sun catchers in the City. Such little things seem so insignificant in the grand scheme of our existence. And yet, I can't look away.

"Because it is mine. Once I put it outside, someone will steal it and make it theirs. What you don't watch is what you lose, Beth. That's a good lesson to take away from here … if we let you go." Moses steeples his fingers together and leans his forearms on his upper thighs, glancing down at Gabe and me like we are little children.

"Why wouldn't you let us go?" Gabe asks.

"Because having a pair of Seers around is a rare thing. We could use some of that knowledge of yours … your gift. And if not that, it might not hurt to just have you around. Like an addition to my collection here."

"I'm not a collectable." I push myself up to stand, making a move to leave, though there's nowhere for me to go.

"Sit down," Moses commands, his voice deepening into something dangerous.

Gabe tugs on the dirty pant leg of my jumpsuit, and I sit back down beside him. Here, I am not the Keeper. I have no power. I am only a Seer, like the rest of the Seers … like I was before the Dreamcatchers came.

"This is how it will work. I will have a tent set up for you beside mine. You will be our 'guests' for a little while. I will even find some scouts to search for those plants you are looking for. Then … we will ransom you and your medicine back to the City." Moses pauses to examine his fingernails, which are all well-manicured. "And they better offer something good. Money is not an object to us here. We need supplies to survive, and that is worth far more than your currency."

"I'm sure they'll figure something out." Gabe doesn't sound so sure of this, though, and I wonder if he knows about the state of the City since I left and since he fell into the coma. Brandon and Elan never really said much about how it is fairing now, and if it recovered from the attacks. If we get back from all of this, I'll have to find out before we head back home.

"For your sakes, I hope they do." Moses nods to Lee, and the latter man steps forward and pulls us both up to our feet by giving us a firm tug on the arm.

"Let's go get you two cleaned up while your tent is being arranged." Lee runs a pointer finger down my shoulder and holds it up for me to see. "You are filthy."

"Everything is filthy here." Gabe struggles to try and free his arm from Lee's grasp, but Lee proves to be stronger and doesn't let him go.

"That might be so, but Moses likes us to be as clean as we can be when in camp. So come on with the both of you." Lee leads us out of the fancy tent, and when I look behind me to take one last look at Moses, he is lost in thought, staring at his sun catcher and the light that has been captured between the glass. I feel much like that light, radiant, but kept a prisoner for no other purpose than to be admired. We have to break out of here. I can't let us sit like pretty little prizes until they figure out what to do with us. At the same time, he said he would find the plant for us. Maybe I'll just have to sit pretty for a little longer … if not to save myself, then to save Echo.

Chapter 14

The sky is the color of pinks and scarlet, bathing Aura in a crimson light. As I walk through the streets, everything is hauntingly quiet, and there is no one, absolutely no one anywhere. I decide to head for the Citizen Settlements. I haven't been back there since we rescued Fortuna, the Seer baby now in the care of Jamie and Irene. An invisible string tugs me in that direction, and I go like the puppet I am, one foot after the other, to the Settlements.

When I get there, the guards are not at the watch station, and the gates have been left open. The wind is the only thing that moves, brushing the dirt up from the ground and swirling it into tiny funnels that dissipate soon after. The tiny shacks that make up the Citizen houses are all shrouded in silence, and when I decide to peek inside one of them, I am met with the most horrible sight: a mother holding her child, both of them rotting and covered with maggots and flies. From the skin that they have left, I can see dried blood under the mother's nose, a sign of the plague.

I reel away from the window and check the next house, hoping to find survivors. How could it be that so quickly the plague could claim so many lives? We've only been gone for a couple of days ...

The next house is no better, and the people inside, four of them, are in worse shape than the mother and child in the previous house. Some of their bones are showing from the rapid decay, and the flies in the house have grown bored and stick to the walls, their wings buzzing some sick melody. I turn away and clutch my stomach, sure that I'm going to vomit, but somehow I manage not to. *I need to keep myself pulled together if I'm to find out what is going on here. Obviously, the rest of the Settlements aren't going to be in much better shape, so I turn to head out. It's still not clear if the Seers can also catch the plague, and I don't want to stick around long enough to find out.*

I decide to go back to the palace to check up on Echo and his mother, but the silence of the streets equals to a deafening warning, as if screaming at me to turn around now and get out of here while I can. But again, I am being pulled along, somewhat against my will, toward the palace in the center of the kingdom. Something moves to the right of me, and when I turn to try and catch it, it is gone, and I am left alone with the quiet once again. Something is definitely not right here. It's the calm before the ambush, though I have no idea what is waiting for me ... if it is anything at all.

As I trudge down the streets toward the palace, that something runs by again, and I barely catch it in my peripheral. When I spin around to follow its movement, I almost lose it. But a touch of its shadow lingers behind, and I hurry off in its direction. I'm chasing ghosts, it feels like, because I have no idea what it is I'm pursuing, but I need to get to it, to capture it and find it out. I can feel the need growing inside of me, like if I don't get to it, then I will be letting something horrible slip out of my grasp.

I round a group of shops that line the end of this street, and in some of them, elaborate and fancy dresses have been arranged on mannequins. Normally, I would stop to get a better look, my curiosity always getting the best of me, but I have no time to quit my pursuit. Even if I stop for a moment, I will lose whatever it is I am chasing, I know.

I pick up speed and start to sprint after my source, and I can feel that I am getting closer, that I'm right on its tail. Whatever this thing is, it runs too quickly, and I'm afraid that if I slow down for just a second, that it will pull way in front of me, and I'll never catch it. I decide to play a trick and run down a side alley to cut it off at the corner, and when the alley spits me out on the other side, I spin around in front of the thing and it collides into me, knocking us both onto the ground.

I tumble over, but manage to grab what seems to be a person as we both hit the ground. I'm not letting it run off again, not if I can help it, and just as soon as our momentum stops, I push it over onto the ground. That's when I realize that it is just a boy, a scraggly little boy with dirty blond hair and big, beady eyes with pupils dilated to the size of quarters. He stares up at me like some rabid sort of beast, then hisses like an animal. It's almost enough to startle me into letting him go, but I hang on tightly to him and give him a little shake.

"What do you want? Why are you following me?"

The boy hisses again and turns his head, biting into my arm. I shriek and yank my arm away from him. With my other hand, I close my fingers around his throat and pin him down to the ground by his neck so that he can't bite me again. "What the hell was that for?"

Another hiss.

I shake him. "Talk to me! I know you can talk!" But really, I don't know if he can talk at all. So far, all it seems the animal boy can do is bite and hiss. Eventually, though, he does talk, and when his mouth opens, his teeth are covered in blood. Is that my blood? I look down at my arm to see how severely I am bleeding, and it is only then do I realize that he managed to take a good chunk of skin out of my wrist. Damn it.

"You said you'd save us."

"And I am trying to." I become sick to my stomach the more I stare at the blood in his mouth. My blood in his mouth.

"You said you would save us ... and now it is too late."

"Why is it too late?"

"Because we are all dead."

I tilt my head. "But you aren't dead."

The boy-animal laughs and tries to pull my arm away from his neck with his bony hands. It's no use, though. He's obviously very weak, and I have the advantage of hovering above him and placing most of my weight onto his scrawny neck. "We are dead, Keeper Beatrice. We have all died because of your failure."

"But I haven't failed."

He laughs again, but this time, it's sardonic and bitter. "Be careful, Keeper Beatrice. If you do fail, you fail all of us ... and we will all die."

And then, he dissipates into a dark, thick shadow that blows away with the next gust of wind. I am left kneeling in the streets of Aura with a heavy warning that expands inside my head until I can hear only ringing in my ears.

I cannot fail them ... but yet, perhaps I already have.

***

When I come to, my head hurts just as it did at the end of my Vision. It was a Vision. The very thought only serves to make my head throb even more, and I cradle it in my hands. By my side, Gabe is sleeping in a pile of satin pillows that have been gathered in the back of our makeshift tent, which has been filled with the most luxurious items. Moses has certainly treated us royally, though his intentions are still unclear to me, and I don't trust any of it. I reach out and shake Gabe's shoulder, and at first, he blindly swats at me, but when I give him another, firm shake, he wakes up and sees my glowing eyes right away.

"A Vision?" His words are sleepy, somewhere between here and his dreams.

Outside, the sun is just coming up, illuminating the gold fabric tent that has been stretched out over us. I can also see the shadows of people milling about, too close to our little home for comfort. News of our capture has probably spread around the camp by now, and no doubt people are starting to come out and see the Seers for themselves.

"Yes. And not a very good one either. It was in Aura, and there was this boy who was obviously sick with the plague, but he was acting strange and … and … rabid." I rub at my wrist where the boy in my Vision had bitten me and taken off a chunk of skin. "He said that I failed him … but then at the end of the Vision, he warned if I did fail them, then everyone in Aura would die."

Gabe tugs on my arm, urging me to lie back down in the comfortable pillows beside him. I do it if only because my head is killing me, and closing my eyes right now seems like a great idea. Nestling my head on one of the cushions, I let my lashes flutter closed and soon after feel Gabe's hand brushing back my hair soothingly.

"Doesn't sound as accurate as your Visions usually are. I wouldn't worry too much about it, Beatrice. We're going to find that stupid plant. And we'll save your stupid husband, and then we can get home."

"Shhhh," I warn Gabe. "Don't say anything too loud. We don't want to give any of these Rogues any more information than we already have."

"You're right." Gabe's hand continues to brush over my hair, his fingers raking through the dark, black locks. "But still. I wouldn't worry too much about it. There has to be another meaning behind it ... perhaps it is just impressing upon you the seriousness of finding the plant."

I shrug a shoulder. "Perhaps."

"But you don't believe that." I open my eyes and find Gabe smirking down at me. He knows me too well.

I shake my head. "I don't. My Visions have been rather clear as of late. I think it's true that they will all die if we don't bring back this plant, and I'll never have the chance to free their Citizens. In the Vision, that was the first place I went—the Settlements—and all the Citizens, every single one of them, were dead."

"And what was your plan after you've freed them? I'm just going to go out on a limb here, Bea, and say that the Dreamcatchers aren't going to love you for taking their slaves away from them." Gabe's fingers unravel from my hair and he props his head up on his hand, looking down at me.

"I was going to invite them back to the City. Or at least try to get the Dreamcatchers on board and show them that they don't need to enslave their Citizens to benefit from them. Could you imagine how much better it would be if they just let their Citizens live and donate their time and resources to the kingdom? I'm sure it would be far more prosperous than how it is run now." I stare up at Gabe, and the glow of my violet eyes illuminates his face, casting it in a lilac haze. "I mean, look at them. The Dreamcatchers are panicking because if the Citizen population dies out, they'll have no way to sustain themselves. They have no people to help heal, or to breed, or to make the products of their kingdom."

Gabe nods, but I can tell that my feelings over this cause aren't ones that he shares. Gabe probably could care less about the Dreamcatchers or Aura. No, he doesn't "probably" care less about them—he just doesn't care. At all. I can see it in the way that he looks away from me that all he really wants is to return home to the Institution, to somewhere he knows and is familiar with.

Instead, we are being kept prisoner in this tent, and I don't know how much the people on the outside can hear, but there are more of them now, and the looming shadow of heads and bodies shifts and moves all at once as they try to get closer in hopes of seeing us.

"This isn't going to be good," I note and close my eyes again, trying to force them to stop glowing, even if it doesn't quite work that way.

"What are they doing?" Gabe pushes himself up to sit and gets to his feet soon afterward. The ground is covered in fur pelts from many different types of animals that I have only ever seen in textbooks. There are some wooden trunks that have been placed in the center of the room, but I have no idea what we'd possibly keep in them. It's not like we came here packed up and ready for a vacation.

I don't get up to follow Gabe because my head is still pounding from the inside out, and I can imagine it cracking like an egg if I try to stand. "Probably trying to see us. Moses said they haven't had Seers here in a long time."

"Strange that they should have ever come out here at all," Gabe mentions as he moves closer to one of the walls with only the fabric between him and the people on the outside. "And how have they not seen Seers before? Certainly they must have them when they have children. All Citizens do."

"Our Citizens were never infected by the serum that the Scientists used to try and save the City." Moses is standing in the doorway of the tent, and as the flap falls, I can see dozens of pairs of legs of the people who are gathering around outside. "Therefore, we do not breed Seers or Dreamcatchers. And those Citizens who have escaped the City and were from the line of the serum, well, they aren't allowed to breed … and if they do, their children are killed. We have no time for these sorts of unnatural games, Seers Beth and Gabriel. We are a community that functions on all being on the same page."

I frown and keep my head turned, trying to hide from Moses that I've recently had a Vision. He'll figure it out, though. Moses, I've realized, is much more observant and attentive than his fellow Rogues, like Lee, who puts up a wonderful front that he's just everything that should be found in a man, but is flawed much like any other person who is full of themselves.

"The people outside wish to see our new prizes, and you'll be presented to them accordingly because I don't need any riots because they are displeased with not being able to have a look at you." Moses walks across the tent and over to the two trunks that are in the middle of the space. "Have you ever heard of India?"

"India?" Gabe echoes the unfamiliar word. I've certainly never heard of it, but I don't want to draw any attention to myself.

"India was a warm country in Asia, across the other side of the world. They had such beautiful things, pink and red fabrics with tiny mirrors sewn into the hem, exotic furnishings, and delicious, spicy foods. Everything about the country was just …

warm. Well, from what I've read and seen in old history books. India was destroyed in the War, much like everything else, and its culture was snuffed out of existence." Moses opens up one of the trunks and pulls out an orange robe-looking piece of clothing. It's more like an over-sized tunic, and is cut with hard angles, probably more suited to fit a man. "But then I started to read about India, and I loved the thought of smelling the spiced incense on the wind, and constantly being surrounded with the colors of the sun, and I based my camp on India and its beauty. Today, you'll dress in traditional Indian clothing, and I'll walk you outside and you'll let the people see you and stare at you and do whatever it is they want without harming you, and then you'll be taken back to your tent and left alone until we have dinner." He hands the garment to Gabe, who takes it reluctantly.

Out of the other trunk, Moses pulls out a light pink dress with the little mirrors sewn into the fabric, just like the ones he so recently spoke about. My clothing is made from two pieces, the second one being some sort of sash that will probably be thrown over my shoulder from the looks of it. "This is a sari. The women of India wore them all the time and fluttered about the streets, filling it with color. You'll look radiant in it, Seer Beth." For the first time, he looks directly over at me and pauses as he hands the sari over. "Your eyes are glowing."

"They do that sometimes," I cut in, hoping he won't ask any more questions.

"You've had a Vision." Moses smiles and comes closer to me to reach a hand out and cup his fingers over my cheek. "Look how beautiful."

"Please don't touch her," Gabe growls lowly.

Moses ignores him though and stares down into my eyes, his gaze deep and curious. It's making me uncomfortable, and I turn my head away from him and step back. "I should get changed."

Moses frowns when eye contact is broken, making it clear that we're not done with each other. "We'll talk more about your Vision over dinner. I will give you about ten minutes to get yourselves dressed, and then I'm coming in for you and taking you outside." He slips out of the tent, leaving Gabe and me behind.

Gabe walks over to where I am and peeks down at my face. "Are you okay?"

"It's fine. He was just looking."

"I don't want him touching you. I don't trust him, and I don't want any men touching you," Gabe mutters and brushes his fingers down the same cheek that Moses held just moments before.

"We should get changed. You go over there and turn the other way, and I'll change here, and only when we are both done will we both turn around. Got it?" Not that I think Gabe will try to turn around and sneak a peek, but I'm just in no mood to deal with such things right now. My head is still killing me, and now I have to wriggle my way into this sari thing and hope that I am putting it on correctly.

I pull my jumpsuit down and step out of it, discarding the one-piece outfit on the floor. I decide to keep my undershirt on, since the sari will probably cover it, and no one will really see it anyway. Pulling the pink fabric down over my head, I shimmy into the dress-like garment and tug it down over my hips. It falls to the length of the floor, the hem stopping just before it so that it doesn't drag when I walk. I sling the second part over my shoulder and sloppily wrap it around my waist, and I'm sure, just as soon as I'm done fiddling around with it, that I'm not wearing this like I'm supposed to be. "Does yours look stupid?" I call over to Gabe and look over my shoulder, forgetting my own rules about not peeking.

Gabe stands facing away from me, though his shirt is off, and I can see the muscles in his back flex as he tries to work the tunic over his broad torso. His clothing isn't as accommodating as my own, and even when he has the tunic pulled down all the way, I can tell it's too tight on him. The hem of his piece falls below his knees, and a pair of loose pants has also been provided for him, I notice, as he steps the rest of the way out of his jumpsuit. I quickly turn back around to look elsewhere. My cheeks flush with heat.

"Probably just as stupid as yours looks, judging by that tone," Gabe laughs, and I hear the rustling of fabric as he probably tries to slip the pants on.

I smirk. "Ready to look at each other?"

I can hear Gabe's smile in his words, "This looks ridiculous."

"Yeah, well. As long as it gets us our plant, I don't care how stupid I look in the end." I adjust the stole that I've wrapped awkwardly around my shoulder and across my chest. "Okay. Turn around."

We both turn around, and Gabe stands there dressed in colors too bright for his normally pallid self. I'm so used to seeing him in black and gray that it comes to me as a shock when I am met with the obnoxiously vibrant color that makes up Gabe's outfit.

But Gabe is staring at me in a whole other way, one that encourages a blush to my cheeks, which are now burning as pink as the accents of my sari. "Wow, Bea. You look beautiful."

"Thanks." I glance around to anywhere that isn't Gabe. "Now what?"

"I guess we wait." Gabe still stares at me, and I'm still trying to avoid his gaze.

"Are you two ready in there? These Rogues are getting restless, and I hate when my people are upset," Moses calls from somewhere outside, and I nod to Gabe, signaling to him that we should be on our way. If anything, it will get him to stop staring at me, and I won't feel so much like a bright orange ball of blushes and shyness.

"Yeah, we're ready." Gabe puts his hand on my lower back and ushers me outside. The simple touch is enough to make the fluttering in my stomach feel that much stronger, and I go with him easily.

Gabe drags the tent flap open and Moses is just outside, ready to show us off. He smiles almost lecherously at me when I appear, and the people outside all gasp in unison at the sight of the pair of us. I hear someone make a comment about our eyes, and I wonder if mine are still glowing from my previous Vision. Wouldn't that just make their day? If we are to be the sideshow, we may as well be a good one and give them something to look at.

"What you see here before you are Seers, straight from the City. These are the people who have decided that they make the rules, the ones that have driven away the Dreamcatcher people for being different than they are," Moses explains, holding a hand back to us as he introduces our history. Or, what he thinks is our history.

"That's not exactly true," Gabe mumbles, but it's loud enough for Moses to pick up, and the older man turns to face us.

"Oh no? And how have you been taught? Why did you drive the Dreamcatchers away if it wasn't because they weren't like you?"

"Because they were too powerful for their own good, and they could have wiped us all out if we didn't get rid of them." Gabe speaks louder, meaning for his words to reach the others who are standing nearby. They exchange glances with one another, and I can read the confusion on their faces.

"That is a unique way of putting it, Seer Gabriel. It's a matter that we can argue later with each other and not in front of these fine people. For many of them, this is the first time that they've ever seen a real Seer before. Look at how they look at you." Moses' hand sweeps from us to them, putting the Rogues on display now.

I look over the many different faces, most of them dirtied and bronzed by the sun, and I commit them to memory. One day, when I get back to the City, I will remember these people and think of a way to right their wrongs. Clearly, they look at Seers as being somewhat of an enemy, just as we've been taught to look at them as being outcasts and not worth our time or resources.

"I guess we can talk about it later." But Gabe doesn't sound very interested. He's always been very invested in his roots as a Seer. Entertaining a conversation about how the Seers were in the wrong is probably not something he truly wishes to do. "So, how long are we going to stand out here?"

Moses smiles patiently at Gabe and lifts his chin to address the crowd again. "Today, I come to you with a mission. These two Seers are looking for a remedy for some illness that has taken over their people. They say they've Seen a plant … would one of you two describe it?"

I nod my head and speak up, sharing with them the limited details about this elusive plant that we must find. "All I Saw was that it had purple leaves that presented themselves to the sun and curled up when the sun was not present. I don't know where it is, exactly, or much else about it, but I do know it is out here somewhere ... which is why we came this way."

"I am tasking you with finding this plant, and when you do, you will not only be awarded personally, but we will ransom the plant and the Seers back to the City for resources that we've needed for a long time. Rations, clean water, all those other things that keep our community well-kept." Moses' words are met with a general murmur that ripples through the crowd, starting at the front and fading off somewhere toward the back. The Rogues all look at each other with a renewed light in their eyes. Not only have they come to see this Seer show, but now they have a chance to make something of themselves, and possibly bring a reward to their whole camp.

I find it to be cruel in a way, especially when there's no knowing how long it will take them to find the plant, or if they will find it at all. Moses has successfully managed to fill his people with a fragile hope, and I can clearly see the way this inspires them by the way their faces light up, aspirations high.

My stomach knots at the thought of failure, and as Moses continues to talk, projecting his voice over the masses of people, I can only think of their suffering if they should fail.

And it will be my fault.

Chapter 15

A couple of days have passed by in which we've done mostly nothing. Each day that passes is another day that I worry about if Echo is still alive. I can only hope that he doesn't succumb to the plague as quickly as his mother did, and that the Dreamcatchers are doing all that they can to keep him alive until I return. If I return.

Gabe and I are only allowed outside of our tent when we are being escorted, and usually that is to dinner and back. The camp has been bustling with a renewed energy since Moses' promise to reward the one who finds the mysterious plant that we need to bring back to Aura. The dirty faces that we looked out at not so long ago seem brilliant and dingy at the same time, and in the gazes of these Rogues there's a furious hope that they are going to be the ones to find the plant and become the savior of their camp. I've been hoping that someone would know something more about the plant in my Vision, because I don't know how much time we have to waste on scavenging miles of arid wasteland in pursuit of it. It might be a game to the Rouges, but I have a whole city of Dreamcatchers and Citizens to save, not to mention Echo.

In a little while, we will be heading to dinner, as usual. I am dressed in a sky-colored dress that is like nothing I've seen before. Attached to the fabric are tiny little mirrors that reflect whatever light hits them, turning me into a glittering spectacle for Lee to leer at. It is what he seems to do best lately, much to Gabe's dismay. A few times, I have thought that Gabe would fly off the handle and let Lee have it for looking at me the way he does, but thankfully, Gabe's kept his temper in check. It's important that we don't get ourselves in trouble here. We are prisoners after all. They don't need to keep us alive if they don't have to.

I pull my hair back in a sleek ponytail, since the tents are humid, and the weight of the black tresses tends to make me miserable. Looking in a cracked mirror, I make sure I'm put together nicely and decide that I am ready to go just as Lee calls to me from outside the tent flaps. "Are you ready, my dear?"

Maker, I hate him.

"Yes." I call back and begin my walk to the door. It feels different without Gabe here, but they took him out of the tent some hours ago with the intention of showing him off to the camp. Sometimes, we go out together, and the people come to stare at us, or yell at us, or curse us for what we are. Most of the time, though, we are walked out one-by-one, probably so that the danger of both of us getting hurt at one time is lessened. The Rogues have so far not acted violently toward us, but I can tell that they are strung tight, and they've been waiting most their lives to get their hands on a Seer to show them exactly what they think about their so-called exile.

Gabe will be at dinner too, and that's the only reason why I step out of the tent and let Lee grab me by my wrist. "There's my lovely girl." He smiles at me and it makes my insides tighten. "How do you like your dress today? You look like an evening star."

I yank on my hand, pulling it out of his grasp. "I can walk on my own," I mumble, ignoring the compliment. I might look like a star, but I feel like a doll that they've been dressing up for their own amusement. I know that is what they are doing, I can see it in the way Moses fills with delight when he sees his two little Seer puppets all dressed up and at his command.

"As you wish, darling." Lee and I walk the short distance to Moses' tent in silence, and as soon as we get there, he pulls open the flaps and a warm rush of rosemary-scented air wafts from the inside. There are Rogues who stand around the inside of the tent holding serving trays and pitchers, their skin slick and dripping with sweat from the unbearable and unrelenting heat of the desert. Gabe is seated on a cushion in front of a table that sits low to the ground. He is wearing baggy, light-fabric pants that match the color of my dress. He doesn't wear a shirt, though, but instead has been adorned with a thick, gold chain necklace that hangs about his neck and looks heavy and uncomfortable.

At the head of the table, Moses sits on his own plush cushion and motions for me to have a seat on the one that is situated to his left side, with Gabe seated to his right. Lee shows me over to my seat and once I lower myself onto the pillow, he takes the place next to me and sits uncomfortably close.

"How are my two little Seers doing today? I hope the heat has not been bothering you too much?" Moses claps his hands twice to signal the start of dinner, and all those who were standing around before become animated and begin to fill our glasses with wine, or dump some questionable-looking food onto our plates. It is a testament to the fact that the Rogues truly do not have much as far as resources go, and though Moses might collect all sorts of dated objects from a world that we'll never know again, that doesn't mean he has the stores of food and other necessities needed to keep his people fed and well.

"Fine," I reply simply as I watch a girl about my age discard a spoonful of some sort of meat onto my plate.

"Just fine?" Moses tsks, taking up his gold goblet with the inset jewels. He motions to me with the cup, then looks at it and smiles. "Do you know where this came from?" he asks us both, then turns it around in his hand, gems sparkling from the light of the hanging lanterns set around the inside perimeter of the tent.

Gabe looks at me for a long while, then looks back to Moses and obliges his question with a simple, "Nope."

"Well, let me tell you a story of the past." Moses sips from the goblet and sets it back down on the table. "There was a time when the world was so divided that no matter where you went, people were all of different religions. Here, on this land we live, there were many types of people with their own beliefs."

"We have been taught about religion at the Institution," I remind Moses.

"Yes, yes. I am sure you've been 'taught' about many things that aren't quite the truth in your Institution. I want you to listen to my truth, though, so do behave and don't interrupt." Moses fixes me with a look that suggests if I speak up again, he won't be as nice to tell me to be quiet. "As I was saying, there were many people with many beliefs, and these beliefs fragmented us as a nation. Everyone wanted to be right, everyone wanted to point fingers at the other person and tell them that they were wrong. And as the years went on, it became worse and worse until eventually it began to fall apart with the rest of the world."

Lee's chewing is loud and obnoxious and fills the silence after Moses' little story. I'm unsure what this has to do with the cup, but eventually Moses begins to speak again, and Lee's chewing is drowned out.

"This is called a chalice. It is from an abandoned church we found during our wanderings. They used to fill this with wine during their religious ceremony and drink from it." Moses laughs at this, finding humor in something that I don't quite understand.

"Can you believe it? This … golden cup with all these gems … I am sure it was worth a lot of money back when it had some meaning. You could probably feed a whole house of people for months on the profit from this thing, but instead, they kept it in a church and drank from it all to put on a show for those who followed that faith."

"And now look," Lee cuts in, gesturing to Moses and the chalice. "It's worth nothing. Just a pretty something to look at." He glances to me. "Just like yourself."

"I am hardly a goblet." I narrow my eyes.

Gabe smirks at my reply, then reaches for his own glass to down all the wine that has been poured for him. His patience is growing thin, I can tell, and if drinking some will help calm his nerves, I am thankful then for the wine.

"No, you are not a goblet, Seer Beth. But what we are trying to say here is that like this chalice, which was once important to someone, you Seers will also fade away and become nothing more than people like us. You will lose your importance, and people will scoff at how much you could have done when you had the chance, but never did." Moses taps his fingers on the golden chalice and extends his hand, gesturing to my plate of food. "Eat. You've hardly touched your plate."

I can't even think about the food on my plate. What if what he is saying is true? Are we not doing enough? Are we not helping as much as we could be, and will it be too late by the time we realize this? I look through my lashes at Gabe, who is pushing his food around on his plate with his fork, not eating it. How can we eat with this burden on our minds? Someone here has to be polite, though. Someone here has to keep us from being dragged into this circus.

I shove a fork-full of the mystery meat into my mouth and chew on it with a blank face. It's salty, too salty, but I suspect they have to make it that way to keep their rations preserved.

"So, are you two a thing?" Lee asks as I chew away at my food.

Gabe looks up between Lee and myself and frowns slightly. "What do you mean?"

"Are you two together or something? I can't quite figure it out. What do you think, Moses?" Lee gulps down some wine from his glass, and just as he puts it down, one of the servers comes over to refill both his glass and Gabe's.

"Seers aren't allowed to be 'together.'" Gabe looks at me when he says this.

"Oh no? Why is that?" Moses cuts in this time, leaning forward in anticipation for the answer. "Seems like sort of a nonsense rule."

Gabe runs a hand back through his greasy, dark hair and stares up at the top of the tent for a moment. I'm sure he's trying to find a diplomatic way to state why Seers can't be together, but I also know that he doesn't believe in the reason why either. While Gabe and I have been best friends since we could remember, it's just recently started to become more, and that was going against the rules all within itself. "Well … we aren't supposed to be together because … " He looks back at me again. "It's forbidden by the Institution."

Moses laughs and slaps a knee with one of his hands. The gold bracelets he wears around his wrist clash together, clicking against each other as they move back and forth. "Well, we know that, Seer Gabe, but surely there is a reason as to why it is forbidden?"

"It is because," I start, trying to save Gabe from the question, "in the past, when Seers were allowed to ... court ... each other, there were consequences that resulted from their unions. New Seers would be born, their powers too great for one body, and they would die before they became of age. So, to end the cycle of Seer children constantly dying, the females were sterilized, and relations have been forbidden within the Institution."

All the females except for the Keeper and her daughter. Except for me.

Gabe's eyes don't leave me, and it is as if, for the first time, he is realizing that I am one of the ones who haven't been sterilized. He drinks from his glass for a long time, and I look down at my lap, hoping the conversation will pass.

"Well, it doesn't seem to have stopped you two from having feelings for each other. How have you managed to get this far without being caught?" Moses motions for a serving girl to refill Gabe's glass just as soon as he puts it down.

"Very carefully." Gabe watches the girl who is refilling his glass and avoids my gaze all together.

Lee points at Gabe and laughs. "So it's true! You do have feelings for Seer Beth." Laughing some more, Lee slaps the table with his hand and everything on it jolts and rattles in place. "So we have a pair of rebel Seers on our hands, it seems, Moses. They aren't so much different than we are."

"Very interesting indeed." Moses seems to muse over this new information, and I immediately ask myself if Gabe has made a mistake in admitting as much to them. "Well, isn't that something? Two little seeds of revolution waiting to be planted back in their

City. But do you think they'd actually try to make a difference? To push a change?"

"Well, maybe they will think about it on their way home." Lee finishes the food on his plate and holds it up in the air. It isn't long before one of the servers comes around to collect it, and his hands fall back onto the table, holding it by the edges. "When they take the plant back." He nods toward the back of the tent, as if indicating that the plant is somewhere back there. Have they found it already?

"Maybe. It would be an interesting experiment indeed." Moses stares at me for a long while, then looks to Gabe, contemplating the both of us for what seems like forever. "Are you two finished with your dinner? It seems you have much to think about now. I can have Lee show you back to your tent."

I nod my head. "Yes. I think we are quite done." I have hardly touched a thing on my plate, and I'll be sorry for it later when my stomach is growling in the middle of the night, but I want nothing more than to be out of this tent. To clear my mind. To stop thinking of myself like a chalice. An empty, worthless chalice, all dressed up for nothing.

Gabe starts to stand, indicating that he's finished, and I follow his lead and push myself up to my feet. My dress falls around my form and down to my knees in graceful ripples of gentle fabric. It catches Moses' attention, and he watches me with renewed interest. It's not the leering that Lee tends to do, but something different. I catch his gaze for an instant, and it's enough to make me blush. I turn quickly and walk after Gabe, who is already on his way out of the tent.

"Think about it, my little seedling. You can be the change the City needs." Moses' words catch me just as I leave the tent, and I pause and almost turn around, but force myself to keep walking.

I could be the change the City needs.

If only he really knew.

Chapter 16

Dinner leaves me feeling exhausted. I am mentally worn down and want nothing more than to go back to my tent and sleep. That is exactly what I plan to do.

Gabe puppy-dogs after me but doesn't say a word. The tension between us is taught, and we are strung out on emotions that the both of us can't bear to understand, or want to understand, for that matter. We know that whenever we return to the City, it will be different. I am already mourning my friendship with Gabe and wishing that I never had to become the Keeper. I don't want to lose what I have with him.

I hold the tent flap up until Gabe is inside, then yawn loudly. "I think I am going to turn in for the night."

"Yeah, me too. It's been a long day and we have a lot to talk about tomorrow." Gabe doesn't mean about our relationship, though. He wants to address the fact that Lee let slip that the plant might have been found already. We could be shipped back to the City at any moment, and that would take us farther away from Aura, where we actually need to end up.

"I suppose we do, don't we?" I don't even bother to change out of my intricate sari before I curl up in a mass of plush pillows, choosing a puffy one to rest my head on.

"You look exhausted." Gabe kneels down next to me and puts his hand on the curve of my hip. When I don't answer, he lies down the rest of the way, spooning the length of my body so that I fit snuggly against his broad form. I welcome the embrace. It makes me feel safe, and it doesn't take long before I drift into sleep. This happens shortly after I feel Gabe kiss the back of my head, his lips in my hair, his breathing hot against my scalp. I could get used to falling asleep like this.

***

Echo is never too far away from me. As soon as I drift into my dreams, he is standing there, his arms crossed over his chest, lips pursed in a frown.

"What's wrong?" I ask him as I casually glance about, taking note that we are standing in his chambers, which are bright from the sunlight that floods the room through the floor-to-ceiling windows.

"I can sense him, you know." Echo's words are, as always, level and soft. It's like anger doesn't know how to get through him, he controls it so well. Even without the tone, I can tell that he's not happy, though. It radiates through his being almost as brightly as the sunlight.

I frown in return. "I don't know what you want me to say, Echo. Gabe has been in my life for far longer than you have ... and he is here with me because I am trying to find something to save your life."

Echo's features soften a touch. "True." Though I don't know which statement he is agreeing with. "I still don't like it."

"And he doesn't like the fact that I am married to you either, Echo, but it's just how things are." I brush my hair back behind my shoulders and sigh, looking off toward the windows. "Honestly, being stuck in the middle is getting to be tiring."

"Well, you can't have us both."

"Don't you think I know that?" I snap.

Echo doesn't flinch. He's so patient and calm and everything that I wonder if I can ever be when I pick up my position as the Keeper again. I have to learn from Echo, observe him, mimic him. Those are things I can ask him for another time, though.

"Are you well?" I change the subject because I'm tired of Echo asking about Gabe and Gabe asking about Echo.

Echo crosses to where I am and takes both of my hands up in his, brushing his thumbs over the bumps of my knuckles. "You need to hurry, Beatrice. There's not much time."

"For ... for everyone? Or, just for you?"

"Both." The one word sends an electric jolt down my spine, and it opens an empty hole inside my stomach. Echo's not been in my life for too long, but I can't imagine him not being there, waiting for me in my dreams. Will it have to be that way when I return back to the City anyway?

I grip his hands in mine and stare up into his pale, blue eyes. "Please hold on, Echo. We are so close ... there's even rumor that the plant has already been found. We just need to come up with a plan to get it and run."

"And if you get caught?" Echo drags his teeth over his bottom lip. "Maybe I shouldn't think that way."

I smile in an effort to lighten the mood. "Probably not."

He leans down and presses his mouth to mine in a light kiss. As I kiss him back, I imagine myself drinking him in, like smoke swirling through a fan and dissipating on the other end. If only I could envelop him, possess him and never have to let him go. If he could live in my dreams forever, and I could just close my eyes and be there with him. As I think about these things, I realize that it's probably a very real possibility that I could always have Echo with me, and I'd not have to let him go.

But would it be fair to Gabe?

Outside of my dream, Gabe is still holding me. I wonder if he knows what I'm dreaming of? Will he know when I wake up, flushed and breathless? Will he understand that I can't help the fact the Echo comes to me in my dreams? It's the way of the Dreamcatcher. Normally, I would be dead by now if I was Caught. Echo wouldn't have bothered to waste all this time on me if he were another sort of Dreamcatcher. But Echo needs me. He loves me. He'd never kill me.

But he might refuse to ever leave me.

Echo wraps his arms around my waist and pulls me close to him. I continue to kiss him back, and can taste a faint, coppery taste of blood. I try to ignore it, but it becomes more and more noticeable, and finally, I have to break the kiss.

I lower my eyes in apology. "I'm sorry."

"It's okay," Echo assures me and kisses my cheek. "I need to go."

When I look at him again, I realize that he's getting paler, and his eyes look like they've sunken into his skull. This is probably what he looks like back home, and if this is any indication of how quickly I need to move, I obviously need to hurry it up.

"Please hold on, Echo."

"For you, Beatrice?" Echo grins a lopsided, somewhat pained grin. "Anything."

***

When I wake up, Gabe is sure enough still holding me. My cheeks are flush, but thankfully, he is still sleeping, and won't ever know that my dreams were the culprit. Or rather, that Echo was.

Urgency races through my veins, and I'm restless. I shift in Gabe's arms and try to think of a way we can break out of here with our precious plant … if we can even find it. So far, we are only running on rumors and not much more, and there's really no trying to find out. The gossip is all we have. No one is going to talk to a couple of sideshow Seers. At least, no one will without telling someone else first.

Our guards are the best source of information that we have. They forget that tents aren't made of brick, and when they drink too much, they talk too much, and Gabe and I find out all sorts of interesting things. The other day, one of the guards told a whole story about a secret speeder path that leads to a ravine with fresh water running through. They keep it secret because if everyone knew, they'd deplete the water source, and there are so very few that are good enough to drink from anymore.

The speeders.

They are small enough and fast enough to get away on. If we could get to the speeders and somehow destroy the rest of them, the Rogues would have no other way of catching up with us. I haven't seen any ships around, and it'd be a small wonder if they were able to maintain one all on their own.

Gabe stirs next to me, nuzzling his chin into my hair. I turn onto my back and look at him and how his hair falls over his eyes and onto his face. Gently, I reach out and tuck the strands back behind one of his ears, smiling faintly at his peaceful, sleeping expression.

That's when it occurs to me that things could change when I get back to the Institution. I am in charge of it now, so why does everything have to stay the same? Why can't I just change what I want to change and move on?

Then, I wouldn't have to lose Gabe. All I'd have to say is that Keepers are allowed to have one partner in their lives—after all, how am I supposed to have the next Keeper if I don't have a partner to be with?

How did the last Keeper? Or the Keeper before that?

I lock away these thoughts for another time and promise myself that I will revisit them later. I forget, sometimes, that I am the leader of the City, even if I've barely had the chance to actually lead it.

Gabe's eyelids flutter open, and he squints his violet eyes, covering them with his hand to protect them from the light. "Bea? Have you been lying there staring at me for a while now?" He smiles, peeking at me through his fingers.

"Something like that." I won't lie. I could stare at Gabe forever.

"You look like you've got a lot on your mind." Gabe yawns and snuggles in closer to me.

"I do. I've been thinking of all sorts of things, but mostly, I've been thinking about what we have to do to get back to where we came from." I'm careful about saying too much, because just like the guards forget that the tent is made from fabric, sometimes I have the habit of forgetting that they can hear us, too. They'll think nothing of us wanting to get back to the City, but if I mention Aura, then I'm sure they'll freak out.

"And what have you thought of?"

"The speeders." I whisper the words between Gabe and I, our mouths already close to each other's. "We need to get to them."

Gabe is watching my mouth more than he's listening to my words. When I fix him with a look and knee him in the leg, he glances back up into my eyes. "Huh? Oh. Right. That's a good idea … except they probably have a ton of them or something. That'll make them easy to find, but it'll also make it easy for them to catch up to us."

"Then we have to destroy the other ones so they can't chase us."

Gabe's foot trails up my ankle. "Right."

I don't think he's paying me his full attention. "Gabe, concentrate on what I am saying. This is important. We are running out of time."

"Okay, okay. So, we have to get to the speeders and destroy them. But how? We don't even know how many there are, or where they are, or if they are under guard or not. I mean, we are taking a huge shot in the dark here."

"It's the only shot we have, Gabe."

"We'll have to try to find out more about where the bikes are kept, then. I don't know how we're going to do that, because as soon as we start asking, they'll be on to us."

This is true. It's not like we can directly ask someone about the speeders. We have no business asking anyone anything at all. "What if you made sure to really look out for them during one of your tours around the camp? You can keep an eye out for people who look like they are about to go on a speeder ride, or for buildings that look like they might house speeders."

"It's the least I can do, but what if it isn't good enough? I mean, I don't know ahead of time where they are going to take me whenever we are paraded around the camps."

I sigh. "Something has to give, Gabe. Right?" It's not the answer he is looking for. It's not good enough, and I know it. We have to do better. We have to get out of this place and back to Echo before he dies.

The morning sun is already hot, and our tent has become humid and nearly unbearable. I unwrap myself from Gabe and crawl over to the trunk filled with foreign clothing to see what it is that I'll wear today. I rifle through the fabric and find an emerald-green tank top made from soft silk. To go with it, I choose a black, floor length skirt that won't stick to me because of the heat.

"Close your eyes, and don't peek," I instruct Gabe, who only smiles at me, but does as he is told.

"As you wish," he grins, and I catch it just before I turn and slip out of my dress and into the tank top. I pull the skirt on and let it rest on my hip bones, then turn back to Gabe.

"Okay. Your turn." I switch places with Gabe and lay back down in the pillows with my arms tucked under my head. I stare up at the ceiling as Gabe changes, thinking about how we are going to manage to break out of this place, and if it can be done at all. What if Lee was tricking us by leading us on to believe the plant was already found? What if it is what they want? And how are we going to get to something that's kept in Moses' tent anyway?

"There." Gabe announces that he is finished, and I look to see what he has chosen. His pants are baggy, much like the ones from the previous night, though this time they are a dark tan color. His shirt is what draws my attention, tight and form-fitting, so much so, I wonder why he is bothering to wear a shirt at all. "You are staring."

"I'm not." I quickly glance away, blushing.

Gabe is probably enjoying the fact that he's caught me looking at him that way, but I don't look back at him to find out. Before I can even return to our conversation about scoping out the speeders, Lee's voice calls to us from the outside. "Are you two ready for your walk today?"

"He treats us as if we are dogs." I frown.

"In a way, I guess we are just pets to them." Gabe offers me his hand, and I slip mine into his firm grasp as he tugs me up off the ground. "Remember to keep an eye out, okay?"

"I wonder where they will take us today." Through the past week, it seems as if they have taken us almost everywhere the camp has to offer. To the mess hall, a long tent set up for community dining, to the residential areas, to the training course, and everywhere else. There can't be much more for us to see in this Maker-forsaken place. It's hardly anything at all to begin with.

"Let's go find out." Gabe escorts me to the tent flaps and pulls one of them back, revealing Lee, ever so cocky, with one hand on his hip, and his greedy eyes on my form.

"You look beautiful today. Moses sure knows how to clothe his ladies, doesn't he?" Lee holds out his hand, and I realize that he expects me to let go of Gabe and follow his lead instead.

I look back at Gabe, and he offers me a single nod. It's best if I just go along with Lee's act than fight against it, and I think Gabe has come to understand that, too. So, I let go of his hand, and I let Lee take hold of my fingers instead.

"I am not his lady."

"Of course not, my darling. You and Seer Gabe here seem to be quite the thing ... but I think we've already discussed this, and it didn't quite go over so well, now did it?" Lee grins so I can see all his yellowed teeth, and I don't offer back any sort of response. He wants to get a rise out of me, and I'm not going to give it to him.

"Moses wanted me to take you to our graveyard today. He said that he thinks it's time for you to see what our suffering eventually leads to." Lee gestures to the west, where the residential area is.

Gabe presses his lips together disapprovingly. "Why doesn't Moses ever take us on these little walks of ours?"

"He's a very busy man, Seer Gabe. Moses has a whole camp to run, people to keep happy, business to manage. He devotes every supper to you two, and that within itself should be an honor. He doesn't usually share his dinner with anyone." Lee begins to lead us in the direction that he gestured, and we start through the dusty paths that snake around tents of every sort, some designated as stores, some as homes, each with its own purpose.

As we pass by, people peek out of their homes to get a better look at us. Though it feels like the whole of the camp has already seen us, there also seems to be more and more Rogues tucked away in corners of the camp that we've not seen before. I've underestimated how many there actually are. I would think, if they all banded together, they could easily march on Aura or the City to make their demands. It would be a huge risk, but the Rogues are known for taking risks. It's not like they haven't tried the approach before, in the past, when their numbers might not have been so big.

It doesn't take long before we come to the edge of the residential area, standing before a plot of dry, arid earth marked with dusty stones that are spaced apart. The graveyard isn't traditional in any sense at all. It's hard to tell one plot from the next, and there aren't any fancy headstones or tombs to be found. Lee pauses at the perimeter and stares out over the many, many graves that stretch out and out until I can no longer tell where the graveyard ends.

"This is it."

"Seems rather droll." Gabe puts himself between Lee and me and crosses his arms over his chest. "What was the point of bringing us here?"

This angers Lee, and his face screws up into a scowl as he violently gestures out to the land in front of us. "The point of it is so you can see just how many people suffer and die in our camps." Lee grabs Gabe by the back of his neck, his fingers locked in a powerful grip, and shoves Gabe toward about a dozen graves that have been dug recently. "These ones are fresh. Most of them children. Sometimes we don't have enough food and the heat is too much for them to hold on."

Gabe wrenches himself free of Lee's grasp and rubs the back of his neck. "Don't you touch me again."

Overhead, I spot the raven, and I wonder how long it's been milling about. I hope it doesn't come down to try and perch on me, though it's never tried before. The raven would probably give away my identity, and I can't afford to have that come out now. I also can't afford Gabe getting into a fight, so I reach out and wrap a hand around his wrist to calm him.

"It's sad." I look to Lee. "And I am sorry that your people have to suffer."

"What is sad, Seer Beth, is that these people, my people, have been shut out for generations. They've struggled to survive for years, and sometimes they do, and sometimes they don't. We could all survive if either Aura or the City would offer their help to us. But they don't. And why?" Lee asks the question, but he doesn't wait for an answer. Instead, he answers for himself. "Because we have been branded as outlaws, unfit for assistance. We are the people who didn't want to conform, or the people who didn't make it to the City in time to be taken into safety. To help rebuild. And now we are out here, fending for ourselves while you Seers and Dreamcatchers get to bask in your splendor."

Gabe laughs. "You think we 'bask in splendor?'" He laughs some more and nudges me in the arm. "The Institution is anything but splendorous, I assure you. The City has its own issues, especially now after the invasion. We might look like we 'bask in splendor' from the outside, but trust me … it is anything but."

I note the disgruntled tone of Gabe's reply. Why shouldn't he be disgruntled, though? After what the Keeper has done to him? After she chased him away from me for months and months. After he's watched his friends die. Why shouldn't he be bitter?

My hand drops from his wrist. I don't want these two to get into a fight, so I walk away from them and over to one of the graves marked with a stone. They both follow after me, as neither of them probably want me to get too far away. Squatting down, I peer at the inscription on the rock, which has been etched with a careful hand in letters with straight, perfect lines. It's a name: Isabelle. And that is it. Just a name on a rock. A name that will fade away as it weathers and Isabelle will be no more. I run my finger across the lettering and then stand once more. "Is this visit over?"

"Yes, I think you get the point." Lee speaks to me, though, his comment not extended to Gabe and his understanding of why we've been brought here. "Let's get you back to your tent. This has been enough for one day."

The raven screeches overhead and circles over a particular area of the camp over and over again. I watch it as we start our walk back, somewhat in the direction of where the raven flies. As we are returning, we take a path we've not been down before, one lined with stalls that sell hand-made goods like clothing, baskets, and pottery. Lee walks ahead of us and every now and then he looks back to make sure we are following close behind. Mostly, though, he's not paying us any mind, which comes in handy when Gabe jabs his elbow into my arm and nods to the left.

I look that way, spotting a long tent, the flaps blowing to and fro in the wind. I can catch glimpses of what is inside, and can count about two dozen, dusty speeders. There are some that have been stationed outside as well, but a group of men are moving them inside as the wind picks up and the dirt and sand is blown up off the ground.

"Seems like a storm is coming in." Lee rounds a corner, missing the look that Gabe and I exchange. We've found where the speeders are kept, and it looks like they are normally put out in the open and are being brought in because of the storm. This might work if we can move quickly, and if there's no one in the tent watching the things.

It doesn't take long for us to get back to our tent, and it's just as well, since dark clouds roll in over us, sucking the light out of the sky. Canvas whips and cracks as the wind moves through the camps, disturbing the tents. Lee pulls back the flap of our tent and waits for us to head inside. "It's going to be a bad one, and they

196

don't pass by quickly. I'll make sure your tent is secured to the ground so you don't end up blowing away. Desert storms aren't pretty things like you are." Lee winks at me and lets the flap fall, leaving Gabe and me alone.

The wind howls louder, and somewhere far away thunder grumbles, vibrating through the ground. It won't be long until the storm is upon us.

"We need to do this now," I say quietly, using the cover of the wind and thunder to mask my voice from the guards outside. Gabe comes closer to me so we can talk about it without having to yell at each other and compromise the plan.

"I think that's a good idea. I don't know how bad these storms really are, but I can't hear a thing going on outside, and I doubt the guards are going to stick it out. They've probably gone back to their own tents." Gabe looks toward the door, and there is nothing to be seen where the lingering shadows of the guards usually are. "I think they've gone already."

"But how are we going to get into Lee's tent?"

"That should be easy enough." Gabe's eyes find mine. "He's got something for you. Why don't you use it to your advantage?"

I stare at Gabe. Hard. "Are you kidding me?"

"I wish I could kid about these things, Bea, but we have to do what we have to do or we're always going to be some sideshow to these people, and we'll never get back home." Gabe reaches out and grabs my arms in his hands, shaking me lightly to get his point across. "You have to do this."

"But … "

"No. No 'but.' You have to get that plant tonight, and we have to get out of here while we still can." Lightning flashes through the darkness, and I wonder how it can still be day outside when it looks like night. A crash of thunder soon follows. The storm is right overhead of us. "Go to him. Remember that you are doing it so we can get back home."

I am doing it for Echo, so he doesn't die.

I nod my head. "Okay. I … I will try. And I will meet you … where?"

"At the speeder tent. There shouldn't be anyone there, and I can hide out for a little while." Gabe lets his hands fall from my arms, but his gaze never leaves mine.

"And if I can't do it?" I stare back at him, hoping that the fear I have for this plan doesn't read in my gaze.

Gabe smiles and leans in to kiss my cheek. "You'll be able to do it," he whispers and pulls away. "I will wait for a half hour. If you don't come by then, I'll come back to the tent."

A half hour. I have a half hour to go to Lee's tent and somehow get my hands on the plant without him knowing. Then there's the getting out of the tent part. I have no idea how any of this is going to work, but if we don't take advantage of the storm while we can, we might never get out of here, just like Gabe said.

Gabe walks over to the tent flaps and carefully peeks out of them. Looking back at me, he says in words I can barely hear, "You can do this, Bea." And then, he slips out and is gone.

I can do this.

Chapter 17

Lee's tent isn't far away, but I feel as if I will never make it as I walk into the wind with my hand up over my eyes. My skirt violently blows around me, whipping in ripples with each gust. By the time I make it to Lee's tent, I'm exhausted, but I have to pull through because Gabe is waiting out there for me, and I can't fail. It's not an option.

Without an invite, I yank open the tent flap and step into the safety of the tent. Lee is laying on the ground on what seems to be a rug made from the hide of some sort of fuzzy animal. He looks up at me in surprise, and his mouth moves, but no words come out at first. Finally, he finds what he wants to say. "What are you doing here?"

"Gabe fell asleep, and I wanted some company." Gooseflesh forms on my arms. Already this is uncomfortable, and I have to question Gabe's logic in subjecting myself to this man.

Of course, the answer only serves to boost Lee's already inflated ego, and he grins widely, motioning for me to join him on the rug. As I walk over, I take note of the things in his tent, trying to figure out where he'd put the plant if he had it. His space isn't as cluttered as Moses' tent, which is filled with knickknacks from all around the place. Instead, Lee's tent is sparse, with a few old trunks that look like they've seen a hundred years, a small cot, and a dresser to keep his clothes. None of these things are fancy or ornate like Moses' trinkets. They are simple and necessary.

"Well, I wouldn't turn down a visit from such a lovely thing. Though, I do wonder how you escaped your tent." Lee smiles at me in a way that makes my stomach wrinkle. The storm becomes more active outside, and flashes of lightning illuminate the tent and then leave us in partial darkness once more.

I look up, indicating the current conditions, as if I could see through the canvas tent. "I don't think they wanted to stay out in this weather, to be honest." I sit down on the fur rug, distancing myself from Lee. Still, I don't feel safe. I could put a million oceans between us and I still wouldn't be comfortable.

"It's just a little storm. I pay them to do a job, and they run off at the first crack of thunder." Lee pours himself something to drink, and the sweet scent of wine drifts my way. "Would you care for some? We don't have much of it around here, but every now and then I like to treat myself to something special." His gaze roams over me when he says this. It feels like thousands of ants are crawling all over my skin, and I quickly break eye contact.

If I am going to do this, though, I need to do it right.

"Yeah, sure." I won't drink much. I need my wits about me, and I've never even had wine before. They don't allow drinking at the Institution. Alcohol is strictly forbidden, so I don't know how much it would take for me to lose control of my faculties. I will be careful.

He pours me a glass and hands it over to me. I cup it in my hands and bring it to my lips to taste. It's a little dry, but there's a touch of raspberry or some sort of fruit that makes it pleasant.

"So what is between you and your Seer friend anyway?" Lee leans back on his palms, relaxed and at ease. The complete opposite of myself.

I play dumb. "What do you mean?"

"You know what I mean." He doesn't fall for it.

Shrugging my shoulders, I sip at the wine again before deciding to answer. "It's complicated, and I'd rather not get into it."

"Well, you are in my tent now, and I want an answer." There's no room in his tone to argue. He is right. I am in his tent, and if I am going to find that plant, I need to play by his rules.

His rules. "I don't know. We aren't allowed to have relationships at the Institution, so whatever we have, I need to move past it before we get us both in trouble." Think, Beatrice. Think. "I guess that is why I am here."

This sparks Lee's attention. "For me?"

I drink a little more wine to make this easier. What was I thinking when I agreed to this plan? What was Gabe thinking to want to put me in this position?

"Yes, for you."

Lee sits up and crawls forward on his hands and knees, making his way over to me. The belt around his waist is laden with weapons—a knife on one side and a pistol on the other. Even when he is relaxing and alone in his tent he is prepared. Perhaps Gabe and I should have been more careful when we set up our camp. Then I wouldn't be in this position.

He leers at me with a lazy grin, and when he gets close enough, he cups my cheek in his palm and stares into my eyes. The thousands of ants that I feel crawling on my skin turn into millions. "You have beautiful eyes, do you know that?"

"They are the same as everyone else's eyes at the Institution. I guess I never paid them much mind." I force myself to look into his eyes after saying this. I need to play the part. I need to get to that plant. I need to save Echo.

How much time has passed by, I wonder? Has it been a half hour? Has Gabe given up on me? I think of everything else besides the man who is now kneeling in front of me, hovering. He is much bigger than I am, and though I am trained in combat, I question if I am able to take him down if I need to.

"You are … gorgeous." His hand leaves my face and he runs his fingers through my hair instead. I shudder and though it gives the impression that I enjoy the touch, really I shudder in revulsion. I don't want him touching me.

Before I can register what is happening, Lee pushes me down on the ground, pinning me to the floor by my shoulders. His mouth pushes over mine, and I try to turn my head to get him away from me, but he holds my face in place with one of his hands, kissing me.

I can't breathe. This isn't going the way it is supposed to go. He's on top of me and over me, and I am trapped. I claw at his arms with my fingernails, but it does nothing. I gasp for air when he pulls away from my face to kiss my neck instead. Just as soon as I open my mouth to scream, his large hand presses over my lips and my scream is muffled and goes unheard. It seems like he's done this before, and I wouldn't put it past him that he has.

I kick with my legs, but Lee goes nowhere. He is a force that is unmovable, and I scold myself for putting me in this situation. I have no one else to blame, and I only have myself to get me out of this.

His knee pushes between my legs in an effort to part them, and that is when it becomes too real. And then I remember.

His knife.

As he continues to kiss at my neck and down to my shoulder, I pull his knife free from its sheath and quickly stab him in the side, digging the blade deep within his skin.

This stops him.

He pulls away from me almost immediately and puts a hand to the gaping wound as blood pours out of it, soaking into his shirt and turning it a beautiful shade of red.

He stares at me in disbelief. "You … you … "

" … will never put myself in this situation again." I hiss and stab him one more time, this time in his gut, and he falls over onto his side, blood pouring out of his mouth.

It's a quiet death. His eyes remain open, but they don't see anymore. The blood pools around his body, and the furs become matted, no longer luxurious.

I need to keep moving. Now is my time.

I scramble off the ground and stumble to my feet. Blood has soaked through my green tank top, and it sticks to my skin. There aren't many places to look, so this should be easy enough now that Lee is out of my way. I start for the trunks first.

Pulling open the lid of the first one, I push around the items inside, but I find nothing of importance, nothing that looks like the plant we were searching for.

Quickly, I move to the other trunk and open it. Sitting on top of everything else inside, is a towel with a leaf sticking out of the side. A purple leaf.

I've found it.

Despite the fact that there's a dead man on the ground behind me, I smile and clutch the plant to my chest, as if it were something as precious as a child. This is what will save Echo and his people. Our people.

Now, to get to Gabe.

Chapter 18

I burst through the tent and into the storm. Sand and dirt blows everywhere, and I shield my eyes to protect them. With swirls of gravel and dust blowing in tiny funnels that whip across the camp, it's hard to see which direction I should go in, and so I trust my instinct and just start running.

I sling a leather messenger bag around my shoulder, one that I stole from Lee's tent. Inside, I've buried the plant deep down to keep it safe. I am the messenger of life, bringing the cure to Aura to save Echo from death. I feel like nothing can stop me as I dart ahead, losing myself in the chaos around me. There is no one else around, as everyone probably retreated into their tents to avoid the stinging wind that scrapes my skin. I can feel tiny pebbles embedding themselves into my arms, but I can't stop running. I need to keep moving.

I need to get to Gabe.

As I round a corner, I can just barely make out the shadow of the long tent where we previously saw the speeders. I don't know how much time has passed by, or if Gabe is even waiting for me still, but I push myself forward, sprinting the last few yards. But just as I get to the entrance of the tent, I hear the knoll of a bell ring out through the thunder and the howling wind. It tolls heavily and ominously, adding to the eerie nature of the storm.

A warning bell.

They are onto us.

I duck into the tent and pull the flaps shut, tying the ropes down to keep the tent from blowing back open. Squinting through the darkness, I am breathless and panicked, and the bell echoes through my head. I can hardly think straight, and just when I hesitate, I hear Gabe calling for me through the darkness.

"Beatrice? Over here! Hurry!"

I trip into something heavy and metal and stub my toes. "Damn it!" I curse and stumble over in the direction of Gabe's voice. Eventually, his hands grab at my waist and he pulls me close to him, embracing me in his arms. "Are you okay?"

"There was a bit of an accident." I breathe the words heavily, trying to catch my breath.

"An accident?" Gabe holds me back at arm's length, and I can barely decipher his face in the darkness.

"I killed Lee."

"What?"

The bell continues to ring. Outside, thunder crashes and the ground shakes under us. "We have to go. I'll explain later, but we have to go now."

Gabe doesn't ask any more questions. He lifts me up and puts me on the nearby speeder, then hands me an assault rifle. "Keep this close. It's loaded and ready."

At first, I'm surprised that we should need to arm ourselves. Then I realize how stupid it is to think that we needn't arm ourselves. They will find us soon. And I'm sure they will have their own guns locked and loaded, too. I hike the gun into my arms and Gabe climbs onto the speeder in front of me. He looks over his shoulder, and I catch the glint of his violet eyes.

"Ready, Bea?"

"Do I have a choice?" I respond back as I lean forward into Gabe and wrap my arms around his waist. "Let's get out of here."

Gabe starts up the speeder, and I can barely hear its engine through the clamor of the wind, thunder, and the ringing of the bell. He pulls his legs up and gets ready to take off through the opposite side of the tent, where the opening hasn't been tightly secured. Just as we start to move, gunfire tears through the canvas of the tent, perforating it with tiny holes that are ripped open more by the wind. Outside, I can catch the shadows of Rogues who are quickly approaching, but I can't tell how far away they are.

Both of us duck down, and the speeder comes to a halt as Gabe fumbles for the gun that he has slung around his shoulder. The assault from the outside doesn't stop, and he drags me off the bike and onto the ground behind it to take cover. "We're going to have to fight them off!" he yells at me through another thunder crash.

I crawl over to the speeder and prop my rifle up onto the seat, opening fire toward the Rogues. If we want to get out of here, there's no time to waste. Gabe sets up next to me and pulls back on his trigger, and though it's hard to see anything in the darkness, when the lightning flashes through the sky, we can catch flickering glimpses of angry, sand-worn faces, and men blindly firing their weapons in our direction.

I continue to squeeze the trigger, and a few of the shadows from the outside drop to the ground, only to be replaced by more. We are outnumbered. How are we ever going to escape?

A bullet wizzes by my ear, and I duck down, only to hear Gabe gasp in pain behind me. I stop firing just long enough to turn and seek him out. "Gabe? Gabe! Are you okay?"

He is somewhere on the ground at first, but then he pulls himself back up and sets his gun on the speeder once more. "I'm hit. They got me in the arm." He sucks a pained breath in through his teeth. "There are too many of them."

He confirms what I've feared. There are too many of them, and only two of us. The whole camp will be after us now. On top of all of that, Gabe is hurt. Needing to get out of here has become more than a priority.

The Rogues breach the tent, ripping down a large chunk of canvas. The wind blows over some speeders that are close to the edges, and a few people trip over them and fall onto each other. They are like the blind leading the blind, as they aimlessly try to seek us out, using the flashes of lightning to guide their way.

"You need to get out of here," Gabe murmurs by my ear, then opens fire again, warding off those who are getting too close to us. Men are screaming, adding to the clamor of everything else.

"But what about you?" I am not leaving without him. I can't leave him behind … not again. Not to these people. They will probably kill Gabe if they get their hands on him, and I would never forgive myself for it.

I'm not given much choice. Gabe picks me up and puts me back onto the speeder. Holding my head in his hands, he looks me in the eyes and then leans in to speak close to my ear. "You have to get out of here. Don't worry about me. I'll catch up."

"I can't leave you!" I yell back at him, then duck down as gunfire rains over our heads, slicing into the canvas behind us and tearing it open. Outside, I can see how the lightning streak across the sky in branched lines of light, stretching outward and touching many different points on the ground. It illuminates the nothingness that spans on forever in every direction, lending it a certain sort of brilliance.

"You have to." Gabe's fingers press into my cheeks and behind my ears, and he pulls me forward, pressing his lips fully against mine. I kiss him back, though it is filled with fear and apprehension, and when he pulls away, I hardly have time to say goodbye before he starts my speeder up. "I'll find you, Bea."

"Gabe … " And then, the Rogues are there, and one of them reaches out to grab my bike to tip it over, but I pull back on the throttle and shoot out of the tent, leaving Gabe behind. I race into the flashing lightning, tears streaming down my cheeks, and an ache in my heart. I can't hear anything from the camp anymore. Maybe the bell is still ringing, but everything has gone mute for me. Though the sand stings my face, all I can feel is the pressure of Gabe's lips on mine, and the sinking despair that tears my heart out of my chest.

I head west, back to Aura, sobbing the whole way, until the storm dissipates, and the clouds give way to a beautiful blue sky. It is as if none of this has happened, though the ever-present absence of Gabe reminds me that it did.

I am the messenger of life. I am the bringer of the cure. I am the Seer who has not only left her friend behind once, but has managed to do it again.

I am nothing without Gabe.

***

When I get to Aura's spaceport, I am quickly met by the guards, who stop my speeder on the edge of the tarmac and practically drag me off its seat. I must look travel-weary and worn, judging by the way they are staring at me. I've forgotten about the blood on my shirt, or the irritated redness to my skin from driving under the hot, desert sun. My hair sticks to the sheen of sweat that covers my arms and face, and I am out of breath, as if I've run this whole way instead.

It doesn't take long before they realize who I am, and almost all at once, they let me go and step back. "Queen Beatrice."

Queen Beatrice. I am a queen now. How could I have forgotten? Not only am I the Keeper of the City and the Abandoner of Friends, but now I am the Queen of Aura.

One of them asks, "Are you hurt?"

I look down at my stained shirt and shake my head. "No." I am not hurting in any physical sense, at least. "I need to get this to your healers."

The guards glance at each other in confusion. "Get what to the healers, Your Highness?"

Have they forgotten so easily why I was sent out into nothingness? I reach into the messenger bag and feel around for the plant, though I can't help but think about Gabe and what has become of him now. Is he already dead? Have they captured him? Are they torturing him?

My fingers brush against the cool leaves of the plant, and I carefully pull it out to let the others see. "I've brought back the cure."

They waste no time getting me into a shuttle to take me to Aura. Everything happens so quickly, and I'm hardly paying attention to any of it. As the shuttle flies over the empty span of land between the spaceport and Aura, I stare out the window and back toward the east, where I've left Gabe behind. How am I ever going to explain this to Elan and Brandon? They will never forgive me. Ever. And if they don't forgive me, how will any of the Seers find it in themselves to accept me back to the City?

I look down to my hands, which cup the little plant with the purple leaves. This plant is going to save the Dreamcatchers from extinction. The plant that will save Echo from his mother's fate. How can something so little mean something so big? And how could it have brought me to kill a man and abandon my best friend?

The shuttle arrives at the gates, and I'm escorted out of it and toward the palace. The first thing I notice is the silence. No one walks the streets, and there's a strange odor that lingers in the air, one that reminds me of the slave camps. The stench of dying.

The guards usher me inside, and the heavy doors shut and lock behind us. The once-busy hallways of the palace are empty. Not even the men and women that make up the royal staff are anywhere to be seen. Our footsteps echo for what seem like forever, the clicking sounds bouncing off the walls with every step.

When we turn the last corner, we stop by a room that I've not been in before. The guards push the doors open, and inside there is a flurry of healers milling about makeshift lab stations that have been sporadically set up around the room. Vials and tubes push putrid-colored liquids into other vials and tubes, an endless maze of an unknown concoction.

I stop just inside and glance at everything and everyone, the plant still cradled in my hands. At first, the room comes to a stop not because of what I am holding, but because of my presence alone, and they all bow in respect, a few of them murmuring "Your Highness" in a formal greeting. But then one of them, a woman with bright red hair, notices the plant, and she bounds forward, startling the guards to react and close up around me in protection.

"She has the plant!" the woman blurts, and the room comes alive once more. "She has the plant!" The healers break out into a unified cheer, and were my heart not so heavy with the fact that Gabe is probably being beaten into a bloody mess right now, I would probably smile and rejoice with them.

Instead, I carefully relinquish the plant to the red-haired woman. "Please hurry and turn this into the cure you were searching for." I lower the tiny plant into the woman's hands, my fingers brushing across the leaves as I pull away and step back. Immediately, she turns to join her peers once more, and the whole lot of healers get to work.

Tiredly, I look to the guard. "I wish to see my husband now." Because I can't possibly stand to see Brandon or Elan right now. I have too much to explain to them, and too little energy to do it. The guards obey and escort me out of the room and through the palace to where Echo's chambers are. Our chambers.

Outside of his room, there are a handful of royal protectors who quickly move aside for me when I approach. As I get closer to the doors, I smell that odor again, the sickly, deathly scent that makes my stomach turn. *Please don't let it be too late.* I wouldn't be able to stand losing Gabe and Echo all in one day.

The room opens up before me, and inside there are a dozen healers bumbling about with herbs and poultices, carafes of water, and trays of untouched food. I can't even see where Echo lies, as his bed is surrounded by people, servants and healers alike, all trying to do their jobs.

I clear my throat and once one of them catches my arrival, the rest of them quickly move out of the way. The bustle of people parts before me as I approach Echo's bed, and when I am but a few steps away, I can see him clearly … and I immediately wish I never looked upon him at all.

He is nothing like how he was in my dream, when he came to visit me last. When I was curled up with Gabe, sleeping beside him. Instead, he is frail, and I can almost see his bones through his paper-thin, transparent skin. His stark blond hair is limp and brittle, and it sticks to his face, which is covered in a fevered sweat. His eyes are closed, and he's still—too still.

I stop by his side and hesitantly put my hand out to rest on his forearm. "Echo?"

My voice brings his eyes open, and though it is not the most handsome of things, he smiles at me, his chapped lips pulling up at the corners. "Beatrice ... "

"I found it. I brought home the plant." I say this immediately, not wanting to put him through any more torture of waiting and wondering if I've failed or not. The news makes him smile even more, but it's quick to fade when he starts to cough, and blood droplets spray into the air. He's slow to cover his mouth, and the tiny dots of red stain the white sheets used to cover him.

"That ... that is wonderful news." Echo puts one of his weak hands over mine and squeezes it. "Hopefully ... they can make the antidote in time ... "

I squeeze his hand back, firm and reassuring. "They will, Echo. They will. I don't want you to worry about it anymore, okay? You need to rest up and get better." Despite myself, I choke on the words, tears rising to my eyes, and I quickly look away. "Just rest up and get better."

It's not clear if Echo had the chance to see the tears or not. But his hand slips off mine and back onto the bed, and he only nods his head in response, too weak to say much more. I can't stand seeing him in this state, but I would be a bad wife if I walked away from my husband to let him suffer here alone. So, I pull over a chair and sit beside his bed, and at some point, I put my head down on the mattress and close my eyes, falling into a restless, broken sleep.

***

Someone throws back the curtains to the windows and the sunlight floods the room, rousing me from my dreamless slumber. I lift my head to find Echo still sleeping, his breaths coming in ragged inhales and exhales. I sigh, then brush my fingers through my hair as I sit up and notice that most of the healers are gone, and Echo and I are practically alone.

There's a knocking at the door, to which I call out, though not too loudly. "Come in."

Jamie and Irene bustle through the door, each of them holding covered silver trays, and each of them sporting smiles as big as their faces, as if oblivious to the fact that Aura is dying.

"It's nice to see you back, Your Highness," Jamie chirps as she sets the tray down on a nearby table. Irene rests hers on a table that is closer to Echo, and they both pull off the lids at the same time, revealing the breakfast underneath. The aroma of eggs and cooked meats mingles with the sickening odor, and it makes my stomach churn. But I smile politely, regardless.

"Thank you. I was getting hungry." I let my gaze fall on Echo, wondering how they've been managing to keep him fed this whole time.

That's when Irene pulls out a thick syringe filled with a pale-yellow something. She hums to herself as she picks up Echo's arm and sticks him with the needle, which brings him to wake almost immediately. Before he has a chance to cry out in pain,

Irene pushes down the plunger and empties the contents into his frail body. "There you go, Your Highness!"

Echo groggily looks to the two women, then turns his head and spots me. It is as if he's forgotten that I have been here the whole night. He probably had forgotten. "Beatrice."

"I'm here, Echo." I motion to Irene to put the tray up on his lap. "Why don't we try to eat a little bit, okay?"

He looks me over and notes the blood on my shirt. "You're hurt?"

I forgot about the blood, and the fact that I probably still look a mess, having fallen asleep in a chair after traveling all this way on a speeder bike. Jamie rushes over and pokes at my side where the red stain has spread into a lazy circle. I put my hands down and stop her from prodding any more. "It's not my blood," I explain to the three of them, then lift up the shirt to let them see that my stomach is quite intact.

"Oooooh." Jamie smiles in relief and goes back to milling about and getting things in order while Irene sets Echo's tray up in a manner that won't be easily tipped over by his mismanaged movements.

"What ... what happened?" Echo insists, even if I really don't want to rehash the story right here and now. Or ever, for that matter.

I lean forward and pick up his fork, dipping it into the scrambled eggs. Lifting the fork to his lips, I wait for Echo to open them so I can scoop the eggs inside. He only parts his mouth just barely enough for me to get the food in there. "There was a scuffle ... when we were trying to leave. A man named Lee tried to force himself on me ... "

"He what?" Echo talks as he chews, and some of the eggs fall out of his mouth. It's not exactly attractive, but Echo himself is looking worse for the wear anyway.

"He had me pressed to the ground, and I couldn't get up. So, I stabbed him. In his gut." I scoop up some more eggs and hold them up to Echo's mouth, but this time, he doesn't open it. He just stares into my eyes, wordless.

"It's okay, Echo. I'm okay. I promise." I reach out with my other hand and brush back his hair, which is greasy and sweaty. But it's all I can do to comfort him and cool the heated hatred that boils in his gaze.

"He shouldn't have dared," Echo grumbles.

"But he did. And now he is dead because of it." I take my hand back and set down the fork, choosing to pick up a piece of toast instead. Ripping off a corner, I lift it back to Echo to eat.

He opens his mouth and accepts the toast, and after chewing on it for a little while, he continues on with the questioning. "And what about Gabe?"

The words twist in my chest like a knife, and I immediately lower my eyes.

"Beatrice?" Echo asks again after swallowing down the bread.

I don't know how long I choose not to answer Echo's question. Time seems to drag by forever at some points, and at others it seems to move so quickly I don't know how to slow it down. In this moment, though, I can't tell if it is speeding up or stopping all together. Part of me wishes it would go backward, so I can be back at the Rogue camp, so that I can pull Gabe up onto my speeder and tell him that I'm not going anywhere without him, and he can't make me. I want to go back and save him.

I feel Echo's hand on mine and it jars me out of my thoughts and back into the present. "I had to leave him behind."

"Why?"

"Because ... " I start, and I want to finish with "Because I am a horrible friend" but I know that won't be enough for Echo. Echo wants the truth, and he's good at finding it. "They were coming after us, and there was a horrible storm, and if we had waited any longer, we would have been caught, and I wouldn't have been able to get the plant back to Aura." I put my head in my hands and shake it, closing my eyes. "Gabe got hit in his arm, and the Rogues were closing in on us. Before I had time to think, he put me on the speeder and told me to go ... and I went. I left him behind ... and I went ... "

There's a silence that fills the air after my words. No one in the room moves or says a word, and I can only hear myself breathing inside of my hands. Or am I crying now? I can't figure it out. When Echo puts both his hands on mine and parts my fingers away from my eyes, the cool air touches the tear tracks that run down my cheeks. "I left him behind, Echo..." I whisper in sad, broken words.

Though he is weak and dying, Echo tugs on my wrists, pulling me into the bed beside him, and he wraps his arms around me to hold me close to him. "You had to do it, Beatrice. You had to bring back the cure ... "

"Brandon and Elan are never going to forgive me."

"I think they would understand, Beatrice. It is not as if you chose to leave Gabe behind, really. You had to." Echo brushes his hand over my hair, petting it down in long, soothing strokes. Jamie and Irene hover by the end of the bed, keeping an eye on their king, though I also see the way they look at me in pity and concern.

"I had to," I repeat after Echo, trying to drill this fact into my head. I had to do it. I had to do it to save Aura. But it doesn't make me feel any better, and I can feel the tears start to well up in my eyes again.

Echo starts to cough violently, and he quickly grabs a cloth napkin that was set down beside his plate of food and presses it to his mouth. I look up to find him pulling the blood-spattered napkin away from his lips, concern in his eyes. "I need that cure." Each word is raspy, and as he speaks, more blood trickles from the corner of his lips and slides down the side of his chin.

Jamie is quick to reach out with a clean cloth and sops up the blood as if it were drool from a baby and nothing more. "We will go check on it, Your Highness." She smiles at Echo as if nothing could possibly be wrong with him just before she turns and drags Irene out of the room with her, tugging the other woman by her arm.

Echo rests his head back on the pillow and goes back to petting down my hair, though I'm sure it's more of a motion to calm himself than to calm me at this point. I don't want to fret too much over him, but I'm worried, and I know at this point it is a race against time. I can't imagine having to leave Gabe behind, only to find out the cure hasn't been made in time, causing me to lose Echo on top of everything else.

I lace my fingers with Echo's and squeeze his hand, but he doesn't squeeze in return. His arm is limp, and his breathing is shallow, and when I prop myself up on my arm to look over him, I realize that I've less time than I thought I did, and that Echo is starting to fade away.

"Please hang in there, Echo ... " I wipe the remaining tears from my cheeks in an effort to pull myself together. I have to be the brave one here. I have to have the strength to pull Echo out of this.

But it's so hard to be brave when you're losing everything you've thought you loved.

Chapter 19

Outside it is dark. Not even the stars can manage to shine through the blanket of blackness that shrouds the world and covers it in shadows. I am standing on a paved street, though the concrete is cracked and in some places ripped up from the earth, making it non-accessible and unusable. Tall, hardy weeds sprout up between the cracks, jutting upward toward the sky in an effort to find the sun, and during the day, it must not be too hard, given that the sun seems to burn hotter than ever after the War, and surviving outside and under it without protection is a feat in itself.

I look behind me and the road stretches into infinity, going places where I can't see. Places I don't know exist. We've been taught that the City is the largest established community left on this continent, that Aura is close to follow with its Dreamcatcher and Citizen inhabitants, and in between here and there are the Rogues, a group of people who never quite made it to either of the other options, stranded forever in the wasteland in the middle. But I feel as if this road doesn't go to any of those options. That it will take me somewhere more, somewhere I've never learned of or seen before, and there's an undeniable urge to follow it to see where it will lead me.

I start to walk north, a direction that always seemed off limits to the rest of the world. I step over the cracks and potholes, at times only narrowly avoiding twisting my ankle or falling onto the ground. Above me, the raven appears and starts to cry, as if warning me to stop and not go any further. I start to wonder if the raven ever had my best intentions in mind. Or is it still loyal to the Keeper previous me?

A deep, orange-y hue swirls into the night sky, casting a burning haze over the Earth, though it does little to actually light up the way and provide clarity where the night has swallowed it up. I watch as the pumpkin color twists and turns, always moving, like some sort of snake slithering its way through the darkness. When I look forward again to see where I am going, there's the shadow of a man standing about a hundred feet in front of me, but I can't make out who it is. The raven cries again, and I startle and quietly curse the damned thing for following me at all.

"Where are you going?" the shadow man asks me, his voice sounding much like someone I know, but I can't quite discern it right now. With each word spoken, it also sounds like the wind is blowing, and I have to listen closely to decipher what is actually being said.

"I don't know. I felt the need to head this way." I point in the direction I was walking. His direction.

"Sometimes, Beatrice, we often don't know where it is we are going, or where we will end up, but we are called to do it anyway. And we go."

I start walking again, approaching the man, whose identity becomes clearer the closer that I get to him. It doesn't take long before I realize that this apparition is none other but Gabe.

"Gabe?" I run the rest of the way to him, no longer careful about watching my step. I just want to close the distance between us, then never let him get that far away from me again. When I bound the last few steps, I wrap my arms around his neck, and he spins me around in a tight hug, and I never want him to put me down. Never. "What are you doing here?"

"Where?" Gabe murmurs into my ear as he gently sets me back onto my feet. "I have no idea where 'here' actually is, to be honest."

And neither do I. But it quickly occurs to me what is happening. I am in a dream, and Gabe is in my dream. Echo has managed to pull both of us together somehow, and here we are, in this dark space, on a road leading to nowhere.

"It is our dream." Though I'm placed back on the ground, my toes safely reaching the road once more, I don't dare let go of Gabe. I hang on to him with a passion and fear that I've not known before. In the back of my mind, though, I know that dreams don't last forever, and at some point, I will be letting go of Gabriel again.

"Our dream?" Gabe asks, confused.

"Echo has put us in each other's dreams. He's Caught you, just as he's Caught me."

Gabe tilts his head up to look at the sky, which is still streaked with that deep, swirling orange that never stops moving. "I've been Caught?"

"It's not as bad as everyone made it out to be, is it?" I laugh, though the laugh is dry, and it doesn't last long at all. I bury my head into the side of Gabe's neck and smell what seems to be dried sweat and blood. I close my eyes. "I'm sorry, Gabe."

Gabe wraps his arms around my lower back, his fingers pressing into the small of my spine. "Don't apologize, Bea. I blame you for nothing."

"Nothing? Not even when I left the City to follow Echo?"

This causes Gabe to pause, but he squeezes me close to him and shakes his head. "Nothing."

A wave of relief surges through me, replacing the twisting knot in my stomach that has been growing and tightening ever since I sped off on the bike, leaving Gabe with the Rogues.

"It will work out. I don't know how, but it will," Gabe assures me, and when I look up at him, I find he's looking down at me, his dark hair falling in front of his eyes, matted with the grime and dirt from the Rogue camp. "I just need you to remember something ... "

I reach out and brush his hair out of his face, waiting for what it is he wants me to take away from this. He reaches out and takes my hand in his, lowering it away from his head, and stares down at me with a seriousness that I've not seen in Gabe for a long, long time. "What is it?"

"Do not forget the City. And remember what the Widow told you ... "

I close my eyes as the Widow's words whisper through my mind: Trust in that which you cannot see.

"I won't forget. I promise."

The sky starts to turn a deeper shade of red and yellow, and the night is quickly becoming overwhelmed. Gabe kisses the side of my head, his lips pressing to my temple, and he holds me close to him once more. "We'll find each other again, Beatrice. I don't know when, but we will ... "

I find no comfort in the prediction, though. This is not a Vision. This is a dream. It is me and Gabe, lost in each other's minds, pulling at straws and guessing at what is going to happen, when really we have no idea what will become of either of us. Echo gave me this dream to comfort me. It is beyond his capabilities to give me a Vision.

As the sky becomes brighter, Gabe becomes fainter and fainter until I can no longer feel his arms around me. The road under my feet has disappeared, and instead I stand in hot, unforgiving sand that soaks up the light and turns it into an unbearable heat. My mouth quickly becomes dry, and it tastes coppery, like blood, but when I lift my fingers up to touch my tongue and pull them away, nothing is there.

"Gabe?" I call out, but no one answers me back. I'm alone in this desert land. Alone with nothing but the burning sun to keep me company. And the raven, which starts to cry out once more, its noise jarring and annoying.

Just when I think it is too much, the dream starts to break apart, and I slip back into the waking world and out of the harshness of the light.

***

When I wake up, there is chaos in the room around me. It is filled with healers, one of which is trying to pry me out of Echo's bed as the others mill about, propping his limp body up, poking and prodding with instruments that I am unfamiliar with. Echo's head lulls to the side, and his eyes are half-lidded, the pupils rolled up into the back of his head.

This isn't good. I search through the people in the room and spot Irene and Jamie huddled in the corner, their fingers by their mouths and panicked expressions on their faces.

"What is happening?" I ask no one in particular, hoping someone will answer me. No one does. I continue to stumble away from the bed and am eventually overcome by the healers, and walk over to stand with Jamie and Irene instead, realizing about halfway through that I've not changed since I got back from the Rogue camp, and that there's blood spattered up and down my left arm, the one that was closest to Echo. Just as I get to them, the doors to Echo's chambers swing open, and another healer dressed in a white robes hurries to Echo's side with a vial in her hands. Behind her, Brandon and Elan appear, looking just as confused as I am sure I do.

"This is a mess," Elan states in his typical, flat tone.

"Is that the cure?" I ask as I look back to the healer with the vial. They are shoving a tube down Echo's throat now, and he doesn't even gag on it. An IV bag has been hooked up to his arm, and the healer with the vial extracts the purple liquid inside with a syringe. I don't know what they are doing to Echo, it all moves too quickly. Suddenly, the syringe is inserted into the tube from the IV drip, and the purple liquid mixes with the other solution, seeping into Echo's vein.

"I think so." Brandon scans the room, and I immediately know who he is searching for: Gabe.

"He's not here." I beat him to it and hope that maybe, just maybe, they will be content with that answer. But by the way Elan's eyes meet with mine, with that "you better explain yourself" expression, I know it won't be enough.

The healers form a circle around Echo's bed and they all hold hands. The number of Dreamcatchers in the room reminds me of the headache building behind my eyes, as I haven't had time to take any serum to protect myself from the pain. Whatever they are doing makes it that much worse, and the pressure starts to build inside my skull. I grab my head with my hands and murmur weakly to Jamie, "I need some serum."

The girl's face turns to one of alarm and she squeaks out a hasty, "Oh!" Then, she scurries off into the crowd of people and out the door.

I continue to hold my head, but watch the healers as they start to chant together. Their words are haunted and drawn out, and I can't decipher what language it is that they are using. They start to sway back and forth, all at once, their movement like an unending, connected wave. It's calming. Mesmerizing. I can't take my eyes away from them.

Soon, Jamie returns with a small cup filled with the liquid that will take my own pain away. I am quick to drink it and hand back the empty glass with a thankful, though concerned smile.

"Where is Gabe?" Elan doesn't seem to care about what is going on in the room right now. He doesn't care that my husband is dying, and all we have is the hope that the cure will work. That Gabe and I didn't make a mistake by leaving Aura to find the plant.

I can pretend to be distracted, but I know Elan will see right through it. He's too bright for his young self. I turn to him and lift my chin, trying my best to summon my position as Keeper over Elan. I have to be the part that I've been forced to play. It's a lesson I've not quite learned yet. "I had to leave Gabe behind. We were being attacked, and he told me to flee before we were both taken down." I don't want Elan to argue me, so I straighten my shoulders and back, pulling myself up a little taller. "I had no choice."

Elan's violet eyes narrow, and he sets me with a look that I will probably never forget. I can sense his disappointment. I have let him down.

Brandon doesn't look any better. He uncomfortably crosses his arms over his broad chest and asks in a quiet voice, "So we lost Gabe?"

Lost. Lost is such a strong word. Lost is what happens when you don't think you can find something again. Lost is almost the same as gone. Gabe is not gone. He can never be gone.

"No. Gabe is not lost. He is at the Rogue camp." The weight is heavy on my shoulders. It's so easy to bend. But I won't. Not even to my fellow Seers.

"It's working!" one of the healers blurts, disrupting the therapeutic chanting.

I break away from Elan, Brandon, Jamie, and Irene, and push through the circle of healers to get to Echo's side. His color is returning to his cheeks, and his eyes move under his lids, though they do not open yet. "Are you sure?" I ask the closest Dreamcatcher.

"He's coming around. Look!" he replies, pointing at Echo just as he opens his eyes, then covers them with his hands to block out the light.

I smile for what seems like the first time all day, then lean over him so he knows that I am here. "Echo? Are you feeling better?" It reminds me of when Echo healed Gabe, how when Gabe opened his eyes for the first time, he saw me … and the ache in my heart pangs through my limbs.

Echo smiles back at me as he pulls his hands away from his face and reaches up to brush his fingers down my cheek. "You did it."

I shake my head, gesturing behind me with a sweep of my arm to indicate the healers who are standing by. "No, no. Your people did this. Not me."

"But they healed me with the cure. The cure that you found. That you Saw in your Vision."

There's nothing to say to this. I don't want the credit of saving Echo. I can't celebrate it the way the healers can. They did not leave their best friend behind to save the husband that I married behind Gabe's back. So, I don't say anything at all, but allow Echo to keep brushing my cheek as he fills with life once more.

Irene claps her hands together and turns to Jamie, Brandon, and Elan. "We should celebrate!"

Elan stares at Irene, shaking his head. "Celebrate the fact that a Seer had to be left behind to save your king?"

The clapping stops, and Irene lowers her eyes, admonished.

"Elan, that's enough," I warn, unable to take any more of his scrutiny. "We will discuss all of that later. But for now, let them rejoice. Their king is saved, Aura is saved, and all those who are sick can now be healed."

"We've already started the mass production of the cure, Your Highness." A healer informs me as he bows deeply, and the rest of them follow suit. "We will leave you to your recovery now."

"Thank you for your help," I reply and watch as they file out of the room in a single line, disappearing into the hall. The room is much quieter now, and as if answering a cue not given, Irene and Jamie slip out after the healers, leaving only me, Echo, Brandon, and Elan in their wake.

I watch the other two Seers with a wary eye, as I know they are upset with me, just as I am disappointed in myself. Brandon looks more hurt than angry, and it's in seeing that pain that hurts me in return.

"We will find him again," Echo speaks, drawing all of our attention. "Don't worry. Your friend's sacrifice will not go unseen. Nor will I let it just … happen."

"And how are we supposed to trust you when you already stole our Keeper away and kept her prisoner in your city?" Elan snaps, his brows drawing together in anger.

"Beatrice came here of her own accord. My mother is the one who kept her prisoner," Echo corrects Elan as he pushes himself up to sit a little straighter. His body is still stiff from the sickness, so I reach out to help him prop himself up against the headboard. "And my mother no longer rules over Aura. I do."

"I will believe your so-called help when I see it. Until then, I don't see why we have any reason to stay here any longer. We came to retrieve our Keeper, and now that she's done her part, I think it is time for us to go home." Elan and Brandon both nod at this declaration, their gazes shifting to rest on me. "After we get Gabe back."

I run a hand back through my hair, dragging the black tresses from around my face as I think this over. Reaching out, I put my hand down on Echo's arm to draw his attention to me. He lifts his pale blue eyes to mine, then squeezes my hand in his own. "They are right, Echo. I will need to go home. But you will need to uphold your promise to me before I can return to the City, and free the Citizens from their captivity."

The king of Aura is silent as this notion runs through his head. I can see the way it tears him apart, not knowing how to let go of a way of life that has existed since Aura was created. Or maybe he doesn't know how to let go of me.

"Let them work with you, and not for you, and I'm sure they will stay. Look at Jamie and Irene, for example. They are slaves of your household, but even if you free them of their fetters, they will probably serve you regardless. They love you and your house. Don't you think the Citizens of Aura will do the same if you gave them the chance to live on their own?" I brush back Echo's hair, my fingers running through the almost-white locks, soothing and calm. How do I make him see that he doesn't need to keep these people against their will?

Brandon apprehensively approaches the bed and asks, "Why do you need them?"

Echo blinks and looks over each of us. "They are the source of healing energy that the Dreamcatchers need to thrive."

"Can't you find this energy in other things? Like the plant that was just used to heal you? You didn't need a Citizen to do that … " Brandon points out, and I realize that I have not thought of this before now.

"There are different types of healing energies. This was a sickness. But sometimes people are physically wounded, like Gabe, and another physical being is needed to help mend them," Echo replies, then looks at me. "If we free the Citizens, and they all decide to leave, then what will we do?"

I press my lips together in thought. I have to answer this carefully, or else Echo will always be too afraid to let his people go. "Echo," I begin, my hand closing over his, "we weren't made to be immortal. Your people might have found a way around this, temporarily, but if you keep at it … it will end in disaster. You, yourself, took me to the Settlements to see the horrible conditions that they are living in. It will only be a matter of time before they rise up against you, rebel, and ultimately destroy everything you've worked so hard to maintain."

Echo looks away from me and to the windows, which are filled with the glow of the harsh sun outside. I am reminded that this is a city of gold, a city filled with a certain evanescence which cannot be described. It is beautiful and consumed with light, the opposite of my home. The opposite of the darkness I am used to.

"Let them be free, Echo. Change Aura for the better. And then, you can come home with me, and help me change the City, too." I whisper the words as we gaze out the window and into the sunlight.

I peer to the side, watching as Elan shifts uncomfortably where he stands at the mention of changing the City, but Brandon smiles and nods his head in agreement.

"And Gabe?" Echo looks up at me. "How are we going to get him back?"

Elan and Brandon are watching me expectantly. There's no way they are going to return to the City without Gabe.

I reach up and pull the bottle cap necklace from under the tank top that I have yet to change out of. I look down and run a thumb over the picture of the raven, remembering when Gabe bought it for me, remembering how defiant he was in the face of the Keeper. He wasn't afraid of loving me then. He's still not afraid.

I can only think of one option.

"We will fight for him."

Chapter 20

The tarmac buzzes with commotion as ships idle in place, waiting for their cargo to be loaded. Most of that cargo consists of Dreamcatchers dressed in combat gear, strapped with weapons, and ready to fight. They disappear into the hull of the vessels, one-by-one, ready to fight for something they've probably never thought of fighting for in their lives: a Seer.

I stand beside Brandon and Elan, all of us also dressed in jumpsuits, guns strapped over our shoulders. The wind blows freely over the flat surface of the spaceport, whipping my long hair around my face and causing the flags of Aura around the perimeter of the tarmac to snap violently back and forth. The sound of the canvas cracking reminds me of the tents that Gabe and I stayed in at the Rogue camp. It makes me ache for him all the more. I want to leave now.

There's no particular fanfare when Echo finally arrives from his escort, the same ship that he used to get me from the City to Aura. It pulls in and lowers its ramp, and two lines of three Dreamcatcher guards emerge first from the ship, preceding Echo, who wears the same combat outfit as we all do. Nothing about him differentiates him as the king, which is good, because I don't need him targeted any more than I need to blow my own cover as Keeper.

All-in-all, there are about ten, mid-sized ships loaded with maybe ten to twenty men and women each. I hope it is enough. The Rogues might not be as technologically advanced as the Dreamcatchers, but they are crafty, and I'm sure they've come up with some sort of plan in case they were ever attacked. They are too smart not to have.

As Echo approaches me, I manage a smile, but it's nervous at best, and he can probably tell. I hook my hair back behind my ears to keep it from blowing in my face. "Are you sure about this?"

"Gabe helped to save my people, and my people will help to save Gabe," Echo replies simply enough, then reaches out to brush a stray strand of hair out of my line of sight. "It's only fair."

"It's a good first step in the right direction of forging a peaceful relationship between the Seers and the Dreamcatchers." I glance up at the ships as their ramps start to close, sealing up their hulls and signaling that they are ready to go.

"Do we have a plan?" Elan asks, always concerned about the logistics of everything.

Echo readily nods his head and motions for us to follow him back onto the vessel that he arrived in. The three of us follow him up into the ship, and after us, the guards load in and seal off the hatch. We are on our way.

"The plan is, we will take them by force." Echo glances between the three of us, saying nothing more.

"That's it?" Elan deadpans.

"That's all we need, Seer Elan. The Rogue camp is located in a wide-open space. By the time they realize we are coming, we will already be upon them. We will have the element of surprise." Echo raises a hand, letting the captain of his crew know to proceed onward. The ship lurches forward, but after the initiate jerk, it's hard to tell if we are moving or not.

Brandon sits forward, resting his elbows on his jumpsuit's kneepads. "And how are we going to find Gabe? And what about all the people who won't be fighting? Like the women and the children?"

As badly as I feel about it, I never thought about the Rogue women and children, who will be stuck in a fight that they didn't start.

"Remember in combat class, Brandon? Sometimes you can't prevent causalities. People are going to get in the way. That's just how war goes." Elan doesn't seem so concerned about who might get caught in his crossfire. He's always been the one to charge forward, but only after coming up with a sound plan. And as I watch him shift in his seat, I can tell he's not comfortable with Echo's plan so far.

"But is this war?" Brandon directs the question at me. "Are we starting a war?"

I hesitate. Are we starting a war? Do I really know the answer to that question? "It's a battle, Brandon. All we can do is be careful that we don't take down the unarmed." Turning to Echo, I fix him with a look. "Can you give those orders? Before we get there? No one is to shoot at anyone who isn't shooting at them?"

"Sounds fair enough." Echo motions to one of the guards, beckoning him over. "Commander, please make sure that the rest of our contingent is aware that we are not shooting at those who are unarmed and not fighting. We are only fighting those who are taking part in the battle."

The Commander salutes Echo and heads off toward the front of the ship, presumably to relay the new orders to the other ships that are following us.

The four of us sit in silence, listening to the humming of the ship as it hovers through the air, its trajectory set for the Rogue camp. I am nervous about what I will find when I get there. I am nervous that we won't be able to get to Gabe ... or that it will be too late when we do. I tug on my sleeve, my fingers tracing the thin line of thread. And then something urges me to look at Brandon, and when I do, he lifts his hands to his head and closes his eyes. A Vision.

I move from my spot next to Echo and kneel down in front of Brandon, putting my hands on his knees. "What is it, Brandon? What do you See?"

Brandon winces, his face screwing up into a pained scowl. It doesn't take long before his hands drop from the sides of his face, the Vision over. His eyes flicker open, the violet orbs glowing, and he looks to me, swallowing hard. "That was strange."

"What was it?" I try to encourage him to share with me, when in actuality, it's his duty to share with me. I am his Keeper. It is expected. But I don't press him.

"Well," Brandon rubs the bridge of his nose with his thumb and pointer finger. "The thing is ... I started to See something, something bright ... and then all of a sudden, everything turned black ... and all I could See was darkness. And then it was over."

Elan's brows knit in concern. "That isn't normal, is it?"

"Not normally, no. I've personally had it happen once, but my Visions aren't quite the same as everyone else's." My admitting as much makes me nervous. What does this mean?

The Commander returns to the back of the ship and announces, "Estimated time of arrival is now ten minutes."

Ten minutes. It felt like it took Gabe and I forever to get to the Rogue camp. Now I'll be there again in a mere ten minutes. Ten minutes and we'll be rescuing Gabe.

"Well, take it easy, Brandon. I need your head in the game when we get to the camp. Okay?" I pat his leg and stand back up, my own mind much heavier now with Brandon's unusual Vision. Sitting back down next to Echo, I take a deep breath and look him over when I notice he's staring at me.

"What is that about?" he asks as he pulls his gun in front of him and checks to make sure everything is working. He pulls the magazine out, looks it over, then slams it back into place with a click.

"I'm not quite sure. I've never heard of a Vision that just … stopped like that." I speak quietly, keeping the conversation between myself and Echo, as I don't want to worry Elan or Brandon any more than they already are. Brandon keeps rubbing his head with his hands, and Elan is whispering something to him, but I can't quite make out what it is they are talking about.

"Do you think it's a bad thing?" Echo wonders.

I tug my necklace out of my jumpsuit and hold it in thought. "If I had to guess? I wouldn't think it was a sign of anything good to come." My violet gaze settles on Echo, watching as his expression falls in concern. "But I don't know what it will be if he didn't actually See anything. It just doesn't seem good."

"Well," Echo starts and pats my leg in an effort to comfort me, "let's not think about it too much. We're going to find Gabe, and then we can fix the whole slave issue … and then we can get you back to the City."

"After we divorce," I remind him.

"What?"

"I am the Keeper, remember? I can't be married … and most certainly not to a Dreamcatcher." I tuck the necklace back under my jumpsuit and reach out to brush Echo's cheek with the back of my fingers. "Especially not the Dreamcatcher King."

Echo sighs and leans back against the hull of the ship. "I thought you said you were going to change things?"

"That might be so, and I really want to, but I can't just return and drop all of this on them. They are already probably mad at me for leaving them to follow you in the first place ... but to return and announce that I'm the Dreamcatcher Queen?" I can't help but to laugh wryly at the very thought. It wouldn't go over well at all. "It would be a disaster, Echo. You and I both know that. And you are the diplomatic one, so I'm sure you get it more than I do."

"I guess." Echo lowers his eyes as my fingers run down the side of his face.

"Let's not think about that now, okay? We have a mission to focus on, and everything else can come after." At least, that is what I am telling myself. Maybe I will regret it later, when there's so much on our plate that we don't know where to start, but I can't afford to waste my energy thinking about it now.

"Five minutes!" the Commander announces, his voice rising above the humming of the ship.

"Well, here's hoping your minimalist plan works, Dreamcatcher." Elan rolls his eyes and grabs for his helmet, shoving it on over his head.

Echo also reaches for his helmet, cradling it between his palms. "Sometimes, the best made plans are ones that aren't complicated with details, Seer Elan."

Elan waves off Echo's words with a vague gesturing of his hand, seemingly uninterested in his philosophy.

"He gets that way before battle," Brandon assures Echo, half-apologizing on Elan's behalf.

Echo shrugs his shoulders and fixes his helmet on his head, ending the conversation. I also prepare myself by slipping my helmet on and pulling the tinted visor down over my eyes. I can still discern Brandon's glowing gaze from behind his own visor, though it is dimming now and will probably be back to normal by the time we touch down.

The windows to the ship are small and only allow for brief glimpses of the outside world. We are moving so quickly that all I can make out is the dark, reddish hue of the miles of sand that stretch out forever in each direction. It's a wonder that we can find the Rogue camp in this vast wasteland at all, and a part of me admires them for being as bold as setting up in the middle of nowhere, with nothing but their numbers to protect them.

Today, it will be found out if numbers alone will keep them safe.

"Brace for impact!" the Commander's warning comes just before the ship touches down, jolting us around in our seats and announcing the end of our journey.

"Well, here goes nothing, right?" Elan jumps up and pulls his gun in front of him. "Let's go get Gabe back!"

We line up behind the Dreamcatcher guards, who stand on the edge of the ramp where it levels with the ship. A loud groaning precedes the hull opening, and sunlight floods the dark space, making me grateful for the tinted visor, else we would all be blinded. As the outside is revealed to us, I note that we are still a few hundred yards away from the camp, the tents dotting the horizon.

The bell sounds.

"That didn't take long," I murmur and reach for my gun, bringing it around front of me.

"Let's go!" Echo gives the order, and the guards descend down the ramp first, followed by Elan and Brandon, then Echo and me. When we are out on the arid, hard ground, I look behind me to see the other ten ships unloading their men and women as well. As soon as all feet are on the ground, the ramps are lifted, and the ships hover once more, heading for the camp. "They will provide overhead support," Echo explains as we move forward as a team toward the camp.

My chest tightens with anticipation. Each time the bell rings, it vibrates through my bones. Somewhere in there, Gabe must know we are coming. I hope he knows we are coming. I would hate for him to think that I've abandoned him for a second time. *No, Gabe. This time, I'm coming back for you. This time, I'm not leaving you behind.*

Our footsteps fall in line with an unheard cadence. We are ready to fight. If we succeed, it will surely never be forgotten. It will change everything, Aura and the City fighting side by side.

But if we fail?

It doesn't take long before someone opens fire. The Rogues. Little sparks of light flash from the tips of their guns, and I can see that first before I can make out the people behind the firing. They are ducked down behind barriers of sandbags piled up on top of one another about waist-high. They have cover. We don't.

"We should have gotten closer!" I blurt, but it's too late. The Dreamcatchers return fire and the percussion of all the guns sounding off at once is deafening. Their ships provide cover fire as we walk forward in a straight line. From time-to-time, those who are in the front are picked off and drop to the ground, screaming as we close in. It won't be much longer until we can take cover behind those same sandbags, firing blindly into the community of tents, if all goes well.

As we get closer to the camp, the bell becomes louder, filling my ears with its warning. A few Dreamcatchers break the battlements first, jumping over the sandbags and firing into the line of dirt-smudged faces. At times, when they are close enough, I witness a Dreamcatcher grab onto a Rogue with their bare hands, and subsequently, I witness the Rogue fall on the ground, eyes white, mind empty. Gone.

I must have stopped walking, since Elan shoves me forward and I lurch in the direction of the others. "Keep up, Bea!"

Right. Keep up.

We press on into the mass of tents. I have no idea where they would be keeping Gabe, but I do have an idea of who might know of his whereabouts. Moses.

"We need to get to the big tent. The one with the guards." I point toward the middle of the camp. "That's where Moses is."

"Moses?" Echo yells from under his helmet, and I can barely hear him over the gunshots and commotion.

"He runs the camp!" I call back and motion for them to follow me. I try to remember the Training Games, and all the street tactics we were taught to defend the City. Stay low. Make use of the structures around you. Blend into your surroundings. Surprise is key.

Though we are hardly in any type of city, I still keep the points in my mind. Ducking low, I decide to head for the middle of the camp, hoping that on the way, there might be some sign of Moses' tent. Echo, Elan, and Brandon follow, and behind them is Echo's small contingent of guards, who clearly do not like having to take up the rear.

A few Rogues suddenly jump out in front of us, but before they can pull back on their triggers, Brandon opens fire, tearing holes into the Rogues' shabby tunics, which start to turn red from their blood. One of them falls forward onto his knees, clawing at his chest, choking on his own blood. He's still for a moment, then tips forward, face planting into the dirt and sand. The others drop soon after.

I blink back at Brandon, who, if I could see his face, I'd imagine was smiling that big, stupid grin of his. But now is not the time for celebration.

We zip down the narrow alley, tents on either side of us. Sometimes, as we pass, I can see women and children huddling in the corners, praying. All of this for Gabe.

It only takes turning one more corner before we find Moses' tent. And of course, true to form, Moses stands out in front of it, rifle held in his hand, smiling.

"There she is." He motions to me with a hand, as if I were a guest he was waiting for this whole time. "Come back to save her darling Gabriel, I assume. If that is really you under there."

I don't bother to yank off my helmet. He can assume who I am all he wants. "The sooner you give him up, the sooner we will be out of your camp."

"It's a little too late for that now, isn't it Seer Beatrice. Or … should I say, Keeper Beatrice?" Moses smirks, and with another gesture of his hand, two guards drag a bloodied and beaten Gabe out, forcing him down to his knees. "You've not only started war between us and the Seers, but it looks like we've a war between us and the Dreamcatchers as well. And it is a pity, really. I was really hoping that we could all get along."

Gabe lifts his head just barely. His eyes are swollen almost shut. It's a wonder he can see anything at all. His face is bruised to the point of being mostly purple and black, and he has cuts down his arms, as if he were trying to defend himself from something at some point. I hurt for him. I left him behind when I could have fought for him in the first place. And now look. Look how broken he is. He stares at me with a distant, vacant gaze, one that slows the racing of my heart, frozen with the fear that I've already lost him.

Echo's guards continue to shoot into the area around us, keeping back some zealous Rogues who try and bound forward to attack. Echo, Elan, Brandon, and I all stand in one line, our sights set on Moses.

"It is what it is now, Moses. There's no going back. All you can do is protect the rest of your people by handing Gabe over. Be a good leader and think of them first." I am desperate to get Gabe away from the Rogues that are holding him. I'm desperate to get him back, period.

"Is that what you did? Did you think a good leader leaves their own behind to save their enemy?" Moses inquires.

I glare at him, thankful for the visor that keeps Moses from seeing my anger.

As I open my mouth to respond, something happens. The ground shakes from under us, and I grab onto Echo and Elan to keep myself standing.

"What … was that?" Brandon looks to the rest of us.

And then, there is a shrill whistle followed by an explosion. Flames rise into the sky, mushrooming into a cloud of smoke. Half of the camp is on fire. But from what?

"What in the hell … " Moses stares behind us, his mouth agape.

I turn to see what it is he is staring at, and that's when I notice the Dreamcatcher ships have all turned, their weapons trained on a ship that is much, much larger than our own. They shoot at it with everything they have, but it doesn't seem to be doing anything at all.

Another shrill whistling noise as a streak of purple-red tears across the sky and rips into the camp, exploding closely enough that it knocks us all to the ground.

Elan rushes to his feet, lunging forward to grab Gabe by his collar while his guards lie stunned on the ground. "Let's go!"

I snap out of it and scream to Echo's soldiers. "Go back to our ship! Go back to our ship!"

Brandon helps with Gabe, hauling him off the ground and throwing him over a shoulder. We don't have long to react before Moses and his own men open fire on us.

"Run! Run!" Echo calls back as we wobbly move across the shaking ground and into what seems to be a wall of pinkish flames. One of the Dreamcatcher ships falls from the sky and lands in the camp in a ball of flames. "Damn it, I hope our ship is still there when we get there."

The same thought runs through my mind. We could be stranded here with whatever it is that is attacking us.

I shoot back at Moses and his men, trying to keep them at bay. When I cast a look over my shoulder to see how far away they are, I barely have time to throw myself on top of Echo as another whistling streak of fire strikes Moses' tent, blowing it to pieces. We both tumble onto the ground, pushed forward by the force of the explosion. I land on my right arm, which catches on a piece of shrapnel and tears open.

Then, I scream. "My arm!"

Echo carefully pushes me off him, then yanks me back to my feet. "We have to keep moving, Beatrice!"

How can I move when every motion sends a jolt of searing pain through my arm and down my body? I shake my head, cradling my bloodied arm to my chest, my gun hanging to my side by its strap. "I've cut myself deep. There's so much blood …"

"We can't worry about that now! Do you want to die here?" Echo pushes me, and I will myself to keep running. No, I don't want to die here. I don't want to die at all.

We jump over the sandbags and make a dash for Echo's ship, which is waiting for us some hundred yards away. It seems so close and so far away all at once. As we close the distance between us and our salvation, the large, mysterious ship in the sky creates a deep, thrumming noise, as if charging something up. It hums and everything stops, save for the Dreamcatcher ships, which continue to shoot.

It demands our attention, and we all slow down, stopping just before Echo's ship to look up into the sky and watch.

"What is it doing?" Elan asks, pulling the visor of his helmet up to get a better look.

Another jolt of pain hits me, but this time, it's not from my arm. No. It's a Vision. A flash of a Vision. A Vision of light. Bright light. Too bright to bear. And then, there is nothing. Blackness.

"Beatrice?" Echo puts a hand on my good arm to check to see if I am okay.

It's just enough time for me to shout, "Close your eyes! Look away!"

The light is too bright when it comes. It swallows everything up, and I have an instant to squeeze my eyes shut as it blankets over the whole area. There's no heat, no telling if the light is still on us or not, so I grab out and feel for Echo and nudge him toward his ship. "On the ship! Keep your eyes closed!"

We scramble in the direction of the ship, and I trip over the ramp on my way inside. I can hear the footsteps upon metal behind me, which means the others have found their way inside, too. "Elan? Brandon? Echo? Gabe?"

"Here!" Elan calls, followed by Brandon and a grunt from Gabe.

Echo bangs his hand on the hull of the ship. "Close it up! Go straight for the City. No stopping! Go, go!"

The ramp pulls up and seals shut. After we are all safely inside, the ship lurches forward and speeds in the direction of the City. We are finally going home.

I tentatively open my eyes and peek around to make sure we are, in fact, all here. And that we are all okay, too. "Help me get my helmet off."

Echo reaches over and tugs the helmet off my head, then stares into my eyes, which are probably glowing from the Vision. "What was that thing?"

"I have no idea." I push on the wound on my arm to try and stop the bleeding, then chew on my lip to abate the pain. "How is Gabe?"

"I'm fine," Gabe mutters, slumped in his seat. Somehow, he manages to smile in my direction, his lips cracked and bloodied. "You came back for me."

"Of course I did." I smile through my pain. "Of course I did …"

The light starts to dim the farther away we get from the mysterious ship. Echo helps to wrap a makeshift tourniquet around the cut, tying it off tightly. I smile through my pain to thank him, and he smiles back heavily. When he is done, I move over to the window to peek back at the burning camp and see that the other Dreamcatcher ships have turned and followed us as well. Some of them are smoking and obviously damaged, but at least they've escaped. Content that we are safe, for now, I sink down into the seat next to Gabe and suck in a deep, calming breath.

That's when I realize that Elan is kneeling in front of Brandon, trying to pry his hands from over his eyes. "Let me see, you big oaf!"

I get back up and walk over to the two of them, concerned. "What is wrong here? Brandon?" I kneel down beside Elan and look up at Brandon's face, hidden behind his very large hands. "Brandon?"

With a final tug, Elan manages to pull Brandon's hands away, and when he looks at us, we can't do anything but stare back in shock.

"I didn't look away in time … " he whispers.

I stare into his eyes, which are no longer violet, but are all black instead, his pupils fully dilated.

"I couldn't look away in time … " Tears form in his eyes, rimming them before falling down his cheeks.

Echo comes to stand by my side, and we are all quiet, unsure of what to do or say.

"I can't see." Brandon reaches out for one of us, and I take his hands in mine to console him. "I can't see … " He repeats himself over and over again and begins to sob. Elan looks away, unable to watch his fellow Seer cry. A Seer who can no longer see.

Whatever that ship was, whomever was in it, they've figured something out that can destroy all of us.

They know how to steal our power.

Chapter 21

Brandon cried the whole way back to the City. On the way, we decided it would be best for only one of the ships to approach, to spare all of us from being blown out of the sky by the Watchmen. Thankfully, Elan was able to negotiate our arrival, and just as soon as the City shield was deactivated, we touched down on the roof of a nearby building.

Now as the ship powers down, I worry about how the Seers will receive me. I worry about the state of Brandon, of Gabe, and what will become of Echo and the other Dreamcatchers once we are back at the Institution. We stand side-by-side in front of the bay door, waiting for it to open, Echo to my left and Gabe barely standing on my right. I cradle my wounded right arm in my left, wincing through the pain, but feeling guilty because I'm certain it doesn't amount to the type of pain Gabe and Brandon are experiencing.

The door cracks open and lowers to the floor, and with every inch of opening, I see the many faces of Seers who have gathered to witness our return. The ones in the front are holding rifles, which are pointed our way. The others are all in their black robes like a unified front—a wall of hesitation, anger, and curiosity.

Here I stand, their Keeper. The Keeper who abandoned them to follow some Dreamcatcher to Maker-Knows-Where. Only the sound of the wind and the resting ship exists around us. They are waiting for me to speak, or perhaps I am waiting for them to show me that they aren't going to take me to be executed by firing squad.

"Bea," Gabe whispers my name in encouragement, but it only serves to remind me of the medical attention he and Brandon are in need of.

"We need medics, please." I call the words to the Seers below us, hoping that the words are neutral enough to not start out on a wrong foot.

A few glances are exchanged to one another, and a few of them finally decide to break off and find a couple of stretchers, which they promptly bring back. As they approach the ship to get Gabe and Brandon, I watch as their brows pull together in pain as they get closer to where Echo and I stand.

I have to continue with the momentum. Now is my chance. I step forward and clear my throat. "My fellow Seers, I know my departure has upset you. I know you do not understand it, and you probably don't care right now about the 'whys' of the matter. But, as you can see, there have been some changes ... some issues ... and I really need you to trust me right now. I really ..." The words get stuck between my brain and my mouth. I take a moment to look into some of their eyes, and I can see the betrayal written all over their faces.

When I continue, I cut right to the important issue at hand. "We will be attacked. Soon. And when we are, we might very well all be dead by the end of it."

The looks of betrayal are replaced with confusion and worry. They begin to murmur amongst themselves, and I keep talking, because if I don't roll with the momentum, they might not ever give me the chance to speak again.

"And it won't be by the Dreamcatchers. Whomever or whatever it is, it has the ability to rob us of our Sight, as it did with

Brandon." My gaze moves to the stretchers as Gabe and Brandon are brought off the ship and away to medical care.

"It is true that I left you to pursue the Dreamcatchers." These words bring an audible whisper of disapproval from the gathered Seers. "And it is true that I have brought the Dreamcatchers back here with me." I glance over my shoulder at Echo, who in turn gives me a solemn nod of his head. "In fact, I've brought back the very King of the Dreamcatchers, Echo. I brought them back because we have no choice right now. We need to coexist and work together or we will cease to exist and die together."

"And how can we trust you now?" one of the Seers calls out above the others, and the rest of them echo their concern in a wave of muttered conversation.

I think over the question, pretending that I am in their shoes, pretending that I am standing before the Keeper who chose to follow the enemy instead of staying behind to help heal the recently attacked City, its Citizens, and its Seers. Getting them to trust me will not be easy. I don't even know if it is possible, but I do know that I have to try, or we will lose everything that we know.

I suck in a deep breath and roll my shoulders back, standing as tall and straight as I possibly can. I think of the Dreamcatcher Queen, and how she so easily demanded the respect, attention, and trust of her fellow Dreamcatchers. I think of the Keeper before me, my mother whom I have never known, and how she didn't expect respect; she commanded it.

And who will I be like?

"I don't know." The not-so-convincing reply leaves my lips in a sigh wrapped in defeat. "I can't make you trust me again. I'm not going to force you to trust me for that matter. The only thing I can do right now is be honest with you." I look back at Echo, staring into those captivating blue eyes of his. He smiles back in encouragement, and I try to calm my fluttering heart. At the end of this, I will have to say goodbye to Echo. He has a kingdom to rule, and I have a City to govern. But for now? For now, I have him.

"The truth is, Echo and I have been joined in marriage." I look away from him and back at the crowd of stunned Seers. "It is a long story, and when we've the time to discuss it all in detail, I will not hide anything from you. Our intent is to end the marriage, but now we've not the time. I put this all before you if only so that you can see that I do not plan on hiding anything from you, my fellow Seers. I never did. So please," I beg, folding my hands together in plight, "please believe me. This City is all that we have."

Elan stands on my right, and the way his hands ball into angry fists tells me that he is feeling much the same as the other Seers. He has yet to forgive me, and I don't expect it to happen anytime soon.

Surprisingly though, he steps forward in front of me and the other Seers. He doesn't seem so small right now, as he has in the past. Elan has had to grow up quickly, as have we all. "Seers! I have witnessed our new enemy with my own eyes. I've also fought alongside the Dreamcatchers in order to rescue one of our own: Seer Gabriel. Our Keeper has been true to her word this whole time. I, too, am still angry with her for leaving us, but now is not the time for my anger! Now is the time to decide! If you want to fight with us, please step forward. If you don't want to fight with us, that is fine. You will have to retreat into the City and find cover, so please don't waste anymore of your time and do it now."

I blink a couple of times, suppressing a surprised smirk. Elan is definitely no longer a little boy. He is fierce and convincing.

My gaze returns to the crowd, waiting to see who will retreat and who will step forward. The Seers exchange unsure glances with each other, some even murmur back and forth, and from time-to-time they look back up at the three of us standing before them, begging for their help.

After an unsure minute or two, a female Seer steps forward and calls out, "I will fight with you." Another steps forward, then another, and soon the whole mass of Seers moves forward in unison, pledging their help in the fight.

Maybe I'm not supposed to show emotion as the Keeper, I don't ever remember my mother showing much emotion aside from impassioned, blind ambition, but tears well up in my eyes, and relief and joy simultaneously swell in my chest. I am rendered breathless, and when I try to say "thank you" no sound comes from my moving lips.

Elan smiles back at me, then sweeps his hand out in an "it's all yours" gesture.

I step forward toward the Seers, and they bow their head in respect for their Keeper.

Chapter 22

After I had the chance to visit the infirmary and let them repair my arm, I call a meeting of advisors and ask for the most talented Seer that we have in combat. The man put before me is probably twice my age. His features are all dark, angular, and sharp, like the glare he uses when he looks at me and Echo.

"Hello, Seer. I am told you are the best soldier we have. Have I been told correctly?" I invite him to sit at the large table that occupies a generous portion of the Keeper's quarters.

"I have many years of experience, My Keeper," the man replies, his words taking on two meanings; no one is ever thrilled to be given orders by someone half their age, and this Seer is probably not all-too-thrilled with speaking to his deserter of a Keeper, the wife of the Dreamcatcher King. He pulls out one of the large, leather and wood chairs and sits.

"And what is your name?" I sit as well, and only then does Echo sit, too.

"Seer Jeremy, My Keeper." His violet stare shifts to Echo, untrusting, and his brows come together as his face contorts in discomfort from the headache that comes with being in close contact with a Dreamcatcher.

I note the exchange and lift my chin just slightly. "You can rest easy, Seer Jeremy. My husband has no intentions on doing any of us harm." I purposely call Echo my husband, even if it is still strange to say. I want them to know that he is on our side, even if our marriage is not meant to last.

To Jeremy, I slide a small bottle of the potion used to take away the pain from the headaches. "Take this. It will help with the pain in your head."

He eyes the liquid with suspicion, but eventually uncorks the bottle and tosses back the contents. The bottle is returned to the table and he stares at me and Echo, waiting.

"What I am going to tell you is going to sound impossible, but it isn't. Seer Brandon is now in the medical bay, being tended to because of this … this thing that has happened. He is the proof that this impossible thing isn't impossible at all." I put my arms on the table and run a hand back through my hair. "There is someone else out there. Someone who is not the Dreamcatchers or the Seers. They have some sort of technology that I can't quite put my finger on."

"What do you mean?" Jeremy asks, somewhat more intrigued now.

Echo chimes in now, adding to the conversation as if he has always belonged here in this room. As if he was always on our side. "They fly in a ship that are much more advanced than our own. While we were on our mission to save Seer Gabriel from the Rogue camp, this ship descended upon us and attacked." He looks between the both of us, pausing there. "The rest of it kind of happened very quickly, but from what I remember, there was a loud noise—"

"A humming noise." I shiver as I recall the horrible, mysterious sound.

"Yes, a humming noise. It got louder and louder, and then Beatrice—er, Your Keeper—told us all to close our eyes, and we did." Echo's words lilt and he mournfully continues, "Well, most of us did. Seer Brandon didn't close his eyes in time. We didn't find out until we retreated to our ships and high-tailed it out of there that he had inadvertently been exposed to this white light that left him completely blind."

"Sounds a little like something we know, doesn't it?" Jeremy folds his hands over the table with a calmness that belays the dire situation we are in.

At first, I don't know what he is alluding to. How could this possibly be like anything I've ever known? I never even knew other people existed in this world aside from the Dreamcatchers, the Seers, the Citizens, and the Rogues. Now, these other people are coming around—in a ship even—and I am supposed to somehow be familiar with their weaponry? A horrible, deceptive device that takes the powers of ...

"The Beacon." My heart sinks like a stone. Pushing my hair back with both of my hands, I exhale a heavy sigh as the consequences of this connection swirl around my mind. "I don't understand ... "

Jeremy says, "I don't either, but it seems strangely similar, doesn't it?"

"Ugh," is my intelligent reply.

The three of us sit in silence until Echo speaks up. "So, what does it mean? If the technology is the same, did the Seers know of these people already? Did they know of you?"

"Just, just stop with the questions for a moment." I rub my temples in worry. Or maybe I am trying to summon the answers to these impossible questions from somewhere deep in my brain. It would be so much easier that way. "We still need a plan."

"We do," Jeremy agrees.

"Somehow, we need to gather some intel on these people. Where they went. Where they are going. What other weapons they might have... " I tick off each point on one of my fingers. "We need to do it as quickly as possible. I don't want to find out later that they are making a B-line to the City while we are all bumbling around like a bunch of fools."

Jeremy nods his head and pulls out a datapad, flicking through the information. I see face after face scroll over the screen as he filters through the Seer directory. "Who do you want to send?"

"Come up with a small team, whomever you think is the stealthiest. Send them back to the Rogue camp to do some reconnaissance. Tell them to look for parts of the ship, take pictures of the remnants of the damage left behind. They must scrutinize everything and anything they think will be important, and they have a day to do it." I shift my gaze to the windows, which open up to a view of the City. "If they can push it to less than a day, that would be even better. Our dome is not fully repaired yet, and until it is, we may as well paint a target on us for this thing."

"Very well, My Keeper." Jeremy stands and bows his head then exits the room with military precision.

Just as soon as Jeremy is gone, I pull off the leader's mask that I put on to convince him I know what I am doing, even if we are both well aware of the fact that I have no idea what I am doing at all.

"I am sure it will be fine, Beatrice. I'll even have the Dreamcatchers help out with the mission. We're going to fix this," Echo assures me and reaches over to put his hand on mine. With his touch, an overwhelming calm comes over me, and I suddenly don't feel so harried any longer. It is almost addictive, this feeling, like an invisible string pulling me close to Echo, or a voice convincing me that even the worst things aren't really so bad after all.

I crave this from him, but I also know that I need to stop myself from feeling this way. When everything is all said and done, Echo and I will go our separate ways ... if we are still alive.

I keep my hand under his, and in my head I count down from ten. I can allow him exactly ten seconds. This arbitrary time limit seems reasonable to me, and it makes it a little easier when I slip my hand out from under his and rise to stand. "I am going to go check on Gabe. You are welcome to stay here if you want. It's probably the safest place for you anyway."

Echo laughs nervously and runs his fingers back through his platinum blond hair. "Yeah, being the leader of the City's sworn enemy probably won't lend me any freedoms, huh?"

I smile with a shrug. "Not like I'm much better, seeing that I'm your wife."

"Touché." Echo grins, his smile melting away my worries.

It's going to be hard to walk away from him when this is all said and done.

***

The infirmary is mostly quiet, the calm before the storm. Being here to see Gabe again is almost surreal, considering that the last time I was here, I practically left him to die so I could run away with Echo. It makes it even harder to understand why Gabe would even give me a second chance. Would I have were I in his shoes?

I find him and Brandon in one of the rooms in the back. Gabe is up out of bed and hovering over Brandon, who sits in a chair, his head hung low. I hear him sniffling, and Gabe is murmuring quiet, comforting words while holding Brandon's hand.

I clear my throat, drawing Gabe's attention to me.

"Who is it?" Brandon's fingers close around Gabe's hand and he looks in my direction, though it's in vain.

Gabe smiles at me, but it is pitiful and sympathetic. "It's just Beatrice, Brandon. Don't worry."

"*Keeper* Beatrice, remember." Brandon lightheartedly corrects Gabe, which eases my worry for him.

"Gabe had it right the first time." I grin and walk to Gabe's side. "Well, sort of. I don't know when you ever call me 'Beatrice' unless you are mad at me or I am in trouble for something." Cocking my head to the side, I look up at Gabe. "Are you mad at me?"

Gabe's smile widens into that devilish grin of his. "Nah."

"Hmm." I tap my chin with a finger, feigning confusion. "So, I have to be in trouble then, right?"

"How could you be in trouble when you are our Keeper?" Brandon laughs. Seems like not much can keep his happy-go-lucky attitude down for long, not even being blinded and nearly killed.

"True." My gaze slips over Gabe's broken and bruised face. His left eye is almost swollen shut, the skin an uneasy twilight blue that fades into a darker purple. There's a large, jagged cut across his right cheek, and where the skin is flayed, it is raw and pink. "Hasn't anyone come to patch you up yet?"

Gabe acts as if he has forgotten that his face looks like he ran into a brick wall at a million miles an hour. A brick wall with jagged, pointed spikes sticking out of it. "Oh, this stuff?" He points to the cut on his cheek. "It's no big deal, Bea. You know me better than that."

I snort and roll my eyes. "Yes, I do know you better than that, which is why I insist a medic come over here right now and patch you up before it gets infected and disgusting and your whole face falls off."

Brandon's vacant eyes go wide, his eyebrows arching in surprise. "His face is going to fall off? Really?"

Gabe starts to laugh and squeezes Brandon's hand again. "No, Brandon. My face isn't going to fall off. This is just Bea's way of being overdramatic so she gets what she wants."

"If I wanted to get what I want, I'd just order them to do it, huh?" I poke Gabe in his ribs, and he smirks again, then leans into me so our arms are pushed against each other.

"No need to order anyone to do anything, Bea. If you want me to be seen, your wish is my command." Gabe waves over to one of the few medics who are lingering off to the side in a huddle, peering our way and whispering to themselves. No doubt, they have lots to say about me, but I'm too busy to care.

One of them rushes over, bows to me first, and then turns to Gabe. "Need me to fix this up for you, Seer Gabriel?"

"Yes, please. I don't need any girls looking my way and admiring another manly scar I've acquired in battle." Gabe lets go of Brandon's hand and mutters the words seriously, but breaks his facade by winking my way. "Just kidding."

"Mmhm." I let the medics do their work, and leave Gabe's side to sit next to Brandon. "How are you holding up?" I take his hand now, seeing as Gabe is no longer holding it.

"It's strange, not being able to see anything. I don't know how to explain it. It's just like someone turned the light off on my whole world, and now I'm just sitting here in this horrible, lonely blackness." Brandon's words are haunting and cause a shiver to ripple over my skin. "I don't like being alone, Bea."

I bring my other hand over his, cradling his fingers between mine. "No one does, Brandon. We are going to find a way to get your vision back, I promise." I really shouldn't promise these things, and Brandon probably knows it, since he only nods sadly in response.

"So, do you have some sort of plan?" Gabe looks at me from the corner of his eyes, keeping his head perfectly still as it is being tended to.

"Yes. Seer Jeremy is putting the team together, and Echo is assembling some Dreamcatchers as well. I am sending them back to the Rogue camp to see what they can find." I hate saying it because I hate the fact that I have to send anyone back to that abysmal place. "Hey … " I call to Gabe, my voice soft.

"Hmm?" He touches his cheek when the medic is done with it, feeling the sticky goop that helps it to heal faster.

"They didn't hurt you too badly, did they?" I feel guilty about it, and how could I not? At every turn, here I am abandoning Gabe over and over again when he needs me the most.

"Please, Bea, you know I'm stronger than that." Gabe brushes my concern off with a wave of his hand, but that's not good enough for me.

"I'm serious," I urge.

Gabe turns to me, his eyes still shadowed in bruises, his face still partially swollen and tender. "I am too. Don't worry about any of that, Bea. You did what you had to do, and I'm not ever going to hold it against you."

"Aren't you two just so sweet together," Brandon mocks with a goofy grin that almost makes one forget that we are in a huge mess. Almost.

Chapter 23

This is the first time the Seers and Dreamcatchers have publicly worked together. This is what I've wanted since I became the Keeper, though it's certainly not under the circumstances I wanted.

Echo, Gabe, Brandon, Elan, and I wait at the gates of the City as three Dreamcatcher ships approach. Not too long ago, we'd be bracing for a war, but right now, I am anxious to hear about what they've found. It's been a day since they've been away at the Rogue camp, searching for anything at all and nothing in particular, and I've not heard from them since their departure.

The ships touch down in front of us and the hatches hiss open. From inside, Jeremy and his group of handpicked Seers start down the ramp toward us. The other ships also open up, reminding me of clams when their shells part and allow for a peek inside. The Dreamcatchers disembark, and the whole group stops behind Jeremy when he gets to me.

"My Keeper." Jeremy bows his head and I return the gesture to them all.

"Seer Jeremy," I begin, sweeping my gaze over this rather curious scene. I smile at it and nudge Echo. "Do you see this?"

Echo grins down at me. "Looks like you did what you wanted to do."

"For now." I don't stop smiling though, even in spite of the gravity of the situation. "With this little group ... but it's amazing all the same."

Gabe clears his throat. Was it jealously?

"Right." I pull my shoulders back, the smile gone. "What

do you have to report, Seer Jeremy?"

Jeremy levels his gaze with mine. His uniform and skin are dusty with dirt from the plains. The sun has bronzed his face enough to leave white circles under his eyes from where he wore protective glasses of some sort. The Dreamcatchers are wearing their helmets, in full military uniform, just as they were when we originally invaded the camp. "You wish to do this here?"

I glance sidelong at Gabe, then turn to Echo. Neither one of them seems opposed to debriefing here, so I nod. "Yes. What did you find?"

Jeremy draws in a slow breath, his chest rising up and staying there. As he exhales, he begins his report. "Carnage. The camp has been wiped off the map, so to speak. Hardly anything exists in that space to even suggest a camp existed there at all. The earth is scorched black, debris and bodies are littered everywhere. Scraps of cloth leftover from the decimated tents are blowing freely in the wind." He draws a hand back through his hair, gripping on to the roots like he is trying to pull the images from his mind.

I swallow, not wanting to hear anymore. That carnage could have been us. It could have been Gabe.

It could still be us.

"Go on," I command, urging him to continue.

"What was particularly concerning were the patterns that were left on the ground. Big, round, perfectly-formed circles of black, and between the circumference … nothing. Not even remnants of the debris around the outside … absolutely nothing." Jeremy tries to paint the image in our minds, and I shudder to think of a weapon powerful enough to eliminate anything. Everything.

"That doesn't sound good at all," Gabe mutters.

"Just wonderful," Elan chimes in, his words dry and without emotion.

"And there weren't any Rogues? They were all eliminated?" Echo asks, glancing to his own commander, who steps up beside Jeremy and pulls off her helmet.

"Your Highness." The Dreamcatcher bows first. "We couldn't find any signs of any life back at the camp. I know when we left there were many people we were fighting, but when we came back … " She exchanges a haunted look with Jeremy. "It is too quiet there. Just the wind moves, everything else is still."

With a shiver, goose bumps form on my arms under the sleeves of my robe. For a minute, no one says anything, and I am grateful, because I'm having a hard time willing my mind to process how we are going to defend ourselves against something that can just make other somethings or someones stop existing.

"Did the trail of debris or the marks left behind seem to lead off in a certain direction?" I ask.

The Dreamcatcher nods her head, but Jeremy is the one who responds. "Yes. They are heading in this direction. We didn't see any signs of them on our way there or back, but they have to be out there somewhere. I suspect they are lingering around in the atmosphere where we can't see them."

Elan looks up into the sky, scanning it through squinted eyes. "Up there?"

"I think, but I don't know for sure." Jeremy holds his holopad out toward me, and I take it. "We recorded our findings on there. Feel free to look through what we have and upload what you need to your own device." He brushes some dust off his sleeve, and a little puff of dirt jumps into the air and dissipates. "With your permission, My Keeper, I'm going to get cleaned up, and then we have lots to talk and think about."

"Yes, please. Everyone is dismissed. I'll call us together again soon." I look down at Jeremy's holopad and brush my thumb over the screen to wake it up. The first picture that shows up is of a giant plot of land with little bits and pieces of this and that scattered everywhere. Hell, those little bits and pieces could be that of people, and I'm grateful that they are too far away to decipher if that is what they really are.

"Gabe, Elan, Echo, do you mind coming back to my quarters with me so we can put together some ideas?" I ask my friends, since I wouldn't dare ever try to order them around.

They agree, and on our way back to my quarters, I can't stop thinking about those pieces, and how if Echo and I weren't quick enough, they could have been pieces of Gabe.

Somewhere along the way, I take Gabe's hand, and he squeezes my fingers tightly.

Somewhere along the way, I glimpse at Echo, and he quickly looks elsewhere, but not soon enough to hide the sorrow in his gaze.

We retreat back to my room and sit down around the too-large table that was probably built for no other reason than to plot over. Echo sits down with the grace of royalty, but Elan and Gabe half-plop down in their chairs with little-to-no poise at all. Gabe kicks the heels of his feet up on the table and brushes a few wisps of his hair out of his eyes, while Elan leans in on his elbows with a look of consternation on his face. Or maybe it's a look of disapproval, as his gaze is pinned solely on Echo.

I clear my throat, redirecting Elan and everyone else's attention back on me. "I want to hear your opinions on the matter. I am not going to make any decisions without your input." I sit down with a sigh. "The truth is, I don't want to make any choices by myself. This is … "

"Too much?" Echo completes my thought with empathy.

"Stupid?" Elan doesn't complete my thought. Nor is he too empathetic. "What more of a plan do you need than to find these fools and go after them?"

"Do you know where they are?" I reach for my bottle cap necklace and run my thumb over the crinkled edges. Elan shakes his head, and I smirk. "That's what I thought. Really, Elan, I need you now. I know you want nothing more than to put these people in their place for doing what they did to Brandon, but I cannot afford to lose any of you, or any more Seers. It is our duty to protect our Citizens, and whatever or whomever this enemy is, they aren't going to stop for any of us."

Gabe's booted feet fall off the table and back onto the floor. He sits up straight, as if he flipped a switch into "serious" mode. "I don't think we should go after them. We don't have the manpower or military power to chase them down and win. Whatever that light is will render us all useless if we got caught up in it."

Elan frowns. "So, we wait?"

"Yes." Gabe glances to Elan and smirks. "I know you'd rather run headlong into the fight, but in this case, it would be better to wait here and fortify the City if they are coming this way."

"And we'll help," Echo says. The very offer is enough for Elan to drop his jaw in disbelief, but I don't think twice about it. How could I, the Dreamcatcher Queen, deny the help of the Dreamcathers, who are technically my people too?

I smile at Echo and reach over to squeeze his hand in thanks. "I never expected otherwise."

"What?" Elan exclaims and stands up, fists balled up at his

sides. "We are just going to let them waltz on in here? Into the City? The same City that we chased them out of just months ago?"

"Yes," I quickly reply. "When I became the Keeper, I made it very clear that my mission is to repair our relationship with the Dreamcatchers so we can work together to free and protect our Citizens. This new enemy, whomever they are, is a threat to all of us, Elan. Seer, Dreamcatcher, and Citizen. If we don't end them, then they will end us. And do you want to be ended?"

Elan mumbles, "No ... "

"I didn't think so." I redirect my attention to Echo. "Can you please issue your orders as soon as possible? Tell your Dreamcatcher army to come here with whatever ships and weapons they can spare."

"Of course, Beatrice. Some will stay back to keep Aura safe, too. Let me go do that now." Echo rises and quickly leaves to find his soldiers.

I watch as Echo disappears out the door and down the hallway before turning back to the other two. "Elan? I want you to go find Seer Jeremy, get his plans from him and get his efforts under way. I am trusting you both, so don't let your temper get in the way, okay?"

"You got it, Bea." Elan takes a few steps toward the exit, but stops and turns to me. "And I mean it. You can count on me."

I smile and let go of my necklace. "I never doubted it, Elan. Not ever."

He smiles a boyish smile and leaves.

Now, it is me and Gabe. I rake my fingers back through my hair and try to let all the wound up parts of me unravel and be calm. "This sucks," I mutter.

"It sure does." Gabe laughs and scoots his chair closer to

mine. He reaches a few of his fingers out and brushes some of my hair back behind my ear and says in a quieter tone, "It's nice to hear Beatrice again."

I glance up into his violet eyes. "What does that mean?"

With a shrug, Gabe rubs his thumb over my cheekbone and down to my chin, which he tilts upward ever so gently. "I don't know. All of this feels like it's been one big … dream."

"Wouldn't that be ironic?" I continue to stare into his eyes, finding comfort in the familiar gaze. "If all of this was just some Dreamcatcher trick and we both woke up and were in our rooms waiting for our morning training to begin?" That weight that comes with a sudden sadness sits on my shoulders. "And Mae and Connie were out there, waiting for the two of us to appear so they could go on nagging us about how in love we are?"

"That would be nice, wouldn't it?" Gabe leans in and brushes his lips against mine. "But would we have us? Like this?"

A shiver passes over me, freeing the tension and drama from deep inside my bones. I shake my head, if only because I don't know the answer, and I don't want to bother coming up with one. I just want to kiss Gabe, and have Gabe kiss me back. Is that too much to ask for?

So, we kiss, and I pour myself into him as if asking him to protect me and keep me with just my lips. We are on the brink of something terrible, but inside Gabe's kiss, I can't remember any of it because it is just too far away.

If I didn't have to come up for air, I wouldn't mind it going on forever. If I didn't have to will myself back into the present, where I am needed to help figure out how to save the City, I'd never leave this room. I break the kiss, and we stare at each other. "We have to get back to work."

Gabe's smile is forgiving when he stands from his chair. "Yes, My Keeper."

I smile, and we leave our kiss behind.

Chapter 24

"Turn the shield off."

The safety engineer stares at me like I'm certifiably insane. "What?"

I point to the screens in front of us, specifically to the one that shows a green, dome-like bubble that arches over a skyline. "Turn it off. We need to have our barriers down so the Dreamcatchers can come and go as they need to."

"Y-yes, My Keeper." The engineer stammers and reluctantly presses on buttons, shutting the shield off. The image on the screen turns from green to red as each section is powered down. I watch a meter drop from one hundred percent to zero, and just like that, the City is naked and vulnerable to anything out there.

"Are you sure this is a good idea, My Keeper?" Jeremy questions, though he does so under his breath, as not to second-guess me so boldly.

"It has to be done. There's no other way to let the Dreamcatchers in and out without manually doing this each and every time. If we need them in an emergency, and no one is here to let them in, then what will they do? Wait on the outside with the enemy until the dome falls?" I turn away from the controls and leave the engineers to their thing. "Echo? How long until your fleet arrives?"

Echo closes his eyes like someone does when they are thinking. But unlike everyone else, Echo does it to sense where the other Dreamcatchers are, even if he could easily radio them through the walkie he wears on his hip. "Not long now. Maybe an hour?"

"Okay, good." With a nod, I glance back to Jeremy, who is now standing over a table with Gabe, Elan, and a few other higher-ranking Seers. The table displays a blueish, 3D holomap. "Has there been any other sightings of our enemy? Any new information?"

Elan points to a place on the map, his pointer finger passing through some of the blue outlines to rest somewhere northeast of the City. "Last night, after our meeting, a group of Seers and Dreamcatchers were sent out to scout the area. They found debris around what looked like what was probably a small camp at some point. We are not sure if this is old or new, but it seemed to match some of the characteristics of a Rogue camp. Or, uh, what is left of it."

"So, they are closer?" Gabe rubs his chin as he surveys the map, and Elan nods.

Echo's radio, and several others in the room, squelch and squeal before emitting a static noise broken with what sounds like a person shouting. Echo grabs it from his hip and holds it up to his ear to try and decipher the words, but nothing is discernible.

"What is happening?" I ask of everyone, expecting someone to be able to explain the sudden burst of noise. The Seers by the controls are all maniacally tapping at buttons, switching from one screen to the next, security camera to security camera, trying to find anything that might show us what is going on.

That's when we hear the loud explosion from outside with a reverberation that shakes the glass windows of the Institution. Echo grabs my wrist and looks down at me. "I am going to the roof. That's where we will be able to see best."

"Are you stupid? You are going to go up on top of the roof of the highest building in the City to see what is going on? Do you want to paint a bullseye on you too while you are at it?" Elan snaps and stalks over to the windows. He presses his palms against the cool glass and peers outside. "I don't see anything."

"That's why I am going up there." As Echo lets go of my wrist, he lightly draws his fingers across my skin. "Stay close to your radios. I'll let you know what I see."

A knot forms in my stomach. Is this his goodbye? A simple "stay close to your radios?"

Echo leaves before I can protest. I stare at the door. Another explosion erupts somewhere in the City, and not even that can jar my thoughts away from the door. I start for it, my red robe rippling around my form with every step.

"Beatrice?" Gabe calls, his footsteps soon following my own.

I stop and spin around, and he nearly collides into me, but I stop him by grabbing onto his arms, fingers pressing into muscle. "Stay here, Gabe. I need you to stay here."

"I'm not that crazy. I let you run after that boy once, I'm not about to do it again." There isn't a smile to follow his words, which makes it all the more apparent that Gabe is not joking around right now. "I'm not going to let you disappear, or get hurt, or leave … "

"I'm not leaving. I won't ever leave you." Why do I make these promises? I search his eyes with my own, hoping to find any inkling or hint that he believes me. "But if anything happens to Echo … " I pause to think about what would happen if we lost Echo. The City isn't going to fall apart all because some Dreamcatcher is gone. What else would I say, though? What else can I say that isn't the truth: that my heart would break, just as it would break if I lost Gabe?

"Stay here, Bea." Gabe pleads.

"I will come back." I tiptoe up to press my lips to Gabe's, breathing in calm. When we break the kiss, I exhale the anxiety that courses through the both of us and let him go. "Help Jeremy. You are Acting Keeper while I am gone."

Gabe doesn't seem to know what to say. His mouth is open, words ready at the gate, but he says nothing as I disappear out the door and make a break for the lift.

I need to get to Echo and bring him back inside. While the lift pulls me up to the rooftop access doors, it shakes violently as another explosion rocks the Institution. The alarms are pulled, and a demanding siren echoes through the building, reminding me of the day the Dreamcatchers invaded. To think, in so short amount of time, Dreamcatchers and Seers are now pulling together to fight someone else's invasion.

The lift stops and a soft chime announces that my destined floor has been reached. The doors part to the rooftop, and with each inch they pull back, I can see black and gray smoke rising into a sky full of oranges and pinks as the sun prepares to set. A ship spirals out of the sky and crashes in a fiery ball of twisted reds, but I can't tell if it was a Dreamcatcher ship, or one of the new enemy's.

Echo stands at the ledge of the rooftop, transfixed. I rush over to him, calling his name. "Echo! Echo! Come back in!"

My voice seems to bring him back to the present, and he turns to me, his eyes wide and filled with tears. "The Dreamcatchers ... "

I grab his hands in mine and cup them with a gentle pull.

"We have to go back inside, Echo."

"Aura is gone," he blurts, the words overlapping each other.

I blink a few times, not understanding. "What do you mean? Why do you think it's gone?"

Echo shakes his head. "I can't feel them anymore, Beatrice. I can't feel them."

I don't know what to say. I open my mouth to reply, but then I see a streak of light fly past the Institution followed by a loud hiss. I pull him down, convinced the light will hit us, but instead it flies over the rooftop and hits a Dreamcatcher ship not too far off in the distance.

"Holy Maker ... " I whisper as the reality of this fight sets in. A larger, more sophisticated ship zips over the top of us, following the trail left by the missile just moments before. Crouched down with Echo, my hands still over his, I look up into his heartbroken, blue eyes and sadness surges through me. It is a deep sadness, one that not just I could create.

Echo's hands move around my wrists and he holds to them tightly, fearfully. He projects himself and the violent storm of emotions into me, and I gasp for air, unable to breathe as it courses through my body. I try to break through it, like a drowning someone desperately swimming for the surface before it is too late.

"Echo ... " I whisper his name, barely able to get it out. He is pulling me deeper, deeper, and soon I fear I will be lost forever. My vision tunnels, and I can only see a fraction of Echo's tragedy-stricken face. Is this what it feels like to be truly Caught? Is this how I will die, at the hands of my husband, who seems to have zoned out in his grief?

Somewhere behind us, there's another loud crash and it knocks us both to the ground. Echo's hands lose grasp of mine, and

I suck in a breath, filling my lungs all at once, just in case I get dragged under again.

What am I doing up here again? I clamor to my feet, wobbling as I find my balance. Echo is doing the same, and before I give him a chance to think about the world that he has just lost, I grab him by his arm and drag him, with all my might, toward the access door. "Come on, Echo. We need to get back inside."

Either I am very strong, or Echo has given up his fight, but we both make it to the door, and just as I throw it open, everything turns white, too bright to see through.

And then everything is black.

***

The soft thrumming of engines purrs under me, lulling me back into unconsciousness. I try to wake myself, but my head hurts too much, and I want nothing more than to go back to sleep. How nice it must be to just give up, to let yourself go. But what would I be giving up if I did just let go? The City needs me. Gabe needs me. Echo needs me. I need to wake up.

When I open my eyes, I can barely see anything. It is fuzzy and one shape blends into the other, like I'm looking at everything through swamp water. I feel around with my hands, trying to figure out where I am. The floor is made of metal and cool to the touch. I reach in front of me, then crawl forward, trying to map out my boundaries, but my every move is painful, like my entire body is one big bruise.

"Echo?" I whisper. "Echo? Echo? Please be here, Echo. Please be here … " I am desperate to find him, as the thought of being alone quickly sends me into a panic. My fingers crush into a wall in front of me, and I suck air in between my teeth, staunching a painful yelp. Where is he? *Please be here, Echo, please be here.*

The clink of a lock releases, and somewhere behind me, I hear the hiss of a door followed by clunky, heavy footsteps. I turn, pressing myself against the wall like a cornered animal, trying to get my feet under me like they taught us in combat class. *Don't let your enemy overtake you. Don't let them have the upper hand. If you are knocked down, getting back up is half the battle—probably the half that will save you.*

I get onto one of my knees before the person in front of me grabs me by the collar of my robe and yanks me up to my feet. This person, a man it seems, is much taller than I am, as my toes no longer touch the ground, and I dangle much like I'd imagine a baby cat from its mother's mouth.

"*You* are the Keeper?" the man asks, his voice heavy, his breath sour. His words though are wrapped in an accent that I am not familiar with. One that reminds me of cinnamon and ginger. It makes his words seem serious, deadly, and alluring all at once.

I fight the urge to vomit as the moisture from his mouth settles on my face. "I am Beatrice."

"How could someone so vile be someone so small?" He jostles me, and I wince, my head pounding from whatever knocked me out. I still can't see well, but it's enough to make out the outline of this giant man's face.

"Who are you?" I demand, summoning my courage all while trying not to think about where Echo might be, and what they might have done to him.

"My name is Jorgen, but aside from that, I am no one that concerns you. Who should concern you is our leader, Kadijah." He turns and walks with me held out in front of him, like I were a piece of trash that he didn't want to handle, but he had to anyway. We leave whatever room I was in, and he takes me through the dim hallways of what seems to be a ship. I recognize the sway and pitch of flight from when Echo took me back to Aura. It reminds me of the way he kissed me then, and how excited I was to be on the edge of something new and daring.

Was it that long ago?

I struggle and kick my legs as I pull at his meaty fingers in a vain effort to get him to drop me. "What do you want with me? Where is Echo?"

"Is that the scrawny boy who was with you?" Jorgen barks a laugh that is just as meaty as his fingers.

I don't know how to take that answer, and it angers me. "Where is he?"

"He is not your concern right now. You are going to Kadijah, and she will quickly show you what you should and shouldn't be caring about, Keeper." Jorgen continues on his way, ascending through the ship by scaling metal stairs embedded into the hull.

What does he plan to do with me? What has he done to Echo? These questions run through my mind as I try to recall anything from our combat classes that would lend some help right now.

We enter what I assume to be the bridge of this ship, a large room with plenty of control panels and about seven people total taking care of each station. I squint and see a huge window that opens up to a view of Dreamcatcher ships zipping around and tangling with the enemy just outside the City walls. Bursts of light rip through the sky and explode against metal, sending fire and shrapnel everywhere. I can't tell whose ships are whose after only watching for a few moments, but I sincerely hope the ones dropping from the sky don't belong to us.

In the middle of the bridge, I spy the outline of a large chair, designed for a general. Jorgen throws me down behind the chair and I land on my hands and knees. I wince with the pain from the impact and try to clamor back to my feet. Unfortunately, I am stopped by Jorgen's boot, which he places squarely in the middle of my back.

"General Kadijah, I have brought you the Keeper," Jorgen announces with a salute.

The chair starts to turn, and when I settle back on the heels of my feet, I watch as this General is revealed. She kneels down before me, close enough for me to focus. I don't know what I expect when I see her; perhaps I wanted to believe that whomever could be wiping hundreds of people off the map would be ugly or scary to look at. Instead, I see skinny black boots that give way to black stockings and long legs. The General wears a tea-length skirt and a matching military-style peacoat. Her hair is also long and black, and as she hooks it behind her ears, I can see the flush of pink that warms her olive-toned skin. She is, simply, beautiful.

"So, here she is," Kadijah speaks, her voice like honey with an accent so thick, it is hard for me to understand her. "You don't have to keep stepping on her, Captain Jorgen. Let her up so I can see all of her." She stands up straight and waits with her hands primly folded in front of her.

Jorgen steps back, the pressure of his foot leaving my back. I rise, though it is not graceful as I am still in plenty of pain. I try hard to look less pitiful than I feel, but when I look down, I can see that my robe is ripped and frayed. As my fingertips brush against my sides, I can feel patches that are burnt and warm.

Kadijah is taller than I am, her presence looming, suffocating. I ball my hands into fists, trying my best to summon the strength and courage to do whatever needs to be done to save who is left of the Dreamcatchers and the City.

But what could I possibly do defenseless and on my own?

"Who are you?" I demand, urging myself to remain civil, even if all of me wants to run from here and find Echo.

"I am General Kadijah. We are from Asia. Do you know where that is?" Kadijah talks to me like I am a child, even if she can't be much older than I am.

"No." The truth is, I don't know where Asia is. Until this very moment, no one was aware that other people existed outside of the Dreamcatchers, the Citizens, the Rogues, and the Seers. No one else on this side of the world, anyway. It all perished with the War, I thought.

"Ah, I thought as much. You know, the way that you people continue to live in destruction over here is quite surprising. It is … how do you say it in your language? Inhibiting. Limiting." Kadijah looks over me and smiles. "It sets humanity back such a long way."

I frown. "What do you know about humanity? You are murdering all these people for no reason. Do you think that is humane?"

"I think you are mistaken if you think that we are here for nothing," Kadijah replies, and her already dark eyes darken even more. "Your people are a disgrace. Outside, you look human enough, but inside you aren't human at all. We have been watching you and the Dreamcatchers for decades, and we decided that you mutants need to be put down once and for all." Despite the glare in her gaze, she smiles, sugary-sweet. "And humanity must be restored to its natural state."

"A mutant? Seriously?" I try to remain focused on her face, but she steps back, fading into a fuzzy blur.

"Seriously. The simple truth of it, Keeper, is that we're not supposed to have these 'gifts' as you call them. People are not supposed to see the future. We are supposed to accept our futures as they come to us."

"And the Dreamcatchers?" I ask, finding it to be almost absurd why I should even pose the suggestion that they are not dangerous. For all these years, the Seers have been training to keep the City safe from the Dreamcatchers. I know how dangerous they can be first hand—but we've moved past that.

Kadijah grins widely, then tilts her head and speaks into a small microphone. "Bring the prisoner up to the Bridge, please." She turns to me once more, walking in my direction. "The Dreamcatchers are even worse." Kadijah reaches out and brushes off some singed thread from my arm. "On the other side of the world, Beatrice, there is life. There are people who are happy living and not knowing what might lie in store for them. But knowing? That is when it gets dangerous. Perhaps, a long time ago, it was thought to be a gift—a way to save people, people who have choice, from their Fate. But really, you cannot escape your Fate. So why bother trying to figure out the end game? Why bother with these 'gifts' gone wrong?"

"Because whether you agree with it or not, we are people. You are killing innocent people over something we cannot control. We were *born* into this. We never chose it for ourselves. And since we have it, why not use it for good? The Seers have been protecting this City for decades because we are able to use our Vision to improve it." A large explosion from outside shakes the ship, and I nearly topple over, but Kadijah steadies me. Some alarms blink and sound from different control boards, but they are silenced with a few frantic finger taps, and it is relatively quiet once more.

"Is this an improvement?" Kadijah motions to the window, the explosions. "Did you not See this?"

"We cannot See everything," I growl lowly, clenching my teeth together in frustration. "And we cannot change everything."

Kadijah, still smiling, stoops down so that we are eye-to-eye with each other. Very quietly, she whispers, "Then why bother having you?"

I slap her square across the face. My palm meets with her cheek, and the sound of the contact echoes through the room. Jorgen races forward and grabs my arm, throwing me down on the ground, reaching for some sort of weapon on his hip, but Kadijah barks an order. "Stand down! Stand down!"

I yank my arm away from Jorgen and stumble away from the two of them. "I am not going to let you destroy us. You aren't just going to stand here and systematically wipe out my friends, my people, my City just because you are on some crazy, stupid mission to fit all of humanity into your idiotic concept of perfection."

"You will not *let* me?" Kadijah laughs, and it reminds me of the way my mother, the former Keeper, would laugh when she was up to absolutely no good. "My girl, can't you see? I don't need you to *let* me. I already *am*."

The Bridge doors open, and two armed guards drag in Echo's crumpled body. They unceremoniously drop him to the ground, and my heart stops beating. Is he alive? "Echo!" I start for him, but Jorgen shoves me, and I crash into a control panel, hitting my head. "Leave him alone!" I moan and shake my head, trying to get ahold of my surroundings again. The room sways, both from the pitch of the ship and because of the spark of dizziness from the blow.

Echo moans and twitches, barely moving. At least he is alive. At least I can still save him.

"General? The Dreamcatcher fleet is down. Permission to approach the City?" one of the other soldiers on the Bridge asks.

Kadijah nods in return. "Permission granted." She saunters over to Echo's broken form and nudges his side with the toe of her boot. "Do you hear that, Dreamcatcher King? We have destroyed your people, and now ... now, we will destroy hers." She kicks him hard against the ribs, and Echo yelps like a battered dog. "And you."

The soldiers who dragged Echo here pull him up by the collar of his jumpsuit. They force him to stand there like that, dangling the way a coat would on a hook.

"Bring the Keeper," Kadijah orders, and before I can fight to get away, Jorgen grabs me and drags me to stand beside Echo. One of the soldiers behind Echo takes out what looks like a nightstick of some sort, but with a metal tip. He flicks it open, extending it fully, and pushes a button that makes it hum with electricity. Jorgen does the same, and I try again, in vain, to pull away from him.

Kadijah stops in front of us both, her head held high. "For the crimes that you have committed against humanity, I sentence you both to death. Your City, right now, is being Cleansed. When we have cured every last one of you pathetic Seers, we will send diplomats out to restructure this nonsense that you call society."

Everyone of Echo's breaths is ragged. When he breathes in, I can hear his lungs whistle, and when he breathes out, he coughs and sputters blood out in front of him.

Behind Kadijah, out the front window, I see bright, white lights, like the lights I saw in my Vision back at the Rogue camp. The light that took away Brandon's Sight.

"No! Stop it! Leave them alone!" I shout in panic, my voice cracking. The lights don't dim or go away though, and Kadijah stands there with a pleased smirk upon her face, relishing in my despair.

"Now, let's put an end to this," she orders and steps back. "Kill them."

Echo grabs my wrist just as the sharp sting of the prod against the base of my spine surges through my limbs, followed by the distinct sensation that someone is ripping me into two pieces.

I scream. I scream, and I scream, and I scream, and I am sure that I won't ever stop screaming until I am dead.

And then, I die.

Chapter 25

Where I go it is peaceful and calm. It is bright white with nothing but a tree with long, reaching branches: Echo's tree from my dreams in the past.

I feel like I am hurting, but there's a familiar numbness that makes the pain dull and practically not there. I walk toward the tree, one step after the next, willing myself to move forward, but it's like I am trudging through the mud, and I can never pull my feet up high enough, no matter how hard I try. A wave of warm, inviting exhaustion comes over me, and I want nothing more than to lay down here in the sunlight and stare up at the sky.

Beatrice …

Echo.

I can't lie down here. I need to keep going. I need to get to him before it is too late.

So I walk. I walk, and I walk, and I walk, and I then I make myself walk some more. The distance between me and the tree closes, and as I near, I am delighted to see Echo standing there, a golden crown upon his head, no bruises, no cuts—healthy and perfect and handsome.

He reaches out and takes my hand, pulling me against his chest. I feel none of that pain from before, not even a dull ache. Instead, I feel the warmth of Echo's presence, and I know I am safe here, under our tree, away from the war raging on wherever we were before.

"Is this a Dream or a Vision?" I ask as I stare up into his blue eyes.

"I think this is a little bit of both, Beatrice." Echo smiles that ever-patient smile as his other hand cups around my cheek. "And I think, when you come out of it, I will be gone." He says the words so plainly, as if they aren't as weighted with the seriousness that they are.

"Gone? What do you mean?" The happiness deflates from me, and Echo's warmth becomes a little less.

"This place, where we are, this is a place Between. This is where we linger before our Fates are made up and we go to ... wherever it is dead people go." Echo brushes his fingers over my lips, and for a moment, I taste blood in my mouth.

Shaking my head, I hold on to Echo's arms, urgently grabbing them in my hands, as if trying to keep him here with me. "No. No, Echo, don't you say that."

Echo takes his hand from my cheek and runs it back through my hair. "In a way, Kadijah is right, Beatrice. Our outcomes are always going to be the same, even if you can see it ahead of time. We can spend our whole lives running from it, but it will be behind us somewhere, trying to catch up."

Anger boils to the surface. "Don't you dare, not for a moment, agree with that horrible Kadijah woman!" I shake him almost violently, as if trying to rid him of such thoughts. This woman is trying to kill him, and he is agreeing with her?

Echo shushes me and takes my head between both of his hands again. We stare at each other in this way, connected in our little space, beneath our little tree, and I know, right in this moment, that this is it. This is all I will have left of Echo whenever I come to. I will have failed him. He will be dead, and I will have failed him.

"You haven't failed me," Echo whispers, as if reading my

mind. *"I hear your thoughts, Beatrice. I have Caught you, and right now, you and I are one person. I am hanging on enough to give you this ... so we can say our goodbyes."*

Tears well up in my eyes, rimming and threatening to spill over. As they fall, they are hot with anger and rage, and the farther they fall from my eyes, the more they cool with despair and misery. "I ... I don't want to say goodbye yet ... not yet ... "

Echo half laughs, which is kind of strange, considering I'm standing here, composure failing. But the laugh is sad underneath, and tears are quick to follow. "No one ever wants to say goodbye, Beatrice."

"Please ... " I beg him just as he pulls me back against him.

Echo kisses the crown of my head, then my cheek, and finally his lips meet mine. His kiss is as desperate as my plea for him not to go. It is all of what we have been through, the drama, the excitement, the disappointment, the fear, the frustration ... the love.

Our love.

He tries to pull back, to break it, but I don't let him. I can't let him. When we are done here, he is no longer going to be mine. He is going to be gone, and I have no idea where I will be. Maybe I will be gone too? My hands slip from his arms and I grab the robes by his chest, clutching him closer. A sob escapes through the kiss, and that is how we part, trembling in each other's arms, on the brink of our final farewell.

"I don't know who I am without you. How can I do this?" I whisper, the words barely audible. I'm afraid that if I acknowledge that he is still here, then someone will take him from me right this moment.

As I raise my gaze to Echo, a single drop of blood trails down his nose and over his mouth, but he doesn't seem aware of it. "You can do it. Without me, you are still the Keeper, you are still the Dreamcatcher Queen. You'll be all the Seers and Dreamcatchers need." He pauses there, wiping his mouth. He stares at his hand, as if shocked to see the blood there, then glances back up at me. "Besides," He lowers his hand, accidentally smearing the blood over the white robe, "you have Gabe. He will love you and protect you just as much as I did."

I can hardly see him through the tears that now flow copiously down my cheeks. I try to brush them away, but they are quickly replaced with more. More blood trickles from the corner of Echo's mouth, and he becomes fainter, like he is fading out of this world and into the next.

Echo starts to laugh as he keeps wiping away at the blood, and I tilt my head, confused. "Why are you laughing?"

"Imagine, Beatrice ... " Echo coughs, and some droplets of blood sputter from his lips and onto my cheek. "Imagine if we were never separated in the first place. I could have had so much more time with you ... "

"No ... no ... " He fades some more, and I reach for him, trying to grab for anything to keep him here. My hands meet with nothing though. "Echo!"

"Just imagine it, Beatrice ... " Echo's words reverberate, just like his name. "Goodbye."

And just like that, Echo is gone.

I sink onto the ground and brush the blood off my face. I look at it on my fingers, a crimson red remnant of the once Dreamcatcher King. After everything that I went through to find a cure to save him and the Auran people ... and now he is gone, just like most of them. In the end, despite my Vision, despite trying to alter their fates, I couldn't save any of them. Fate won.

   "Goodbye."

Chapter 26

I wake up, and in this fuzzy instance of time, when Echo is still gripping onto my hand and I am lucid enough to realize what I have to do, I reach out and grab onto Kadijah with my other hand.

She becomes still, frozen in this moment of agony with Echo and me. It takes everything in me to keep hold of her, even as Jorgen attempts to yank me away. But he can't. There is something, some force, that is greater than him right now, and it keeps me standing and bonded with Echo and Kadijah.

I still scream, but to me, it is muffled and far away. Jorgen is pulling on me, and the Bridge crew has come to Kadijah's aid, but as soon as they make contact with her, they too become frozen, linked in this death surge.

This must be what it is like to be truly Caught.

Jorgen pulls on my arm, his bare skin touching my own, and he is Caught as well.

You are the Dreamcatcher Queen, Beatrice.

Echo's words envelop me, filling me with confidence. His hand finally drops from mine, and his body falls forward onto the ground. As soon as his touch leaves me, I, and everyone else, collapse as well.

I cry out when I hit the ground, bringing my hands up to hold my aching head. Everyone around me is still. Too still. I sob and crawl on my hands and knees toward Kadijah's fallen form and struggle to flip her over, to see her face, her eyes. Her gaze is black and hollow, the way the Dreamcatcher victims look after being Caught. I hurry and check the rest of them, to find that they too are all dead—shells of themselves and nothing more.

Finally, now that I know we are safe, I move to Echo, but I know even before I get to him that he is also dead. He told me he would be. Sitting beside him, I gently pull his head into my lap and cradle him against me. The cries that leave me rack my whole body in agony before bubbling forth. They echo through the empty Bridge, and I imagine they are loud enough to travel down the halls, spreading my sorrow to whomever can hear it.

"I love you, Echo," I whisper against his ear, which is already turning cold. I brush his hair out of his face, the tips of his blond tresses now red and caked in blood. Lowering my lips to his, I kiss him one last time, remembering his words to me in our last moments together, suspended between reality, a Dream and a Vision.

It is as much as I let myself mourn and be angry. I need to get out of this place and save whatever is left of my City.

I grab a gun off one of the fallen bodies and stumble my way to the control panel where before people were manning the instruments that control every aspect of this ship. I study the many buttons, screens, and levers, not knowing where to even begin.

"I need to put this ship down," I speak aloud to myself in an effort to keep calm. If Echo weren't lying dead on the ground over there, he'd be beside me, helping me to end this. But that's not the case, and I am on my own to figure it out.

A ship flashes by the large, control window, and I jump back, startled. I tiptoe to the glass to peer over the edge to see where it went, and just as soon as I find it, another ship—it looks like a Dreamcatcher ship—blasts it out of the sky. The remnants of the craft rain down just outside the City in streaks of metal and fire.

I also need to stop them from fighting. But how?

From just outside, I hear footsteps clanking on the floor, so I duck and rush over to the Bridge door, standing just to the side, out of view. It slides open with a hiss, and a woman steps through, weapon drawn. "General?"

I have an instant to react, and I take it by lunging forward and knocking the woman down onto the ground. We tumble together and she fumbles her gun just as we come to a stop. It is too far for her to reach. The Maker must be on my side.

I press the barrel of my gun against her head and put my other hand over her mouth. "Don't make a noise, or I will shoot you right here and now." I don't know if this will work, but I have killed before, and if I have to kill again, I will in order to save the City. To save my friends. To save Gabe.

Thankfully, she abides by my order. Her gaze stops on my violet eyes, and I see in her features the sudden realization of who she is dealing with. Maybe she knows that I am supposed to be dead. From here, she can't see Kadijah's lifeless body, or the pile of other soldiers who were Caught in the process. She can't see the blank faces and lifeless eyes.

"This is what you're going to do. You are going to get on the radio, and you are going to order the fighter ships to fall back. Then, you are going to land this thing." I remind her of the tenuous position she is in by pressing the cool metal against her temple. "And if you do anything other than that, I will put a bullet in your head. You got it?"

She nods her head before I take my hand away. "Get up and do it." I stand and pull her up with me. Putting the gun to the back of her head, I push her forward toward the controls. "Hurry up."

This woman is obviously more familiar with the panels of

technology that goes way over my head. She deftly moves her fingers over the controls and pushes a button that opens the line for her to speak. "This is Lieutenant Khan ordering all ships to fall back and stop fighting. I repeat, all ships are hereby ordered to fall back and stop fighting."

Before she can do anything else, I jerk her away from the other controls for safety's sake and jab the gun into the base of her spine. It is now that she notices the all-too-still forms of Kadijah, Echo, Jorgen, and the others. Her mouth opens and she looks back at me in horror. "You … you killed them."

"Not exactly, but they are dead none-the-less. Your leader and my husband." I speak softly like one would speak around a sleeping child. If only Echo were sleeping though.

"How could you?" the lieutenant whispers, trembling.

"How could I? How could *I*?" It is a simple enough question, but enough to push me over the edge and I start to shout, "Do you see him? Do you see him? Look what she did. Look!" With a shove, I send the woman tumbling to the ground, and she lands in the pile of dead bodies with a thud. She scrambles, horrified, trying to get up, but before she can, I take a few strides to where she is freaking out and I push her head down near Echo's where she can see the blood crusting on his lips, the bruises around his swollen eyes, the many cuts that pepper his face. I want her to see it all.

"Let me go!" Khan screams, struggling against the grip of my fingers through her hair. "Let me go!"

"Why? You tell me why I should let you go!" Just when I cannot take seeing Echo's corpse any longer, I fling Khan to the side. She scrambles away from me, but I keep the gun sight on her the whole time. "If you can give me a good reason, I'll let you go.

But if not, I will end you like your people are ending mine."

The young lieutenant backs into a wall with nowhere else to go. I close in on her, watching her pathetic little self cower in fear and wait for her answer.

Khan says her words very deliberately, but as carefully as one can with a gun pointed at them. "Because, if you don't let me go, you are no better than any of us. You will be the monster that everyone thinks the Keeper is."

I remember my mother, and the callous, cold way that she executed Paradigm. I remember the way she looked at me, Gabe, and Echo and never hesitated to try and kill us all. I close my palms around the grip of the gun, fingers trembling. It would be so easy to end this woman. Maybe it will even make losing Echo feel a little less painful.

But it won't, and I know it won't. Khan is right. I would be no better than my mother. I would be the Keeper they have all heard that I am—a Keeper that is nothing like me. I lower the gun just slightly.

"Do you know how to land the ship?" I ask, trying not to betray the grief that is eating away inside.

Khan seems to breathe a little easier and answers in an exhale. "Yes."

"Then land it, and once we have touched down, you are going to escort me safely back to the ground. And then you are going to turn this ship around and go away. Far, far away … and don't come back." I glance out the front window and watch as the few Dreamcatcher ships regroup, both of us hovering at a standoff. I don't know how long they will wait there, trying to figure out their next step, so I have to move fast.

Lieutenant Khan nods her agreement. I keep my gun

trained on her as she calmly walks back across the Bridge. She stops behind the Captain's helm and activates a screen to the right of a yoke. The ship rumbles as her fingers dance across the screen, and I watch the horizon rise as we begin our descent.

"Open the hatch," I order, sidestepping over to a large circular door on the ground, just beyond where Echo's body lies. I am so close to being free.

I kneel down and with my free hand, grab the collar of Echo's jumpsuit. "I'm not leaving you behind," I tell him, as if he can hear me.

The circular door starts to retract, sliding into the hull, disappearing a little bit at a time to reveal the arid ground a few feet beneath us. Dirt and dust is kicked up the closer the craft gets to the ground, and I lift my other arm up over my eyes to shield them from the debris. *Almost there. Almost there.*

I prepare to jump, but a loud, soul-piercing alarm sounds. The ship lurches, and I fall backward onto my butt, sending the gun across the ground.

"SELF DESTRUCTION MODE ACTIVATED. SELF DESTRUCTION WILL OCCUR IN THIRTY SECONDS," the computerized voice announces as the alarm screeches over and over again.

Khan scoops up the gun and fires at me. "Your people must be eliminated for the good of the human race!"

"You little bitch!" I yell back and flinch as the bullets hit the metal floor around me. I am lucky she's not a good shot, but if I stay here any longer, she might just land one of them. I hook my fingers back around Echo's collar and shuffle to the door, which is now closing shut.

Another shot is fired, and this one rips past my arm, tearing what is left of my battered robe, slicing my skin. My sight goes red in pain. Instinctively, I let go of Echo and grab my arm, covering the bleeding wound.

"SELF DESTRUCTION IN TWENTY SECONDS."

The ship lurches. Khan fires again.

I lose balance and tumble out the door, falling for what seems like forever before I hit the ground. Some part of me crunches, but I don't know what or where is hurt anymore.

I lost him. I lost him again. "Echo … " Rolling over on my back, I watch as the ship speeds forward toward the city, knocking a couple of Dreamcatcher ships out of the way in their wake. I turn onto my side, clawing at the ground. "No … no … "

But it is too late. The ship explodes, and as the bright white light engulfs everything around me, I duck my head and close my eyes.

An unnerving warmth washes over me, and for just a moment, I've forgotten that most of the City is gone, that Gabe is gone … that everyone I've known is gone, and I succumb to the strange, warm comfort.

Chapter 27

"Beatrice?"

The sound of my name sounds so far away, but each time it is said, I am lured closer and closer to consciousness. I don't know who is calling me, but my heart wants it to be Echo, and my brain reminds me that I'll never hear Echo speak my name again.

"Beatrice? Beatrice?

I don't want to wake up. I didn't even think it was possible until now. My body is willing me to open my eyes, to face the fact that my world, as I knew it, has been destroyed. But when I open my eyes, what will I be opening them to? Where am I? Who am I?

"She is waking up!" another male voice exclaims, and he sounds excited.

My eyelashes flutter, and I squint against the bright lights that are everywhere. My first instinct is to cover my eyes with my arms, but as soon as I move them, I regret it. The pain is unbearable, and I pitifully cry out. The suffering is enough to jolt me back into the "fight" mode of "fight or flight." I focus my eyes on the ceiling, the metal beams that run lengthwise across the room. It looks familiar.

The infirmary. I'm in the infirmary.

Brandon's face comes into view, and he grins down at me with that big, goofy smile of his. "Hey, Bea."

"Brandon? You're alive?" I ask, my voice raspy as I try and contain the pain.

Brandon opens his mouth to respond, but Elan's voice delivers the answer. "We should be asking the same of you. You look dead enough." He comes to my side, next to Brandon, and smiles as well. "It's good to see you awake. The doctors weren't sure you were going to make it."

Brandon nudges Elan. "You shouldn't tell her that. She's been through a lot, you know."

"We all have, Brandon. A little bit of truth never hurt anyone." Elan crosses his arms over his chest and surveys me with … Are his eyes blue?

I squint again, trying to make them out. Maybe I am just not thinking clearly enough yet. Maybe I am seeing things. But when I look at Brandon, I notice the very same thing, and I know I can't be that out of it.

"Your eyes … " I whisper to them.

"Yeah, about that … " Elan starts, but he is cut off by someone else who is suddenly shouting through the infirmary.

"Beatrice!"

Gabe!

I didn't lose him!

I struggle in an attempt to lift my head. I want to see him. I want to know that he is real and this all isn't some cruel trick. So, I call to him, but each time his name leaves my mouth, I feel panicked and scared, as if someone will find him and kill him too. "Gabe? Gabe? Gabe!"

He pushes aside a privacy curtain and practically crashes into me, and even if it hurts like hell, I would hurt ten times more if it meant I could be in Gabe's arms. He wraps himself around me, enveloping me, surrounding me with himself, and as soon as I feel safe, all of the misery and grief pours from me in uncontrollable sobbing.

"Echo is dead," I whisper into Gabe's neck. My fingers press into his back as I pull myself closer to him. "He is dead."

Gabe nods his head, brushing his hand down my hair in a calming motion. "I'm sorry, Beatrice." And he is. I can hear the sorrow in his voice, perhaps because he knows it hurts me, or perhaps because Echo saved his life twice, and Gabe didn't have the chance to return the favor.

"I tried to save his body, but she was shooting at me, and the ship—" But Gabe doesn't let me finish the line of excuses. He lifts my chin, tilting my head up so that I look into his now blue eyes.

"You tried your best. We all did. No more excuses." Gabe leans in and brushes his lips against mine. In a whisper, he adds, "I was terrified that you didn't make it out of that ship in time, Bea. I kept thinking about being here without you ... " His words taper off.

"We were all scared, Beatrice. But now you are here! And it will be better," Brandon interjects into our moment. I smile, because I can't not smile. Brandon always has a way to turn a dire situation into something that just isn't so bad.

I pull back to look into Gabe's eyes again, because I can't stop staring at their intense, blue hue. They are gorgeous, captivating, but unsettling. "Why are your eyes blue?"

"The Light did it" Elan says from over where he sits on a windowsill, off to the side and away from all the emotional, lovey-dovey stuff. His arms are crossed over his chest, and he swings one of his legs over and over again.

"Did what?" I look between the three of them, confused.

Brandon points to his eyes with a grin. "Well, it made me see again." But then his grin fades and he looks to Gabe and Elan to fill in whatever he can't seem to say.

"But it took all of our Sight." Gabe brushes my hair back

behind one of my ears, his gaze sad.

"All of you?" I question, afraid of the answer.

"All of the Seers." Elan jumps off the ledge, his booted feet thudding on the floor. He cracks his knuckles, and turns to stare out the window. He gaze is far away and disconnected like he is looking at everything and nothing at all. It is, in one word, heartbreaking.

I rake my fingers back through my knotted hair, hoping to find some sense in what they are telling me. Seers without Sight? "How? I … I don't understand."

Gabe gently and calmly pulls one of my hands away from my head and holds it. "When the ship exploded, the light that it released … well, it took away everyone's Vision. We couldn't look away in time. It happened so suddenly, so quickly, and the light was everywhere. And now, we are just Citizens. The Institution serves no more purpose … the City … " Gabe's words trail off as tears catch in his throat.

Things can change so much in just a day. I have lost Echo, my friends and people have lost their Sight, and nothing is the same. Kadijah got her way, even in death. She has levelled everyone.

Everyone but me.

"The City, Gabe, is still the City. It is broken now, but it is still ours." I squeeze my hands around his and gaze up into his eyes. "And you are still you, and Elan is still Elan, and Brandon is still Brandon, and I—"

I hear him, then. Echo echoing. *You are the Dreamcatcher Queen. You are the Keeper. You are the Dreamcatcher Queen. You are the Keeper …*

In a whisper, I repeat the words aloud. "I am the

Dreamcatcher Queen. I am the Keeper." I say it again and again, until the words make me smile. It is like he is still alive somewhere. Somewhere inside of me. Mine. "I am the Keeper."

Gabe smiles back at my words and hugs me close to him. "You are."

As I let go of Gabe, Elan wanders back to my side, and Brandon gathers around as well. They all look to me, as a leader, as their friend, and I stare up at each one of them and their lost gazes.

Elan asks, "So now what?"

Through the nearby window, the smoke rises into the air, some of it black, some of it brown, and some of it white—all different stages of burning. Outside, the City is in shambles, the people no doubt trying to reorient themselves, find the living from the dead, and put their lives back together. They are probably waiting for me to come to them, to tell them it will be okay, to explain what has just happened. They still need me, just like the Seers still need me. We all need each other.

I stand up, wincing in pain from my fall, and I limp over to the window to view the destruction outside. I don't need to look for long; I know that it is bad. I know that we are all hurting the same as the other Seers and Citizens and however many Dreamcatchers have survived.

"Now we rebuild. We will put this City back together the best we can. We will offer the Dreamcatcher refugees a place to live beside us, along with the Citizens." My fingers brush over the singed and tattered edges of my red robe, and then I close them into a fist, determined. "We will be exactly how it was supposed to be all of this time, long ago, before the Institution became something it wasn't ever supposed to be."

"And how do we start that?" Brandon questions.

I stare through the glass, looking at the violet-eyed reflection that glances back at me. "The only way we can, Brandon," I reply, putting a palm to the cool glass. "Brick-by-brick."

Chapter 28

I brush my hair in front of the mirror, dragging the bristles down in a slow, measured motion. There are dark bags under my eyes, cuts across my face, and bruises all over my body. I don't look pretty or righteous or in any way as graceful as the Keeper should be. Instead, I look like something just chewed me up and spit me out. At least, though, I don't look broken. I can be bruised, but I can't be broken. I can't be defeated.

A woman peeks her head in and clears her throat. "My Keeper? We will be ready to air in just a few moments. Is everything okay?"

I look over my shoulder at her as she hangs in the doorway of the green room. She's young, maybe not too much older than me, and filled with energy. She practically bounces on her toes as she waits for my reply. What is even more impressive, though, is that I have no idea if she's a Seer, a Dreamcatcher, or a Citizen. She is just … her. A person. Shouldn't we all be "just people?"

"Yes, I'm sorry. I was just thinking." I smile back at her. "I'm ready."

"Great!" the woman chirps. "I am going to check on just one thing, and then we'll get you mic'd up and ready to go!" Before she exits, she folds her hands in front of her waist and bounces on her toes. "I just want to let you know, off the record, that I think all these changes you are going to do are … well … they are exactly what we need."

"You do?"

"Yes, My Keeper. The Citizens, we've all wanted this for a

long time. Just to coexist. To help. We want the City to be as much ours as it is yours." She smiles shyly.

Her words mean so much to me now, after all that has happened, all that we fought for, and all that we've lost. I was doubting doing this, a televised address to the City, informing them that everything we were doing is going to change, and that everyone will coexist as equals now that the Seers have lost their Vision. The people here haven't lived life like this for decades; it will be a huge change, a difficult change, but sometimes the changes that are needed are the ones that are the hardest to make.

"And now the City will be all ours, as it was always supposed to be." I smile as the woman's shyness melts away into pure, confident exuberance.

She claps her hands together, then scurries out to do whatever it is she has to do before my speech goes live.

I turn back to the window and watch as helicopters fly by. There are a few Dreamcatcher ships that are left, and they hover around the perimeter, keeping guard just in case any more of Kadijah's people return. Just a year or so ago, this scene wouldn't have even been possible, and now we are on the brink of a new beginning.

A million, million lights twinkle in the darkness, some of them brighter than others. It is beautiful, despite the fact that we have to rebuild once more. Sometimes, it is the rebuilding that is most beautiful of all.

The door opens again, and I glance over my shoulder to find Gabe and his handsome grin. "Hey, Gabe."

"Hey, Bea," he replies, as if nothing had ever changed from when we were sitting in classes together until now. Behind him, Irene and Jamie both bumble through the door carrying large cases.

"We are going to get you all nice and pretty for your appearance, Queen Beatrice," Irene announces with a smile that matches Jamie's. I smile in return, tears springing to my eyes.

I jump to my feet and rush over to them with open arms. "Jamie? Irene? Thank the Maker, you're both alive!" We all embrace each other, and in this moment, I can feel Echo's presence, reminding me that I did not fail by Aura. I might not have been able to save it all, but I saved parts of it, and that is better than nothing.

We let each other go, and the two young women smile at me through their own tears. "Thanks to you, Your Highness."

Gabe stops behind me, puts his hands on my hips, and rests his chin on my shoulder. "So, this is it, huh?" Irene and Jamie giggle and move away to get to work.

I nod and watch Gabe's reflection in the glass. "This is it."

"No turning back?"

"Who'd want to turn back?" I smirk, leaning back into him. "We have to move forward now."

Gabe nods, his chin rubbing into my shoulder, then he turns his head and kisses my cheek. "After today, you will be just Beatrice again, and not the Keeper."

I turn around, my hands on his chest, and look up into his eyes. "And you will be just Gabe, and not a Seer."

"And this will be just a city, not the City." He plays along with me, tugging me closer by the hips.

"Just how it is supposed to be." I tiptoe up and press my lips to his, kissing him without the anxiety of the world falling apart around us. I slip my hands into his hands, intertwining my fingers around his, and I relish in the closeness and simplicity of just standing by Gabe and not having to worry about keeping the

Institution, the City, the Seers, the Citizens, and the Dreamcatchers together anymore.

The door opens just a sliver, and the young woman returns, poking her head in again with a wave. "We are ready for you, Keeper. Are you ready?"

I take a deep breath and close my eyes. I See Echo there, standing in Aura in front of the palace, draped in gold, with a gold crown which reflects the golden rays of the sun. My grip tightens around Gabe's hand to keep me steady as I lose myself to the Vision, and I want to lose myself to it. It is brief, though, and just as Echo smiles, the Vision ends, and I open my glowing violet eyes.

"What did you See?" Gabe asks, his words curious, but I can also hear that he mourns the fact that this is not a power that he will use again.

I shake my head and smile. "It was Echo." Letting go of Gabe's hand, I start toward the door, which will lead me out to the first day of a new life in this world.

Gabe follows after me, and when he reaches my side, he takes my hand again. "Echo? What did he say? What did he do?"

I smile. "He didn't say anything. He just smiled." And that is all I say, because it is all he needs to know.

Confidently, I lift my head, squeeze Gabe's hand, and we both walk through the door, into something unknown and beautiful.

Into the future.

Acknowledgements

Thank you first and foremost to my readers, friends, and family who have been patient and stuck by me through this process. A long time has passed between LUMINOSITY and LUCIDITY. In this period of time, a lot of life changes have happened, for better and for worse. I thought about giving up on this project, but because you didn't give up on me, I couldn't possibly give up on you. From the bottom of my heart, thank you so much for helping me through this journey.

My number one cheerleader has been my husband, though. Brandon saw me through the tears, the frustration, the defeat, and he held me up through it all and made me keep going. That is what I love most about my husband—he will never, ever, ever let me fall. Thank you, Brandon, for motivating me to continue after my dreams.

Between books, my son, Kaiden, was born. We fought hard to be blessed with his smiles, cuddles and unconditional love, and it was all worth it. My Buggy is my life, and he inspires me to continue writing, because if I can obtain my dreams, then he will see he can obtain his own.

I'd like to thank Robin C., Maciej C., and Dustin S. for their patience with me. They have seen me through some tough times, but all the while, they have constantly supported my writing career.

To Cameron, Jaime A. and Kerry A., you are all the best. These last three years have tested me, but you three never stopped telling me that LUCIDITY was still possible. You worked with me, let me rant, let me cry, gave me invaluable advice, and remained understanding through it all. I am probably one, little person in a myriad of authors that you reach out to every day, but please know that you inspired this one little person to remain on her path.

Finally, I want to thank my students. For eight years, I have devoted myself to you. For eight years, you have been "my children." For eight years, I've known no other joy than being your teacher. Nothing brings me more elation than to put my book in your hands and watch as you realize that I—your teacher—wrote it. I see opportunities alight in your eyes, I observe as doors open in your mind as you realize that you are just as capable for following your heart and achieving your goals as I am. As I move on as a writer, I leave behind hundreds of little lives that have filled my heart and soul with a gratitude and appreciation and a purpose that I couldn't imagine being without. Please, always remember that if you don't feel worthy of anything or anyone in your lives, that you are and always have been worthy to me.